The Pattern Shop
Mariah Friend

Pocket Lamp Press

First Edition

Cover design by Peter Selgin

Author photo by Ashley Gurley

Published by Pocket Lamp Press ISBN: 979-8-9932149-1-7 [paperback] ISBN:
979-8-9932149-2-4 [hardcover] ISBN: 979-8-9932149-0-0 [ebook]

Author's Note

This story is fiction—inspired by the textures, smells, and colors of the places I've been while searching for home. I recognize that the ability to move freely between borders is a liberty withheld from many, and one I do not take lightly. I also acknowledge the complexity and limitations of telling stories about places where I was a guest. Eleanorah's journey is one of learning to question the systems, beliefs, and privileges that cause harm. It is messy, imperfect, and sincere.

I've changed names, timelines, and details to protect privacy and serve the narrative. What remains true is the heart of what my travels taught me—no matter who we are or where we're from, *we belong to each other*.

For those still searching—it's never too late to choose home.

For my family, both here and gone, your love is my legacy
and
"My" Lucas–for showing me love isn't something you pin down,
it's something you set free

For when our hearts are open, Providence makes straight our path.

—Unknown

Prologue

"**P**attern making is full of possibilities, an art that includes all shapes and sizes," she whispered, rehearsing the lines from *The Manual* she'd heard her grandfather repeat. "But all patterns, with rare exceptions, are simply different combinations of straight lines and circles." The familiar phrase helped steady her racing heart. Eleanorah quickly gathered her things, bracing herself for the walk toward the front of the bus. Only a few more seconds and she'd be safe.

"Have fun at the factory, Raggedy Ann!" one of the boys from her third-grade class bellowed with glee. "Maybe if you work overtime you can buy some new shoes," the popular girl with perfect blonde hair said, pointing to where the seams from Eleanorah's oversized red rain boots had started coming apart. A chorus of laughter echoed down the aisle.

Eleanorah ignored them as best she could, her fierce amber eyes focused straight ahead, wishing she were invisible.

Freezing rain pummeled the empty parking lot as the school bus sighed and lowered its wheels. Eleanorah pulled her raincoat over her hair and ran toward the shelter of her grandfather's shop. Built in the mid-1980s, just a few years before she was born, it was hardly visible against the overcast skies. Made of steel and tin, the foundry blended in with the various factories nearby, their gray smoke mingling with the clouds. The only thing separating it from the others was the carving of a small tree above the entrance, its tangled roots and branches enclosed in a golden circle that gleamed despite the lack of sunlight.

The door was unlocked but heavy. Eleanorah pushed her way inside with the full weight of her body. Immediately feeling the warmth, her eyes adjusted to the dim light filtering through tall, narrow windows. Particles of dust danced in the air like snowflakes, tickling her nose, carrying the scent of fresh wood shavings.

A low hum stopped in the distance. "*Mo chuisle*, is that you?"

The lyrical words resonated through the shop like a prism of color. Her Grandpa Joseph was the only one who called her that, like a secret language between them. He told her it meant "pulse of my heart" in Gaelic, and that his grandfather used to call him that, too.

"Yes, Grandpa!" Eleanorah followed a trail of chalky footsteps through rows of scattered tools and machinery until she found him hunched over a workbench. His glasses balanced on the tip of his nose, an array of parts and papers strewn about, as if a grand adventure were about to begin.

"There's my favorite granddaughter!" His smile stretched to his earlobes. She ran toward him and he scooped her up, lifting her high above his head. Laughing, she spread her arms wide, as if she had wings.

"How was school?" He set her down gently.

Eleanorah's brow furrowed. She hated her new school and wanted to stay home, like she used to before "The Year of The Explosion," when her dad lost his job and her mom had to go back to work. The first few weeks she'd come home every day, begging her mother to change her mind, and keep homeschooling. Eleanorah tried to explain that the other kids were mean and constantly made fun of her long, red hair, and hand-me-down clothes, something she couldn't change even if she wanted to.

Her grandfather's eyes softened. "Would you like to see what I'm making?" He pulled a small item from his front pocket, brushing the sawdust away with his thumb. "Can you keep a secret?" He lowered his voice for dramatic effect, motioning her closer. "I'm making this for your grandmother's birthday, as a surprise."

A smooth, mahogany heart, carved from two small pieces of wood, rested in his palm. In the middle, where the two halves came together, was a butterfly.

"When it's finished, it's going to be a necklace," he beamed. "Would you like to hold it?"

She nodded, cupping it carefully with tingling fingers. "What kind of butterfly is it?"

"It's a monarch. See?" He tilted the heart in her hands, watching the light catch the gold and orange shimmer of wings. "They're your grandma's favorite. Every spring she waits for them to come back after a long winter."

It was her Grandma Esther who taught Eleanorah the names of the flowers and how to sing to them, too. Like sweet honeysuckle and lavender colored lilacs. Sticky milkweed, meadow sage, verbe-

nas, and bright red zinnias. Her grandfather took care to plant them
every year so that her grandmother, who was bound to a wheelchair,
could watch the bees and butterflies flit from one petal to the next
through the window.

"Where do the monarchs go in the wintertime?" she wondered.

"They fly south to stay warm and hibernate. Did you know they
can fly 50-100 miles in one day? Some of them fly as far as Mexico
to a special forest of oyamel trees."

Eleanorah imagined flying away with them. Maybe there was
somewhere with other kids who looked more like her. A family she
fit in with.

"But...how do they find their way back when it's spring again?"

He paused.

"They listen, I think. To the wind and the currents. To the flight
patterns of their ancestors. The butterflies that fly south in the winter are not the same ones that fly north in the spring. But somehow,
they're connected."

"So the ones that leave never come back?" Her eyes blurred with
tears.

"No," he spoke kindly. "They die and something new is born in
their place."

She rubbed her eyes and gazed into his. A calm blue, like tidal
pools.

"With great love comes great freedom. It's important to remember where we've come from, Ellie. Even if we choose not to go back,"
he said. "The patterns show us who we used to be and who we can
become. That's why I'm giving your grandmother this gift. When

we truly love someone, we must give them wings to fly and trust they will find their way back to us, even if it's in a new form."

She looked again at the butterfly in her hands.

Would she ever have a pair of wings that belonged just to her? Or someone who loved her enough to let her go?

Her grandfather made her feel like anything was possible, but how would she know the way? And what about the rule about not leaving Independence? She'd been taught in Sunday school Missouri was the only safe place to be when the end times came. Her family had given up everything to move to there before she was born. What would they think if she left?

"I tell you what," he said, placing his hands on her shoulders. "I have a few more molds to cast before the shop closes. What do you say we go and get some ice cream before I take you home? You can wait for me in the office and work on your homework until I'm finished. I won't be much longer."

Eleanorah handed the heart back reluctantly.

"Thank you, mo chuisle." He patted her head tenderly, tucking it into his flannel shirt pocket, next to his suspenders.

She backed away slowly until she was far enough away she hoped he wouldn't notice her watching as he brought the patterns to life with each wave of his hand, like an orchestra conductor. Imitating his gestures with frantic waves of her small fingers, pushing and pulling imaginary buttons and levers, it was hard to keep up! Still, she did her best, trying to keep her balance as her body swayed back and forth, listening to the music.

Suddenly, the sing-song of the machinery stopped.

"Ellie."

She froze in place.

"Why don't you wait for me in the office?" Her grandfather prodded, his voice sterner this time. "You can draw another picture of the family tree if you like. I thought the last one you did was really good. I'll be finished soon."

A switch flipped, and the instruments started pulsing again. Eleanorah wandered toward the office, marking a trail through the dusty machines, grazing the tops of cold blades and lifeless steel, imagining the secret combinations that brought them to life. Her grandfather had taught her the names of the materials he used to make molds: resin, fiberglass, wax, and some of the heavy metals. But he hadn't shown her the formulas that made each one come out exactly like the next.

"Ellie, be careful," her grandfather warned, his back still turned. "Best not to play with those. I don't want you getting hurt."

She withdrew her hands and put them in her pockets. *It's not fair,* she thought. *All of the boys in the family know about pattern making. Why not me?* She plopped down behind her grandfather's long desk and listened to the rain hitting the tin roof. It was coming down heavier, now.

Fluorescent bulbs buzzed above her head. She kicked her feet and swiveled the chair, her gaze wandering to a portrait of their family tree on the wall behind the desk. The tree was similar to the symbol outside the door, but unlike the other tree, this one didn't have any roots. The branches—all identical, were uniform and straight. She reached out her hand, watching her reflection mirrored in the glass. *Where did she fit in?*

"Family is a funny thing, Ellie," her grandmother mused whenever she asked why the portrait looked so strange. Something about her grandmother's sadness kept Eleanorah from asking more.

She stared at the tree, her lips pursed tight, trying to keep the questions inside. The branches of the family tree swayed, rustled by an invisible wind. When she closed her eyes, she could almost hear the whisper of leaves, sharing their secrets.

What do you see? they asked.

She squinted at the places where the paint had started to fade. Was it her imagination (she did have an imagination) or were there shadows of absent branches waving, ever so slightly? Eleanorah reached for her colored pencils and a piece of paper, mapping out the missing limbs with a sense of urgency, trying to capture what she saw.

She drew until her wrist hurt, until the colors spilled off the page and onto the desk like overflowing rivers. When she finished, she held the tree in front of her with both hands, looking back and forth between the painting and her drawing. A hot tear ran down her cheek. Her picture looked nothing like the images she saw when she closed her eyes. She wasn't an artist. Not even close.

She bit her lip. If only she could read *The Manual*. If only she knew how to make the molds and follow the patterns like her grandfather. If she could make the machines come to life and prove she belonged, maybe everything else would make sense, too.

Eleanorah ran back toward the rooms full of metal and plastic and glass. Her fingers wrapped around black and white buttons, prodding. "Ouch!" She yelped, yanking her hand free from a small wedge of space where the blades of a saw cut pieces of wood in half. A flap of skin hung loosely over a sharp cut, exposing the tender flesh beneath. Instinctively, she put her finger in her mouth, tasting metal on her tongue for the very first time. Shocked by this discovery, Eleanorah stood mesmerized, immovable.

Her grandfather raced into the room. "Oh, Ellie." He knelt, gazing into her eyes turned snowstorm. "Sometimes our desire to have all the answers can cause us the greatest pain. Don't forget to listen to your heart, too," he whispered. Wrapping her in his arms, he tried to protect her from what was to come. But it was too late.

A crimson drop of blood hit the floor, leaving a rouge stain on the cold cement.

Solitude is the profoundest fact of the human condition. Man is the only being who knows he is alone, and the only one who seeks out another.

—Octavio Paz

1

La soledad

So, this is the place where men become gods. Eleanorah stood on the edge of the uneven platform and shielded her gaze, looking down the steep steps of the Pyramid of the Sun. Her hazel eyes flashed toward the horizon, a spark of rebellion igniting. She wasn't supposed to be here, *but here she was.* The sweat on her face evaporated, leaving salty tributaries running down her cheeks. It was the first day of spring—just a few months away from her twenty-first birthday, but it already felt like mid-July.

A soft breeze blew a piece of crimson hair free from its plaited position on her forehead. In a forest not far, oyamel trees waited for orange and black wings to land among outstretched limbs. Despite the heat, her arms prickled with goosebumps.

When an opportunity presented itself to study in Morelia, the location of the Monarch migration her grandfather told her about all those years ago, an excitement she couldn't explain bubbled to the surface. She was on track to finish nursing school in Chicago, but lately found herself staring through the drawn blinds in the classroom at the loud, bustling city—unable to focus on learning the chemical compounds and sterile, individual parts that were supposed to make a life.

A drumbeat from somewhere in the distance throbbed in her temples, making her dizzy. Its melody swarmed into her consciousness, throwing back the curtains and opening the dusty windows of her heart, unveiling a plethora of color and iridescent prisms; a fragile hope, dancing in the light. She shook her head, certain she was imagining things.

"¿Quieres agua?" A voice interrupted her from the left, near her shoulder.

She turned shyly and reached for the plastic bottle, noticing how their hands slightly touched in the process. "Gracias," she said, grateful for the cool beads of condensation dripping down her fingers.

"Es increíble..." she said, lacking the correct vocabulary to describe the changes taking place inside of her.

Andrés nodded slightly, coffee-brown eyes fixed on the view.

"¿Qué piensas?" He shifted his gaze toward her.

"Hmm?"

"¿En qué piensas Eleanorah?" Andrés asked again, studying her complexion for clues. "Are you thinking of me?" He teased, bringing a warm flush to her cheeks.

She paused to consider him for a moment, secretly admitting she *did* think of him more often than she expected. An international studies major and relative of one of her Spanish teachers, Andrés was hired as their guide for weekend excursions and cultural outings around town. Almost twenty-five, he was four years Eleanorah's senior but had a baby face pocketed with acne scars. Except for his uncanny ability to grow a full, thick beard in half a day, there was little physical evidence he'd matured past the age of fifteen.

Yet, Andrés possessed a calm she was immediately drawn to. When he found out she'd gotten lost walking home one night, he started walking her home every evening, as if it wasn't in the opposite direction of where he lived, pointing out the best *panaderías* on the way, and introducing her to street slang not in any of her textbooks. He was serious, but unlike Eleanorah, he wore a childlike playfulness about his shoulders that readily shook with laughter.

He made her feel like she belonged.

After two months of walking together, her Spanish had improved significantly. She knew her way around the *barrios* better, too. Surprisingly, this hadn't stopped their evening strolls. Convinced at first he was simply doing his job, she came to nervously look forward to the part of the day when they could break apart from the rest of the group and meander past the *parques*, listening for the evening cathedral bells echoing through the city. She told herself they were just friends, but occasionally felt a sharp ache when she thought of returning to Chicago.

"Oh, I don't know. I guess I'm wishing I could stay here forever. There's something about it that makes me feel so alive, even though we're surrounded by all of these tombs. When I'm here, I feel like...like I'm finally free. Like I've been living in this dark room, and suddenly someone turned on all the lights."

Andrés nodded thoughtfully.

"What is your home like, back in the U.S.?"

Eleanorah laughed nervously. "It's...complicated, I guess."

She pictured the old farmhouse where she grew up with her two older brothers. Nestled in a small clearing, she imagined the possibility in her parents' eyes when they drove up the gravel driveway and saw the dilapidated ranch with plenty of space to grow a garden and build a family.

How long did it take before the hope disappeared?

She sighed. "My family is...I don't know, *algo especial*."

She ignored his quizzical smile, waiting for an explanation. She wasn't in the mood to get into all of the details—her struggle to understand a faith rooted in illusion, or the conflict she felt when she finally left Independence.

"It's just...hard. It's easier to be away. Easier to make my own decisions, I guess."

"I think I know what you mean. Parents want us to be a certain way and they have certain...expectations?"

She rolled her eyes. "*Exacto*. My Mom always wanted me to be a nurse but my parents couldn't afford to send me to a four year college. I applied to Loyola without telling them and got a full ride. I figured it was the only way they'd give me permission to really leave home.

"And now I'm here." She shrugged mischievously. It felt good to admit the truth to someone who wouldn't make her feel guilty for it. Andrés smiled, clearly agreeing with her decision.

"Come on, let's go catch up with the rest of the group. We need some more water." She walked toward the edge but paused, eyeing the vertical descent suspiciously.

"It's better if you go this way." He turned backward and started to move down the steps, one at a time. "Here, take my hand. It's okay. We'll take it slow," he promised, noticing the anxious look on her face.

"I'm okay." She sat down stubbornly. "There's not a chance I'm going backwards."

"Como quieras." He withdrew his hand and watched her a few feet above him, making her way alone.

"Come on, *ándale*!" Eleanorah's Spanish professor waved them over hurriedly. "¡Ándale, vamos todos! To the bus!"

Eleanorah took one last hurried look at the pyramids and volcanoes, tuning her ear to the sound of distant rumbling, the spirits of the warriors soaking through her skin. The air-conditioned bus was a welcome relief from the fading heat of the afternoon sun, but she wasn't ready to leave quite yet.

"Do you see those two peaks?" Andrés pointed out the window as they began to move. "They're called Popocatépetl and Iztaccíhuatl. My grandmother used to tell me their story whenever we visited the pyramids. It's an old Aztec legend."

"I don't know it," she admitted, leaning closer to see through the smog.

"Deeply in love," he said, deepening his voice for dramatic effect. "Popo was sent to battle to prove himself worthy of the beautiful princess Izta. But while he was gone, an enemy warrior sent false news of his death in battle. Heartbroken with loss, Izta died from grief, never to see him again."

"Really?" Eleanorah asked. "Was he really all that? I mean, weren't there other warriors she could have married?"

"Of course," he said with a smile. "But that's not the point of the story. Hearing news of his beloved's death," he continued his serious narrative tone, "Popocatepetl climbed to the very top of that mountain you see there, and built the princess a special resting place. Lying down beside her, he swore he'd never leave. Now you see Izta is covered in ice, eternally frozen in time, but Popo can be seen smoking from time to time, protecting his sleeping princess," he finished with a whisper.

"Just so we're clear, I wouldn't wait. Or die from heartbreak." She rolled her eyes, elbowing him playfully.

"No," he said smiling. "I don't think you would."

The sun set behind the sleeping princess and her warrior, darkening them both. Eleanorah leaned back and closed her eyes. Suddenly, she was very tired. The harder she squeezed her lids together, the more bloodshot her eyes became, the heat penetrating.

Hail howled, pummeling the roof and the sliding doors of the basement where she lay next to her mother, reading in bed. Mice ran around freely, in the light, in the dark. Together, they captured one and set it free, drove two miles in the storm to let it out in an empty field. It was free, and alone.

I think the others are searching for it. I think they know something is missing, she wanted to say.

She listened to their incessant squeaking in her pajamas under the covers. They were replaceable, multiplying by the second, but that one mattered. It mattered. The words choked in her throat.

Her mother's suitcase lay open at the end of her bed upstairs but she hadn't slept with Eleanorah's father there in weeks. The clothes were folded neatly, a new toothbrush tucked into one of the pockets. Her hairbrush rested on top.

"I almost didn't come home last night," she confessed, sobbing. "Where is home?" she asked. "Where is my home? Where is it?" Her whole body heaved with grief.

"Mom, mom!" Eleanorah shouted. "It's here, it's right here. You're home, with us." She shook her mother, begging her to wake her up.

"Mom!" Eleanorah cried, barely a whisper above the hum of the air conditioning.

"¿Estás bien?"

Someone was tapping her shoulder. She batted her eyelashes open and looked around. Her sense of smell came back first. Dried sweat. Mango juice. Hand sanitizer. Hair gel. She was holding her knees to her chest, curled in a fetal position, shivering.

It must have been another bad dream. She'd had them as a child, nightmares about snakes crawling on the ceiling, only to wake up to the sound of slithering above her head. *Were they dreams or a memory?*

"I think so," she answered groggily, unfolding her limbs and straightening them out again.

"Are you sure?" Andrés' eyes were full of concern.

"Yeah. Sí," she said, embarrassed that he'd seen her that way. "I'm alright. I must've slept longer than I thought. What time is it? Are we almost back to the hotel?"

"Sí, señorita." His face relaxed. "We're the last ones. Everyone else is already gone, looking for a taqueria for dinner. If we hurry we can join them. Do you want to go?"

She looked around the empty bus gratefully. The driver was the only one still seated toward the front, eyeing them impatiently. "Nah. It might be nice to hang back this time."

"You read my mind. So…" He gestured whimsically. "¿Adonde vamos?"

Street lamps flickered on. Dark green eucalyptus and tall cypress trees lowered themselves with a bow over stone pathways, their branches arching and swaying like the spine of an old man bent toward the inevitable fate of gravity. The city was aged, but not lifeless. Defied, not defeated.

Its landscape was unfamiliar, but she knew it, somehow. The wide avenues and the hum of electricity in the air. The open-air smell of marketplaces where chickens lost their heads, the honeyed fragrance of purple-blooming jacaranda trees. She took it all in, a palette of sounds and sights she painted on her body, invisible tattoos in secret places only she could recall.

The streets were full, yet not crowded. *"Andar en la calle"* was a favorite Mexican pastime that had no purpose or intention other than walking casually in the open streets at leisure. When Eleanorah first arrived, she didn't understand the concept at all. Where was everybody going? Why were they walking so slowly? Why didn't anybody want to take a car anywhere to get around? It took her several weeks to adjust to the carefree cadence.

"¿Quieres que nos sentemos un rato?"

"Sure," Eleanorah said, realizing they had been walking for some time in silence.

Andrés pointed to a park bench under the soft light of a warm street lamp and took a deep breath. "I have a question, something I need to ask you." His dark eyes blended in with the evening's shadows.

Maybe he could feel it, too. A growing nervousness; a feeling she'd been trying to ignore for several weeks every time they were alone together.

Eleanorah waited, afraid to speak.

"You know we wear each other well," he began. "I feel like I can be myself with you."

She met his gaze hesitatingly.

"I think you're beautiful, you know. You're special. Do you know that? There's something about you that catches my attention. I can't explain it." He paused and reached for her clammy hand.

"I want to be more than friends."

A single, monotonous beat thundered in the lull between words. Broad, colorful feathers waved a sweet, smoke perfume through the expectant air. A warrior's cry rose, and fell on the breeze. The sound rang in her ears. The rhythm of bare feet hitting the ground mirrored the pounding in her heart.

Andrés squeezed her fingers gently, bringing her back to the elongated pause, the unanswered question between them. Eleanorah wanted to say yes. She wanted to let herself relax into his arms, into the space he was trying to bridge so carefully between them. Something held her back.

"If you want to stay friends, I understand," he spoke quietly. "We can still take coffee together, we can still go to the movies. I'll still walk you home every night. Nothing has to change if you don't want it to," he said with enough sincerity she believed him.

"Okay, I'll think about it." Only two months remained of her time in Morelia. She couldn't think of spending it with anyone other than him. But what did it mean for her future?

The drums grew louder.

"You will?" His voice carried such a note of optimism she couldn't help but blush. He let go of her hand and stood up, only to offer it again. "Do you want to go see the dancers?"

"Is that what that is?" She was distracted, maybe from the noise, the butterflies in her stomach, the heat of the day. "Yes, let's do it. I'd like to see the Zócalo at night."

"As you wish, señorita." The dark beard covering his mouth never quite succeeded in hiding his smile.

They made a turn down a narrow street and suddenly the wide, ancient plaza opened up before them. To their right was the National Palace, a fortress built on the destruction of the Aztec empire, evidence of its existence still there—gray and black bits of rubble excavated reluctantly beneath centuries of forgetting.

They'd visited remnants of the Templo Mayor earlier at high noon when the sunlight was stern and the Zócalo had an atmosphere of officiality about it. Soldiers marched in and out of its corridors, and tourists moved in a swarm-like fashion, eager to see the murals painted by Diego Rivera in the arches of the main patio.

Now, however, the plaza had a completely different feeling. It was softer, less stout, and strict. Whatever spirit lay dormant in the heat of the day rose slowly, rippling in the moonlight. *Concheros* huddled together in tight circles along the dark edges of the street. Drums beat, not in unison, but not separately either. Shells clanked and clattered as bare feet rose and fell against the asphalt.

It was as if they'd traveled back in time. As if history were no longer a statement of chronological events, linear, and fixed. Rather, a thin, waving veil that could be lifted and moved aside.

Or, left hanging in place, impenetrable.

***

Eleanorah could not sleep. She tossed and turned in the hotel room in Mexico City, thinking of Andrés and his unanswered question. Back in her own bed in Morelia, the insomnia continued.

The neighbor's dog barked incessantly. The air outside barely stirred the transparent, floor-length curtains hanging over the open window. She stared at the magnificently painted burnt orange walls, turned black in the absence of light.

Rummaging through her belongings, she pulled out a stack of photographs from home. There was a picture of her parents on Valentine's Day from maybe twenty years ago, she guessed by her mother's large-framed glasses, and big curls that kissed her cheeks. She was wearing a red jumper, sitting on her father's knee by the fireplace. It was one of Eleanorah's favorites because they both looked so happy.

Another one showed them posing with Laurel, the Australian shepherd that was a Christmas gift from her father to her mother the year before Eleanorah was born. Their faces glowed, and they showed all their teeth. But their smiles were alien to her.

Eleanorah felt her eyes brim with tears. She wanted to warn them somehow. Ask them to try harder. Stop them from what was coming, protect them.

Was it a lie then? Was it now? If the ending is predetermined, was the beginning something to avoid?

They were still together, if you could call it that. But her mother would leave. Eleanorah grew up in the shadow of this knowing; the question wasn't really *if*, it was *when*.

The dog stopped barking. She put the photos away and took a freshly folded towel out of the armoire. She opened the bathroom door and turned on the light. The tile and walls were orange, just like her bedroom. The water in the shower ran cold with a brief interlude of heat Eleanorah had learned to time perfectly. She let it run for a few moments and undressed, shivering.

The water was what she needed. It rushed over her like a permission slip. She carefully unbraided her long hair and sat on the wet tile, letting it fall freely down her back until all the heat was gone, and her whole body shook with sobs.

***

"Ellie, is that you?" Her mother's voice was interrupted by static.

She didn't know whether to laugh or cry with relief. The first three times she called home, an annoyingly cheery voice came on the line, repeating that the call could not be completed. The fourth time, a dull, disconnected tone rang ambivalently in her ear.

"Hi, Mom." Her voice quivered.

She'd used up all but eighteen minutes on the international calling card her school sold for twenty pesos each. A list of smells and sights and sounds clicked through her mind like slides on a broken projector. They were too fast and too fragmented to form into words. She didn't know what to say. There wasn't enough time.

The noise of laughter echoed distantly in the background. "We're having a party for your Aunt's birthday," her mother explained. "How are you? I tried calling your house all day yesterday and couldn't get through. I've been so worried!"

"I'm okay. Feeling a little homesick today," she admitted.

"Well, you're more than halfway through, right?"

Eleanorah flinched.

"How are your classes? Do you like your host family? What have you been doing when you're not in school?" Her mother raced through the checklist eagerly.

"My classes are okay. I like some of them more than others, but I really like our conversation class and the fieldtrips we take. We went to Mexico City last weekend. It was just, so incredible.

"And my parents are actually really lovely," she said, smiling. "I wish you could meet them. Maru is the best cook and Antonio is always egging me on to try the hottest peppers. He thinks it's funny when my face turns red. He's always telling me I need a Mexican boyfriend." Her heart fluttered nervously.

"Hmmm...So what do you do when you're not in class?"

"Well," Eleanorah said, hesitating. "We go out to different street cafés or restaurants. We walk around *el centro* a lot, by the cathedral. Andrés has been taking us to all the *fútbol* matches, which is really fun. On weekends we've been going to different cities with Professor Sofía, but she left last week to go back to Chicago, so we're more on our own now. Sometimes the girls and I go dancing together and practice our salsa lessons."

"I see."

Eleanorah could tell from her tone that her mother was biting her lip.

She let out a slow exhale. "Be very careful, Ellie. You're not drinking when you go out, are you?"

Eleanorah glanced at the bottle of watermelon-flavored Bacardi on her dresser and considered her options. She thought of the piña coladas, the countless rum and cokes. The tall, light-colored cervezas they drank at the soccer games, *dos por uno*. It did not take long for her to learn what she liked. The sweetness of the piña, and the strawberry daiquiris. The lime and salt of the margaritas. Indios and Modelos in glass bottles but not Sol and *never* Corona.

She was the youngest in the group and had something to prove. Besides, she loved to dance—to salsa, old pop hits, and a new kind of music she was learning called *reggaeton*. She wasn't good at it, just like she wasn't necessarily good at drinking, either. But she didn't need to be. The boys she danced with were experts at guiding her hips, twirling, kissing, and picking up the tab.

"Ellie? Are you still there?"

She could lie. She could say she hadn't had a drop of alcohol the whole time. But why should she? It was legal here. She was almost twenty-one and a junior in college. She wasn't living under her parents' roof anymore, why should she have to follow their ridiculous rules?

"You're not trustworthy." "You're a rotten egg." "You're disobedient!" Her mother's angry accusations rattled through her memory, filling the silence.

Whenever her father wasn't around, her mother hurled all of her fury and Eleanorah against the wall, like a hurricane. Wading deep into a pool of helplessness, her mother reached for anything she could wrap her hands around to keep her afloat. Everything but a life raft.

Over time, Eleanorah learned to absorb her mother's pain like a coral reef in polluted water, growing algae in her hair and layers of fat around her middle. She'd accepted her mother's resentment, collecting it in her own chest, hoping it would finally make her happy. It didn't.

She took a deep breath.

"Yes, I am. And I'm not sorry about it," she added, stubbornly.

Of all the incredible experiences she was having—everything she was learning and seeing and doing, she was naive to think her mother would be proud. Of course, she would pick up on the one thing Eleanorah was doing that she disapproved of and make a big deal about it. All she wanted was to tell her about Andrés, to ask her advice, to cry, admit she was homesick, and experience her mother's comfort.

"Well, you should be sorry about it. That's not how I raised you, Eleanorah. Your father and I are very worried. I had a feeling you were getting carried away but of course, he didn't believe me.

"I convinced him we should visit during your Spring Break. We already applied to get our passports renewed. I think you need some extra parental support," she said, tersely.

"You mean supervision." Eleanorah's temper flared.

The phone started beeping.

"Well, I don't think it would hurt. You're supposed to take summer classes when you get back, so you'll still graduate on time for nursing school. Do you think you'll be able to study pathophysiology properly if you're drinking all summer? You might be of legal age in Mexico, but you're not here."

"Mom!"

The beeping was more frequent now.

"This is something you've been working so hard for. Have you even thought about your nursing classes? We've come too far for you to risk it all on a boy and drinking."

"I'm not risking anything! I'm old enough to make my own choices, and I don't want you or Dad coming to visit. I've already made other plans with my friends for Spring Break. I won't even be in Morelia.

"Mom?"

The dull sound of a dial tone broke the silence.

Eleanorah hung up the phone and sat very still. Voices from downstairs floated up the spiral staircase. It smelled like *frijoles* and *pollo*. In a few minutes, the doorbell would ring, and she'd hear Andrés ask Antonio for her by name. In a few minutes, they'd step outside together, a world away from her mother.

She hung up the phone and decided she would be free as long as she could.

***

The doorbell rang at exactly 7:58 p.m., surprisingly punctual for a culture with no way of saying, "Hurry up!" Whose romantic language allowed for things like blaming the keys for losing themselves, the vase for breaking itself, and in general, reflected a more forgiving light than someone like Eleanorah was used to.

Yet, for all the occasions Andrés had walked from his house by el centro toward Eleanorah's, just so they could walk back to the square together, he had always been on time. It was one of many things she appreciated about him.

"¡Qué le vaya bien!" Antonio ushered the young couple outside with a wave, his mustache curled in an upward smile.

"¿Hola, cómo estás?" Andrés kissed her lightly on the cheek.

"Hmm, *más o menos bien*." She wished her hand wasn't so sweaty but pressed it into his anyway.

"¿Qué pasó? Veo que estás, inquieta?" His eyes studied her face that way that he did. Not probing, not quite searching. More like a patient knowing.

"Yeah." She looked at the brightly painted houses as they passed, colors she'd never see back home. Tangerine and lemon. Turquoise and dark green.

"I got into a sort of fight with my mom," she admitted. "She asked me if I'd been drinking, and I told her the truth."

"Ah, mi Izta." He placed his hand on the small of her back and guided her across the street, moving the weight of her book bag full of journals and travel guides off her shoulders and onto his.

She felt herself melt toward him, the way she had when her grandfather called her "mo chuisle." It was incredible how a simple nickname or term of endearment could change everything. Here, being Itza meant she was part of the landscape, a fable woven into the fabric of their shared understanding. At home, it meant she was connected to a past through the fragile threads of language, and family.

"She's worried about my summer classes and getting off track for nursing school. I think she's disappointed in me." Eleanorah looked away to keep the tears from falling.

"I see," he said, a hint of recognition in his eyes. "It's normal for parents to be worried. Did you tell her I'm watching out for you?"

Eleanorah's pale cheeks reddened, remembering the first night out they'd had as a group, dancing well into the morning. She'd been enjoying the company of a boy whose name she couldn't remember, her friends dragging her away under protest. The next day, she found out Andrés had been the one to pick up the tab they'd all forgotten, a first impression she still regretted making.

"No, the time on my card ran out before I had the chance."

The pressure around her waist went slack, and she noticed Andrés's jaw tighten slightly.

"Have you decided if you're going to come with us to Chiapas?" She asked, changing the subject.

"No, not yet. My family is going to *la playa* with *mis primos*. We go every year around Semana Santa."

Her heart sank. "That sounds fun!" She tried to hide her disappointment as they walked along the beautifully arched aqueducts leading them toward her favorite part of the city. Following Avenida Morelos, the wide street opened up into a plaza with the pink, colonial cathedral at its center, its two towers tall enough to be seen from any point in Morelia.

In a few moments, they'd meet their friends at Café Europa, a bohemian spot full of students and expats watching fútbol matches and drinking *micheladas* they'd claimed as their own while trying on their new vocabulary and identities, eating a piece of decadent chocolate cake, and smoking a cigarette or sipping delicate cups of espresso. Eleanorah wondered at the familiarity of it all, how in a few weeks' time, they'd formed routines and habits she could have never dreamed of.

Andrés located the group first and moved to greet them each with the customary kiss on the cheek. Eleanorah followed after him, excited to plan their trip. Now that Professor Sofía was back in Chicago, they had a little more freedom to explore on their own, a chance Eleanorah wanted to take full advantage of. "We were just starting to look at our route." Bella, a sweet, blonde-haired girl from

Wisconsin scooted over so they could slide into the booth next to the window.

"We're trying to decide if we have time to go to Oaxaca or not." Esteban wiped his glasses on his shirt and took a sip from a tall glass of light-colored beer.

"Oooh, I'd love to visit Oaxaca. Isn't it close to Guatemala?"

"Sí, es" Andrés nodded, pointing to the wrinkled map on the table. "What's the plan so far?"

"Well, if we start in Morelia, and head south, we'll pass through D.F. Then we can veer east, toward the coast, and pass through Puebla before we stop in Veracruz, where we thought we'd spend a day at the beach," Bella said, consulting her notes. "Then, we're thinking of heading south to Chiapas to visit San Cristóbal de las Casas, Palenque, and Las Aguas Azules," she concluded.

"That sounds amazing." Eleanorah gave Andrés an encouraging, sideways glance.

"Have you decided if you're coming, man? It'd be great to have you along, you know. Just in case we get into any trouble with your *compadres,*" Juan, dressed in his usual Celtics jersey and basketball shorts, said jokingly.

Andrés thumbed through the guidebook with a grin. "You've done a good job planning it."

Eleanorah nodded and elbowed him playfully. "What did you tell me your mom is always saying about traveling?"

"Ah. *Se dice: 'Antes de que viajes por otro país, conoce tu patria.'* Before you visit another country, get to know your homeland."

"I like that." Esteban raised his almost empty glass. "Cheers to getting to know Mexico!"

"¡Por Mexico!"

They drank in unison, licking light foam from their smiling lips.

***

"¿Tienes frio?" He moved closer so that their shoulders touched.

She shivered involuntarily. "No, I'm just excited about our road trip! I'm glad you decided to come."

"Me, too."

It was just before midnight. The evening had a balmy quality about it, as if they were floating on a gentle sea breeze. Their feet led the way easily while they talked, gesturing with their hands, bumping into each other, adding to the hum of the air, letting off little sparks of electricity.

Before she realized it, they were in front of her house.

"Buenas noches." He leaned in slightly to kiss her on the cheek.

Before she could think, Eleanorah turned toward him so that he grazed her lips, instead. Surprised, he moved back and started to apologize. She dropped her keys, pulling him closer.

"I want to be more than friends, too," she said.

Andrés didn't respond. Pressing his body into hers, he walked them slowly back against the wall. Cupping her face in both hands, he kissed her insistently, biting her lower lip as he exhaled. She returned his kiss earnestly, placing her hands in the back pockets of his jeans, tugging him toward her so there was no more distance between them.

"Por fin," he whispered.

***

The rented gray minivan bumped along curves and potholes, lurching up and down mountains covered with a deep, green chlorophyll. Eleanorah noticed how the steep ridges pulled in heat from the coastline, dancing with the hazy fog as the sun set between their peaks. Encouraged by the fading light, the steam rose and shifted into the valleys, giving off a low hiss she couldn't quite translate.

They followed a southern route outlined by Bella's red ink pen, trailing the path of the conquistadores like bloodhounds, chasing their own scent. *Where were the fallen?* Their innocent eyes scanned the horizon for proof, for pardon.

They saw ghosts in the congestion of El Distrito Federal, heard drumming feet marching to awaken the dead. In the twilight of broken temples and closed palaces, they tiptoed through history, pupils dilated wide to let in the light. It was murky.

They waded in further, the moonlight cast shadows of depth they couldn't perceive the first time they visited. The buried vessels beneath their feet were clay jars full of islands and waterways, canals, and fury, waiting to burst. Crushed vertebrae are meant to stand tall; Eleanorah straightened her posture and tried to make up the difference.

In Veracruz, they toured apparitions still wearing abandoned chains decorating the dungeons of San Juan Ulúa. The damp cell walls trickled with revolt. In humid hallways, the whipped ocean breeze stamped its harrowed warning on their youthful naivety. Her strength wavered.

In San Cristobal, they asked for penance, surrounded by children of the *muertos* and *desaparecidos,* begging for tokens. Like corruptible saints, they handed out *curaciónes* with nervous laughter, offering the empty-handed ignorance of their adolescence, with the best of intentions.

The van jerked suddenly on its descent down the mountain, slowing nauseatingly as it passed over another speed bump. Eleanorah closed her eyes, trying to steady her stomach. There was one about every kilometer now, making it impossible to traverse the switchbacks in any hurry.

"Sorry guys." Esteban apologized from the driver's seat, pressing his foot on the gas again.

They were in the state of Chiapas now, on their way to Palenque. The landscape was beautiful, but there was a haunting quality about it. Eleanorah moved nervously in her seat, trying to ease the cramped, disgruntled feeling of the last few hours.

Juan put a Red Hot Chili Peppers' CD in the player and turned up the volume, belting along. It was day three of their adventure, and he was still wearing the same jersey and basketball shorts from the first day, which annoyed Eleanorah more than she wanted to admit. Bella took up the middle seat, assembling peanut butter and jelly sandwiches for lunch. Andrés and Eleanorah sat in the back, sprawled out as much as the confined space would allow.

"Quieres café?" Andrés handed her a lukewarm styrofoam cup of coffee. "I had Juan get some for us earlier. I didn't want to wake you."

She took it gratefully. The past few days had been a lot. Andrés was even more attentive than usual and they'd hardly had a moment when they weren't together. She wasn't used to the closeness; it was easy to confuse intimacy for claustrophobia. She was learning to accept his affection but couldn't quite keep herself from looking for an escape route, just in case.

Suddenly, the brakes squealed. Coffee sloshed over the cup and onto her lap as she reached instinctively toward the middle seat, bracing herself. "What the....?" Juan turned the music down.

Esteban remained silent in the driver's seat and kept his foot on the brakes, looking straight ahead at the road in front of them. A large, thick rope blocked their passage, held in place by a band of women with babies on their backs and baskets in their hands. A few of them stood resolutely at each end while the others swarmed the van, knocking on the windows.

The van rocked back and forth as they pushed up against the doors. Dressed in long skirts and colorful blouses tucked in at the waist, they motioned to their handmade tortillas, their turquoise jewelry, their separation, and asked for a price.

Some of them had ribbons in their hair, others, strands of gray pulled back in a low bun with wisps of coal black stuck to their determined faces. A few of them wore red handkerchiefs around their necks, tied in a triangle so that they hung down to meet the collar of their shirts.

They surrounded them, demanding compensation.

Andrés leaned forward. "Roll down your window and give them some of this," he advised.

Juan took the crumpled pesos, watching the women in a state of shock.

"Here, let me do it." Esteban grabbed the bills. "Hola, we'll uh, take a few waters," he stuttered in Spanish.

The woman closest to him signaled to another carrying a basket of perspiring, plastic water bottles. She counted out five and waited. Bella put more money in Esteban's hands, and the woman nodded again. As soon as they took the water, the rope lifted from the grill of their van, disappearing as quickly as it came.

Eleanorah watched the women recede into a borderless landscape. The van regained its speed slowly, eyes trained toward the thick jungle interspersed with cleared land and spotted cows. Reaching out her hand, she pressed her fingers against the window. It seemed as if they were part of a painting, only she was the one stuck behind the glass.

"I bet those women were Zapatistas," she mused out loud.

"I think you're right. Or at least their husbands are. What do you know about the Zapatistas?" Andrés asked, curiously.

Everything Eleanorah knew about the rebels and Subcomandante Marcos she'd learned from her Mexican History class, in Chicago. Seated in a small room in a brick building with artificial lights, she'd read his speech declaring war on the Mexican government.

Focusing with difficulty, she'd highlighted the following in her thick textbook:

"We are a product of 500 years of struggle...but today we say, ¡Ya basta! ENOUGH IS ENOUGH."

The black and white photo accompanying this declaration showed a young-looking man with dark eyes. He wore a beret and a cloth mask that covered his mouth and nose with a hole just large enough to smoke a pipe, which he was never without.

"The uprising started the same day the North American Free Trade Agreement was signed, on January 1, 1994," her professor explained. "It was called the 'Act of Freedom' by the Clinton Administration."

Unfortunately, it was mislabeled. There were contingencies, she learned. Cheaper, subsidized corn from the U.S. flooded the Mexican market, and indigenous farmers with small land holdings who cultivated maíz and depended on it for their subsistence could not compete. They could neither sell their native corn nor afford to buy the imported version. Lacking their traditional way of earning a living, the cartels took advantage, offering, and then demanding that they cultivate a different kind of crop.

Subcomandante Marcos insisted it was a warrant of death for his people.

Eleanorah could still feel the current of power and urgency in his message. *Enough already.* There is enough, and we want our portion. We want peace and food for our children. We want the kind of freedom that doesn't starve our souls and steal our livelihood.

Enough is enough.

It circulated through her again now, raising the small hairs on her arms, searching for an outlet for a grief she could not claim as her own but felt in the back of her eyeballs. Like the way a photograph used to leave a burned image imprinted in the optic nerves of the photographer.

FLASH! It's there. FLASH! They're gone.

"We didn't go to war to kill or be killed." She heard the crackling recording of his radio address through gritted teeth and a clenched fist. "We went to war in order to be heard...The dispossessed, we are millions, and thereby call upon our brothers and sisters to join this struggle as the only path, so that we will not die. After decades of oppression, today we say, *ya basta*!"

His words unlocked a secret combination and set her feet in search of reclamation. Her heart became a battle cry, rallying the shadowed places within, still afraid of too much light.

"I know they're a group of rebels that live in this area, mostly in Chiapas," Eleanorah answered Andrés, trying to formulate her words carefully. "They took their name from Emiliano Zapata in honor of what he stood for during the Mexican Revolution."

"¡Tierra y libertad!" Andrés quoted, looking out the window at the setting sun.

"Yeah. 'Give me liberty, or give me death,'" she said, thoughtfully.

There was a cost to freedom, one she wasn't sure she was ready to pay. Until now, she'd cautiously retreated from her own dreams, choosing instead what she thought she could control. Studying life instead of living it with both feet on the muddy ground—shouting, running, muscles aching, alive.

Freedom or restraint? Either way she chose, there was a leave-taking.

She rested her head back on Andrés' sturdy shoulder, wondering if he felt like her, looking from the outside in. He returned the gesture. A heaviness between them that wasn't there before started to grow.

The revolution had begun.

***

They arrived in the outskirts of Palenque by nightfall, the way marked by statues of jaguars and large stone heads from the Olmec civilization, missing their bodies. It gave Eleanorah an uncanny feeling, like the echoes of phantom branches from her family tree. The roads were smaller and more narrow now, and the jungle encroached upon them on all sides, demanding more space, more life.

"There's a place with cabañas a few miles ahead," Bella advised. It's gotten good ratings. I say we check it out and stop for the night."

The cabañas were hut-like rooms with tall ceilings and a tarpaulin roof, one for Eleanorah and Bella, the other for the boys. Torches punctuated the dark sky with smoky, orange light. They unpacked their things and walked down the path to the small bar with a few round tables and chairs, thick vines, and twisted tree trunks framing its entrance.

Drawing closer, they saw men and women dancing topless, swirling through rings of fire, weaving in and out of the flames with confidence, their bare feet stepping lightly on the earth. Eleanorah squeezed Andrés' hand and let it go, moving toward one of the tables close to the edge of the circle. The fire dancers' energy was magnetic. Their graceful, risky movements pulled her in, answering a question she didn't know she'd been asking.

"¿Do you want something to drink, señorita?"

"¿Señorita?"

She looked at the menu, shaking her head several times to focus. "I'll have your coffee with Kahlua. Gracias," she responded apologetically.

"¿Estás bien?" Andrés asked, worriedly. "You've been a little off since this afternoon."

"Sí, claro," she replied, annoyed at the interruption.

A new performer ignited a hoop and jumped through the flames with an elegance Eleanorah could not imagine. She observed his tan torso, highlighted by the shadows and fire. He turned to meet her gaze, balancing the hoop above his head, his cool, black eyes steady, reflecting the light.

Tell me, my love. What do you see?

Eleanorah looked around, turning toward Andrés to see if it was his voice in her ear. But he was talking to someone at the table next to them, laughing in Spanish. Esteban and Juan were at the bar, ordering more drinks. Bella had gone to the bathroom. She focused again on the figure with fire. He seemed farther away now, like an evaporating heat, dissipating slowly until it was gone.

What do you see? The words faded but were still distinct.

FLASH! It's there. FLASH! They're gone.

She took a sip of her coffee and closed her eyes, letting the aroma fill her nostrils. The branches of the tree waved, and whispered in the night. She didn't know what she saw, except that she did.

The last of the poi dancers extinguished their flames, blanketing the air in an enchanted darkness. Eleanorah and Andrés left their empty glasses on the table and walked slowly toward the cabaña, hanging back from the rest of the group like usual.

"¿Realmente me quieres?" Andrés pulled her back into the shadows, just before they reached the doorway.

"What?"

"Do you really love me?" His eyes contained an expression of anger Eleanorah had never seen before.

"Yes, of course. I love you." Her tongue stumbled, the weight of the syllables shifting from the roof of her mouth to the whisper of her lips, struggling with the accent. But it was true. She knew it the moment she said it. She did love him.

He looked away. "I saw you watching that guy all night." His voice trembled.

She stared at him, confused.

"You know who I'm talking about. The fire dancer. You couldn't take your eyes off of him."

She blushed unwillingly. He was right. But it was more than his attractiveness that stirred her. It was something deeper, something she couldn't put into words but had felt ever since she stood on top of the Temple of the Sun.

At first, she thought it was Andrés. Her experiences in Mexico were entangled with her feelings for him. Love for one only increased the other. But after tonight, she had a growing suspicion it was something more.

"Andy," she said, taking a chance and using a name only she could get away with calling him. "I love you. I didn't mean it. Really, I didn't."

The line in his jaw softened. He searched her eyes for signs of betrayal. She stared back, wordlessly offering all the reassurance she could muster.

"I'm sorry, I was wrong. ¿Me perdonas?" he asked, relaxing into her embrace, resting his chin on her shoulder.

She pulled away just enough to press their noses together.

"Of course, always."

"Thank you. You are my ice maiden, my Izta," he whispered, brushing the top of her forehead tenderly with his lips.

But she was a volcano.

***

They stood outside the pale orange door, facing each other in silence, a gloom settling over them. Their walk to her house was sluggish, the stubbornness of their feet longing to prolong the inevitable. The day before, Andrés had looked for her all over the city, as if she were already gone.

Tracing the usual patterns of their rambling, he searched for her in the upstairs room of Café Europa, stopping by the school where she studied Octavio Paz and post-modern Spanish literature. He'd peered into rooms at La Cruz Roja, where she helped doctors care for crying babies, and stitch gaping wounds. But *las enfermeras* simply shook their heads. She was not there.

"If that's not love, I don't know what is," he confided when he finally found her on the way home from an errand.

Or, 'If that's not love, I don't know what it is.' She toyed with the discrete translation of this sentence over, and over. *Which one did he mean?*

Their time was running out. The moment she'd been avoiding since she arrived in Morelia four months ago was here. It was the last time he would walk her home in his worn, Puma tennis shoes and Cubs baseball cap. The last time she'd pick out his sing-song whistle in a crowd and know it was for her.

"I bought a one-way ticket to Chicago." He squeezed her hand. "I have an aunt there and some family. I have some things to finish up here, my thesis to turn in, but..."

Her eyes widened.

"It's not the end," he murmured, kissing her passionately. "It's just a pause. I'll visit you in Chicago, *te prometo*. I have an American passport, I can stay as long as I want," he added earnestly.

"It's just a pause," Eleanorah repeated, slipping her hands underneath his shirt to feel the warmth of his skin, breathing him in as deeply as she could without letting a sob break loose.

"Let's go upstairs." He nodded to her bedroom window, holding her face in both hands, kissing her lips and her neck, slowly making his way down to the top of her shoulder.

She returned his kiss and then pulled away.

Her desire had rules. She reached for him through a caged heart, wanting him near, and fearing it at the same time. "I'm sorry, we can't. My parents..." She glanced up toward their bedroom, across the hall from hers.

It was half an alibi.

"Entiendo." He kissed her on the cheek. "I've wanted you since that night in Palenque," he admitted. "And I won't stop."

Eleanorah considered the unspoken possibility. Bella and some others were spending the rest of the summer in Mexico, easily extending their student visas another ninety days. She could, too.

"I'm sorry, I have to go." she said, looking down at her feet.

He pulled her close, caressing her cheek one last time. "Goodnight *mi amor. Hasta pronto,"* he vowed, taking her in one last time before turning away.

Eleanorah didn't wait to see him walk alone down the sidewalk, looking over his shoulder toward the girl he loved. She didn't see him stand on the curb before willing his feet to cross the street, out of sight. Her hand was already on the knob, the keys in the door, racing to get to the other side to feel some relief, to put space between them before it was too late.

It was too late. She sank onto the cold tile floor, knees to her chest, back against the closed door. As hard as she tried, she could not control the tide of tears forming saltwater scars on fragile skin.

***

Eleanorah gripped the steering wheel tightly, caffeine pulsing through her veins. She barely remembered the taxi ride to the international airport, or telling Maru and Antonio goodbye, less than twenty-four hours ago. By the time her alarm went off at 5:30 a.m. for her early departure, she'd only slept a few hours, tossing, and turning, replaying her fumbled farewell with Andrés.

What made her go when all she wanted to do was stay?

Swaths of purple clover she couldn't see in the dark dotted empty fields waiting to be planted with corn, a familiar landscape, and yet forlorn at the same time. She'd landed at O'Hare just in time to pick up their family's old rusty blue station wagon she'd inherited, making the overnight drive through the plains of Illinois and Iowa, finally crossing into Missouri. She was still hundreds of miles from home, even farther from where she wanted to be.

When her father first asked her to come with them on their family road trip to Colorado before her summer classes began, she refused. She wanted to be in Chicago as soon as possible, waiting for Andrés. Or, even better, still in Morelia by his side. The thought of driving through the entire state of Kansas, trapped in a car with her family after the freedom she experienced in Mexico, made her want to run in the opposite direction.

Eleanorah sighed and looked out the window, forced to slow down through a one-stoplight town. The beginning of summer always brought bittersweet waves of nostalgia—of a childhood chasing fireflies with her brothers in the backyard, the lingering scent of fireworks in the sky on her birthday, the cacophony of cicadas in late summer, and swarms of June bugs darting around the porch light, sometimes landing in her long, reddish hair.

It was easy to get lost in time and space. The black pavement mirrored the midnight sky, stretched like a canvas with holes where the light fell through. A Red Hot Chili Peppers song came on the radio. She rolled down the window and turned up the volume, her voice rising with the lead singer, the wind pressing against her fingers more forcefully the faster she drove. In the dark, it took little effort to imagine she was still in Chiapas, careening through the hills, her friends in the front seat, singing along.

The slow crunch of the gravel driveway brought her back into her body. A yawning sunrise kissed puffy, gray clouds with a red tinge, like a pale woman splashing a bright streak of rouge across her cheek. The sugar maple in the front yard was putting on leaves, partially hiding the white farmhouse with peeling paint and sideways shutters.

Eleanorah removed her seat belt with shaking hands. It was unseasonably cool. Smoke from the chimney meant there was a fire in the fireplace, likely started by her father the night before. She tiptoed inside and made her way to the worn couch facing the warmth from the stove, finally closing her eyes.

Her mother's voice woke her after what seemed like days. "Ellie, it's time to go, honey. Why didn't you tell us when you got home? We were worried all night," she scolded.

"I'm sorry, I just got in early this morning. I didn't want to wake you. What time is it now?"

"It's already 9:30." She clucked her tongue. "Your father just finished packing the car. Are your bags ready?"

"Yeah, they're still in my car," Eleanorah said, resting her head back on the pillow.

"We're all together again, we're here, we're here. We're all together again, we're here, we're here...!" Her father's cheerful singing came from the kitchen. "Good morning Pumpkin! Are you ready?" His face appeared above hers, shining.

Eleanorah winced. His exuberance made her angry without knowing why.

"Maybe I should just stay here, you guys go ahead. I'm so tired..." her voice shook unwillingly.

"I know you're tired, Ellie." Her dad sobered. "But you can sleep in the car on the way. Once we get there you'll feel better. It won't be the same without you." He sat down, waiting patiently until she opened her eyes again.

"Please come? For me?"

His gentle encouragement was enough to change her mind. They'd always had a soft spot for each other. She was the youngest and only daughter—when she and her mother inevitably got into it, he'd always tried to make up the difference.

"Okay." She sat up, slowly. "Alright, Dad. I'll come."

"Hooray!" Her brothers cheered from the kitchen, raiding the fridge one last time before piling into the cargo van, arms full of snacks and tangled headphones for the ride.

It wasn't until she left home for college that they started paying her more attention, sending letters with a few dollar bills tucked inside or drawing funny cartoons that made her laugh. They'd both chosen to stay home and work in her grandfather's pattern shop, learning the new computerized modeling systems that were taking over the industry, but she sensed they were proud of her for leaving.

"Missed ya, sis!" Micah, her middle brother, ruffled her hair affectionately before climbing into the backseat.

"Missed you too." She glanced back before folding her pillow against the window. She wished her brothers would ask about her time in Mexico or take their headphones off long enough to notice she was not okay.

In the front, her parents crooned along with John Denver too loudly, speeding through the prairie on a reverse pilgrimage to the mountains. Eleanorah watched as sunflowers strained their necks toward the noonday sun. The paved roads covered wagon ruts and westward trails littered with dreams and possibilities. The worn highways were as familiar as the lines across their palms; a thrown rope connected to a life raft when they were almost always drowning.

The wide open sky invited space for unanswered questions, its cloudless, piercing blue refusing to shelter her burgeoning uncertainty. For years, Eleanorah wondered why they couldn't return to Colorado permanently. Truthfully, the small grouping of cabins they rented near the White River with her grandparents and cousins felt more like home. The fresh air smelled of sage and gutted fish and clear mountain streams. It wasn't thick and humid, like in the Midwest. It didn't stink of cows or hay or stagnant, moss-covered ponds. It didn't hiss and pop, and crowd one's thoughts with chaotic sounds, hard to distinguish one from the other.

She resented her parents for staying in Missouri. By the time Eleanorah was born, her entire extended family, and hundreds of others had relocated to Independence, believing it was where Jesus would make his triumphant second coming. The New Jerusalem, or *Zion,* was supposed to be a land of milk and honey, according to the earliest prophet of their church. It was the promised antidote to all of their earthly problems, a future utopia meant just for them.

All they had to do was get there.

That was over twenty-five years ago and nothing had happened. Except for a downturn in business at the pattern shop, her parents' constant fighting about money, and her brothers' sweeping avoidance of anything that might cause additional conflict. At this point, their faith was the only thing holding them together. Once it fully unraveled...

Eleanorah rolled down the window and took huge, gaping breaths. The music was too loud. They were going too fast.

"Dad. Dad! I changed my mind. I don't want to go. Please. Please, can you take me back? I can't do this."

"Eleanorah Violet, what in the world is going on?" Her mother turned from the passenger seat, a romance novel in her lap.

"I can't..." She choked and locked eyes with her father in the rearview mirror.

He was the reason she was in the backseat in the first place. It was the first family trip they'd taken together in years, and something told her, the last. There was a thundering in her eardrums she couldn't explain. With every highway mile, the sound grew louder, as if they were about to go over a waterfall with nothing to hold on to.

"Ellie," her father responded calmly. "It's going to be okay. I'm sorry, but we've gone too far to turn around."

***

The next morning, Eleanorah removed the eye mask she'd worn for the duration of their road trip and took in the familiar sounds of the old cabin. Bacon grease sizzled in a cast-iron frying pan. Floorboards whined a familiar melody. Feet dressed in thick, wool socks padded in and out of rooms. A crisp, mountain breeze entered through swinging screen doors, stirring the stale, musty air when they slammed shut.

A thick quilt covered her body. Two empty spaces in the beds next to her and the scent of Folger's revealed she was the last one to rise. She stared at the ceiling, listening for voices, but heard none. Just the happy gurgling of water moving swiftly around smooth rocks. She pulled her favorite sweater snuggly over her shoulders, making her way to the kitchen in search of the coffee pot.

"Morning, Ellie."

She jumped. Her grandfather's voice was soft, yet startling. He sat at the table eating a handful of his favorite red hot candies, his reading glasses perched at the end of his nose. Eleanorah relaxed and moved to squeeze his shoulder, inhaling the sweet scent of cinnamon.

"Morning, Grandpa," she said, emptying the pot into a ceramic mug. "Where's everyone else?"

"Your mother went into town to get a few groceries. Your grandmother is still sleeping. Everyone else went down to the river to catch some fish."

Eleanorah sighed with relief.

"You didn't feel like going?" He raised his eyebrows.

"Not really." She sat cross legged in a rickety chair next to him. "I don't really feel like doing much of anything lately," she added reluctantly. "To be honest, I'm having a hard time being back. I miss Mexico. If it weren't for my scholarships, I would have stayed."

"I see. Are you looking forward to your classes?"

"I mean, I was," she said, hesitating. "I worked so hard to get into Loyola's nursing program but now I'm not so sure it's what I really want." She shrugged. "I didn't expect to love traveling so much. It's made it a lot harder to be here." She paused, taking a sip of bitter, black liquid.

"Grandpa, how do you keep believing in this vision of a better future when all the evidence points to the contrary?" The question tumbled out of her mouth before she could stop it.

"What if everyone would have been happier if we'd stayed here, in Colorado? I mean, Mom and Dad were so convinced that Jesus was coming they left everything to move to the middle of nowhere. So did everyone else in our family. And now what? What if we've been fooled by this whole idea of building some future paradise together? You and Grandma have been waiting for the second coming for years, and things with our family only seem to be getting worse."

She thought of the night of the accidental detonation at the ammunition plant and how her father lost his job the very next day. She was only seven but still remembered it vividly. "The Year of the Explosion," she and her brothers nicknamed it. That was the year the yelling began. The year a visible rift between her parents began to grow and hadn't stopped. The year she knew that as much as she loved them, she couldn't stay.

Tears rolled down her cheeks, plopping onto her arm.

Her grandfather reached across the table, squeezing her fingers.

"I don't have the answers, Ellie. To be honest, sometimes I'm not sure what to believe. Ultimately, these things are out of our hands. We can't control what's to come or how it will come. All we have are the prophecies and the patterns. How we choose to use them is up to us."

"And what about the pattern shop?" she asked. What will become of it if we stop getting orders? They're using computers now to make everything. We don't even need *The Manual*."

"You may be right, mo chuisle." He leaned back in his chair thoughtfully. "People want predictability. Certainty. Computer generated molds without room for human error. Formulas they can mass produce.

"But we must be careful not to trade our spirit for a sense of safety." His blue eyes twinkled. "We can't always anticipate the last orbit around the sun, the last ring around a tree, or how the cycles and seasons will shape us. Some patterns are more ancient than others.

"'To every thing there is a season, and a time to every purpose under the heaven. A time to be born, and a time to die; a time to plant, and a time to pluck up that which is planted...A time to love, and a time to hate; a time of war, and a time of peace," he paraphrased his favorite verse from Ecclesiastes.

"'He hath made every thing beautiful in his time: also he hath set the world in their heart, so that no man can find out the work that God maketh from the beginning to the end.'"

He met her gaze with compassion. "Nature has its own intelligence, Ellie, filled with wisdom that machines can't replicate. Those are the patterns we must follow, the prophecies that will always ring true."

Eleanorah recalled the magic and mystery of her grandfather's pattern shop, pitted against her yearning for safety and certainty. She'd inherited a vision of the future turned sour the longer it remained unfulfilled, determined to eschew anything that required belief in the unseen, no matter how real it appeared.

She sniffled, blowing her nose into the neatly folded handkerchief her grandfather pulled from his pocket. "But what if God is just an idea we've made up to feel better about ourselves? What if it's just a story, and we're all telling different versions of it, pretending we're the ones with the ultimate truth, but none of it is real? What if all of our dreams are just fantasies?"

"You're right," he said, taking a deep breath. "There's no way to know if what we believe is true. Our dreams can certainly be misleading. Sometimes, they don't happen the way we think they will," he said, pausing. "But can I tell you a secret? In my life, I've learned that the courage it takes to pursue your dreams, the ones that lie deep within your heart, is the only proof you'll need they're real."

***

Wind gently rustled the old trees planted just outside of the library. The college was emptier, now. Most of her friends, with the exception of Margot, were still at home or working at different summer camps around the country until school started again in the fall. In a way, she preferred it like this. Walking alone through mostly vacant buildings, she could relive their time together undisturbed.

"It's not the end. It's just a pause. I'll visit you in Chicago, *te prometo.*"

Fragments of dandelions floated in the air. The low grumble of a lawn mower's blade spread their weightless seeds as it cut clean, even rows. She wanted to believe he would come.

Did she still believe him?

The hum of machinery outside the library window was drowned out by the sound of her heart, beating out of time. The compass spun. The hourglass flipped. The waves of Lake Michigan did not contain the ocean, did not smell of voyages or rebels. Did not howl with the cries of La Llorona.

But Eleanorah still heard them.

She waited for Andrés, escaping the reality of their distance by creating a new scenery for their love——sidewalks marked with the graffitied crowns of the Latin Kings. Busy outdoor cafés close enough to the lake to feel the cool breeze. Holding hands on The 'L', and feeling the sturdiness of him next to her. She envisioned baseball games at Wrigley Field, sharing messy hot dogs, and cheering for the Cubs in Spanish and English. She pictured discovering their favorite pub and drinking Mexican beer with their friends in Lincoln Square, blowing off steam together in between exams, and study groups.

She wanted to meet his aunt. She wanted to show him so many things, for him to see Chicago through her eyes, the way she'd seen Morelia through his. She wanted to make space for him. She wanted their love to be real, instead of a lingering *fantasma*.

Me haces falta, she thought. You are missing from me.

He was still working on his thesis, he explained. There were delays with his professor, he lamented. The sun was hot, and nothing happened in a hurry in Mexico. The timeline for his arrival went through several revisions.

Her phone vibrated—another missed call from Margot, wanting to go over their notes together. She clenched her fists. The table in front of her was covered in textbooks and loose diagrams. Scribbled definitions for the sympathetic and parasympathetic nervous systems. One for regulating the body's instinct for fight or flight, the other for rest, and repair. But she could do neither.

All she could think of was him.

Instead of reaching out, she'd fed the black hole of his absence by reading Sylvia Plath and listening to Damien Rice's "Coconut Skins" on repeat. Called herself delicate without explaining why. Increasingly, she found herself drawn to the windows of the salmon-colored building next to the lake where she cared for an elderly woman named Mrs. Santos after class. Thoughts of her body falling from the balcony while Mrs. Santos took her afternoon nap came unwittingly. She began staring at the street below, wondering if it was far enough for finality.

After finishing *The Bell Jar*, she picked up a dog-eared copy of *Mrs. Dalloway*, consumed it late into the night, and then immediately began *The Awakening*, by Kate Chopin.

These women knew something she didn't.

It could be peaceful, calm. A drive to the shore, something heavy and dear to hold onto, like a Bible. One last confession. One last glance at the blinking city lights, the sturdy skyline she loved so much. The blank canvas of dark water stretched out before her. Barefoot, simple, quiet. So quiet. Waves of peace, swallowing her whole.

It was the details that kept her from action, so far. How much weight would she need to drown? How high would she need to jump? The calculations, and the possibility that she wouldn't die, robbed her of the relief the Nothingness first offered, then tempted, now shouted.

Margot knocked on the study room door and poked her head through, her curly blonde hair bouncing as she spoke. "Hey girl, I've been looking for you. I'm going over the study guide for our pathophysiology test tomorrow, do you want to join?"

Her voice was light and bubbly. Once in a while, you could hear a slight Minnesotan accent in certain words she pronounced with a drawn-out vowel sound. For example, bag, coat, or vague. She was the only one in Eleanorah's nursing class who was around for the summer, making up a few courses after spending the spring semester in Sweden.

Eleanorah quickly rearranged the scattered pieces of paper into a neat pile, afraid that if she opened her mouth, a scream might come out.

"Are you okay?" Margot prodded, her smile shifting into a concerned frown. "Why don't we go out tonight?" She shifted tactics, noticing Eleanorah's overwhelm. "As soon as we're done studying, we can walk to The Wood and have a few drinks, my treat. We haven't hung out in a while, it'll be fun!" She enthused, her face brightening again.

They hadn't hung out in a while because Eleanorah kept pretending she wasn't home. Whenever she heard the screen on her back door next to the dumpster in the alleyway across from the boys' dormitory creak open, she froze. She sat as still as possible while the knocking continued, wishing she were invisible. But Margot was not someone who gave up easily.

"Okay," Eleanorah agreed, attempting a smile.

***

A yellow glare oozed through the window of the living room. It leaked from tall streetlights, dripping across her forehead and shoulders. She tried inhaling deeply, fully, but the effort was futile. Her head throbbed. She moaned and rolled over, away from the window. The pounding continued. There was a buildup of carbon dioxide, a sweet aftertaste still on her tongue.

Like migratory birds headed south for winter, she watched pieces of her sanity flapping their wings. They vibrated like a black, speckled cloud, hovering in an icy gray sky. She wanted to follow them, and float away.

"Ellie, Ellie."

A persistent nagging brought the blinding light back. She pushed hard against the intrusion. Someone was shaking her, a heavy and annoying presence wanting her to stop floating, flying with the birds.

"Ellie, come on. You can't sleep here. I have a bed for you. Please. Come on, let's get you into bed." Margot was on her knees, close to her ear. Eleanorah felt her warm breath against her face.

"I'm sleeping right here." She curled her limbs into a ball in the open suitcase—- vintage, like the one her mother left out so everyone could see the neatly packed clothes and new toothbrush, waiting to take her somewhere far away. Her mother's suitcase was hard on the outside, not easy to knock around. It conveyed the possibility of leaving, so she didn't have to.

"I'm sleeping right here. This is all I need. Right here..."

She fell back asleep and dreamt of running, lactic acid causing tired muscles to ache, spasm. She wanted to stop, to rest, but something was chasing her. It wouldn't let her stop.

She shivered, pulling something soft and warm up to her chin.

"That's my grandmother's," a voice said from far away. "I didn't want you to be cold last night, so I covered you up. I hope that's okay."

Eleanorah squinted her eyes open. The harsh light from the streetlights had been replaced by the warmth of a sunny summer morning. Late, probably.

"How are you feeling?" Margot was beside her again.

"Like hell," she muttered, under sticky breath.

"I made a pot of coffee, would you like some?"

Eleanorah pushed herself up to a seat, shielding her eyes from the sun. She was still crumpled inside the suitcase. Standing was an immediate regret. The wine and Benadryl from the night before danced in her system, making her swoon more than walk toward the small table near the second-story window in the kitchen.

Margot set a mug of hot liquid in front of her and sat down. "Do you want to talk about it?"

Eleanorah took a sip and held the steam close to her nose, breathing in a hint of vanilla, and stared out the window.

"Okay, I'll go first," Margot sighed. "Sometimes I feel like I just want to invite you in for some tea and run a hot bath for you, but you won't take off your damn shoes."

"What shoes?" Eleanorah frowned, bending over to tighten the laces.

***

"Is everything okay? I feel like something is wrong. Please, tell me if I'm mistaken," Andrés begged.

She read his email several times, blinking at the screen. A new semester had started, and with it a swell of students roaming the campus with all the energy she could no longer muster.

Incrementally, so that she hardly noticed, her memories (both past and future) had mutated, making edits to their story she never asked for, yet once they were in place, she accepted them as truth. The result was that her capacity to envision the worst increased every day he was not there.

Paranoia disguised itself as logic. It stole her sleep, convincing her she didn't belong. Not to Andrés, not to this city, not to her own body.

Increasingly agitated, she hurled her growing panic at him in the form of accusations, voicing fears she couldn't call back, ashamed she couldn't hold them inside. Lying. Negligence. Broken promises. Fact and fiction, tangled together. If she'd learned anything from her mother, it had to be somebody else's fault.

"You broke my heart." She erupted furiously one afternoon in late September.

"I understand." She heard the hurt in his voice, felt him slump as if with a broken wing from miles away. "Can we still stay in contact? ¿Como amigos?" he asked, tentatively.

"No." She summoned all of her willpower, straightening her spine for the first time in months.

***

The leaves turned. First lemon drop yellow, then chimney red. The city transformed into a carpet of color against a backdrop of gray buildings.

Eleanorah walked up the stairs to the Brown Line Station and joined the other commuters, craning their necks like question marks, waiting. A streak of white headlights appeared. The signal sounded and doors opened, bodies funneling in and out of the crowded train cars. Eleanorah followed them, squeezing into a faded dark blue seat, worn in the middle.

The woman next to her ran weathered fingers over a strand of rosary beads. Eyes closed, she moved her mouth silently. In the aisle, a young boy and his mother conversed excitedly in Spanish. Pushed against the metal pole, their hands inside warm gloves, they clung to its stability as they rattled over tracks.

Here, in this confined space, Eleanorah could observe without being observed. The anonymity was comforting, an opportunity to disappear in plain sight. She studied the map without knowing where she was going. She was just going.

"Clark and Lake, doors open on the left," the familiar voice came overhead. The wheels screeched to a halt. "Con permiso." Eleanorah moved past the young boy and his mother, startled by how easily the words took flight from her mouth.

Some habits were hard to shake. Like how she still listened for his whistle while walking down a crowded street. How she longed for the color turquoise. Or how she refused to wear enough layers in winter, attracting the chagrin of more seasoned Chicagoans who wagged their fingers at her bare hands and head with warning. After almost four years in the city, she still hadn't gotten the formula right.

A high-pitched gust of wind whistled through the air. She should be going over her pharmacology notes or spending more time in the microbiology lab. But truthfully, she couldn't bear it. The Cloud Gate appeared on the left, a shiny, reflective thing people from all over the world came to see, the curved contours offering hints of shadow or wisps of light.

She inspected herself in its image, scanning her body like she would a patient, looking for color, for rebound, for fight. Her nose was red. Cheeks, pale. Lips cracked. She furrowed her forehead, making temporary wrinkles across her face. Her hair needed a trim—even a hat couldn't hide that fact. But her eyes. Her eyes glimmered, ever so slightly.

She shrugged and turned against the flow of traffic, shuttering her view from the sterile concrete. Instead, she imagined bare earth and warm air saturated with spices and static electricity. She ached for the chaos and dirt of Mexico, its streets colored with chicken feet and bright tiles, with blood, and curves and appetite.

"Reverse culture shock," a graduate student at the college's health center pronounced the diagnosis calmly, with a hint of compassion in her eyes. She'd been visiting her once a week since the beginning of the semester, though she disagreed with her conclusion. Shock was the body's way of protecting itself from the pain of unexpected trauma. A shutting down of non-essential parts to preserve the main organs necessary for survival.

But this sort of self-preservation was supposed to be temporary. Either you bounced back, or you didn't. The body and soul's capacity for adaptation were limited. It was never meant to be a chronic condition.

She curled her toes, willing the circulation back into them. Whatever the next station, she would take it northbound near the end of the Red Line and make a pot of tea as soon as she walked in the door. Marching briskly with renewed urgency, a building on her right made her pause. Coloring outside the lines, it introduced itself into the busy street like an open invitation, its windows forming a transparent prism. She moved to go around it, then stopped, reading the words printed above the entrance. "Let there be light," it declared.

A man pushed the door open before she could turn away. He wore a buttoned-down shirt and a hat with flannel flaps to cover his ears. "Welcome to the Spertus Museum," he said, placing a brochure in her hands.

On the cover was a black and white photograph of a young girl with bushy hair and an open-mouthed smile. Her gaze wasn't focused on the photographer, but off to the side, full of joy. Eleanorah read the caption, "Anne Frank: A History for Today," and almost dropped the paper.

Images came, and with them an unwelcome paralysis. She saw flashbacks of starving prisoners wearing loose pajamas, crowded over a bowl of mush on the floor. Folded bodies hiding in trunks of cars. Barbed wire with crossbones warning visitors not to stray from the sidewalk or look too closely at the mass graves just below the surface.

"May I help you?" the man at the door asked kindly. "In addition to the Anne Frank exhibit, we have a newer one, just to the left. The Smallest Witnesses, arrived last week." He pointed around the corner to a room with drawings on the wall.

She looked up, startled. "Thank you," she said, willing her feet in the direction he suggested, instead of running back outside.

The room was small. The drawings, photocopied images on grid paper, were made with crayons by school children. There were figures on camels and horses carrying guns almost as large as the men who pointed them at huts with smoke billowing from their rooftops. Women and children were running, some of them with red pouring out of their bellies. Some drawings had radios and cell phones next to helicopters.

Eleanorah focused on the plaque next to one of the drawings.

It quoted Jamil, a twelve-year-old boy from the Darfur region of Sudan. "The Janjaweed came on camels, and horses, very fast. Sometimes two on one camel, with guns. Many soldiers, with guns. This one is a machine gun. They were shooting us."

The gallery lights focused on another image, a primitive yet detailed portrayal of brutality. A woman lay on the ground with red scribbled across her face. On the same page was what looked like a telephone or radio, larger than her body. "We needed help. There was no one to protect us," the children told the interpreters who gave them the crayons and paper, a way to tell their story.

Eleanorah turned away, nausea and anger billowing in her gut. She trembled. There were some things she did not want the light to show.

***

The BOOM and the echo. The CLAP and the shaking. They were there from the beginning. She noticed the noise like people notice the hum of their old refrigerator. You just stop, after a while. You tune it out. You adapt.

The wings of the plane tilted toward the ground. The sound of the wheels coming down from the belly of the motor reverberated, constricting and pulling tightly around her navel. A translucent reflection revealed itself in the small oval window. In her forehead, she saw the last beams of sunlight. In her eyes, wisps of moving clouds.

Yet.

There were some things she was afraid of adapting to.

The smell of smoke. The rush of blood escaping her body. The way her shoulders surrendered to the heaviness of gravity. The acute sensation of impending loss.

What good is it to hear the echo of the gunshot before it's fired?

The runway rose quickly toward the plane, and the wheels made staggering contact. She closed her notebook, forcing her gaze out the window. Red and green blinking lights poked holes through the dusk, sending signals she couldn't decipher.

"Welcome to Kansas City, ladies and gentlemen. Current temperature is 31 degrees Fahrenheit. The time is 6:32 p.m.. Please remember to stay in your seats until the pilot turns off the seatbelt sign. Happy Holidays, and enjoy your stay in the City of Fountains!"

Eleanorah grimaced slightly at the cheerful voice announcing their arrival and braced herself for the 45-minute trip from the airport to Independence, a drive she preferred in the opposite direction only.

The seatbelt light went off with a ding. She closed her eyes as passengers began getting up and claiming their bags filled with presents from the overhead bins, chatting casually while they waited in the aisle. But she stayed in her seat. The urge to escape overwhelmed her, making it difficult to breathe.

"Mom and Dad are splitting up. I think it's for real this time," Micah called to inform her, just after Thanksgiving. His voice was calm, almost absentminded.

"What happened?" Eleanorah snapped unintentionally, as if maybe it was his fault, something he should've seen or prevented.

"I don't know. Mom just started packing up all of the silverware one day and told us she was going to Mutti's, down the road."

Eleanorah had let out a soft groan as she sank to the kitchen floor.

Mutti was her Grandpa Filibert's nickname for their Grandma Helena. It meant "Mother" and was one of the only remaining signs of their German heritage. Like her relationship with her mother, her relationship with her grandmother was complicated. Mutti was equal parts zest and anxiety with a stubborn streak as wide as the Mississippi River and a tenacious faith that might've been admirable had it not been so unbearable.

Her fear, on the other hand, leaned toward the paranoid. She worried constantly. About the natural disasters that might strike or how her daughters were raising their children.

She was especially worried about the end times. Forced to flee her home and spit-out on an unfamiliar continent as a young girl in 1939, she was certain they were already here. Eleanorah blamed Mutti for giving their mom a place to run away to. For fearing the worst, and sometimes being right.

"Are you there now?" Eleanorah tried to keep the irritation from her voice.

"Yeah..." Micah's voice answered guiltily. "Mom's already filed the papers. She wants to sell the house."

A waterfall you hear coming. A roar you can't outrun. How can it be a surprise?

A few weeks later, her older brother Jeremiah called.

"Ellie...I'm sorry to have to tell you this," he said, breaking into sobs. "Our—our house caught on fire last night. It was an accident. Dad was burning a pile of brush in the backyard. He left and went into town. He thought he'd put it out. When he came back..." His voice cracked from the smoke. "We're all okay, but the house is..."

A blaze of flames licking the rooftop. Hungry, like wolves. Eleanorah watched it burn from a distance, helpless. It was no one's fault. It was everyone's fault.

She shook her head and unbuckled her seatbelt, willing herself to be brave.

Eleanorah located her father just outside the terminal, his blue and white ski cap bobbing above the crowd. She would recognize that hat anywhere. As a child, she used to open up all of his dresser drawers, searching for the stash of quarters he kept in a mug full of change. Somewhere nestled in between neatly folded socks and dark pairs of underwear was the blue and white ski cap, a small tag sticking out of the side.

By now it was ragged and worn, like the lines on his face.

It was unusual to see him there. He was not known for his promptness. Or his ability to answer a phone call on the first try. For this reason and many others, Eleanorah hesitated to rely on him to do things like pick her up from the airport or take her to an appointment. Time eluded him. His personality was unencumbered by the burden it imposed on others.

Her mother would say he was distracted, aloof, inconsiderate. Eleanorah preferred to think of him as well-meaning. A free spirit. Unhurried.

He saw Eleanorah and smiled, holding his arms out wide for one of his famous bear hugs, like he used to when she was small enough he could wrap her up entirely. She set her bags down and fell into his chest. It was the safest she'd felt in a long, long time.

"It's good to see you, Pumpkin." His voice wavered with emotion.

"You too, Daddy. How are you feeling?"

She pulled away and scrutinized his eyes. There was frost around the edges. He was pale. He'd lost weight, too. Her arms reached more easily around him, and some strength was gone. His shoulders rounded as if it took too much energy to stand up straight, to fight against gravity, to walk tall.

"I'm just glad you're here," he said, mustering an optimistic smile.

Micah poked his head around the corner. "Hey, Sis."

Eleanorah pulled him into a fierce hug. Others walked around, hurrying to catch flights or embrace lovers. Fir wreaths decorated doorways and "Baby, it's cold outside," played on the speakers, interrupted by frequent announcements from the airlines. The airport was full of people going or coming home but they stood transfixed, in between.

"You cut your hair." Eleanorah ran her fingers through his unusually buzzed dark brown locks, raising an eyebrow. Micah nodded without answering the unspoken question. He slipped his elbow through Eleanorah's, and they made their way through the crowd to the baggage claim, blinking "Chicago."

"Where's Jeremiah, I thought he was coming too?"

Micah shook his head. "Hanging out with his girlfriend." He rolled his eyes. "They moved in together when mom moved out."

Eleanorah raised her eyebrows. "I guess he took advantage of the distraction?"

"Yeah," he said with a grin. "It's hard for Mom and Dad to have much of an opinion about what we do at this point. I'll tell you more later." He glanced over his shoulder at their father, who grabbed Eleanorah's bags from the carousel.

"Ready to go? We brought the truck." Micah pointed toward the exit doors, strung with lights.

Eleanorah stood and looked around the airport one last time. Oversized snowflakes hung next to advertisements for barbecue restaurants and a mural of jazz legends. Lights from the runway danced through floor-to-ceiling windows in a dreamlike quality. A memory projected onto a white sheet, the shapes and figures moving like wall puppets. Fluid. Floating.

She wanted to reach out and touch them. Ask them how to become part of their world. How to pass through to the other side. She studied the sound of their laughter, the expressions of faces turned upwards in teeth-showing smiles.

And then she turned and walked into the night.

***

A series of shots went off in the distance, accompanied by red flares. Eleanorah shuddered, a reaction that surprised her. Growing up next to the ammunition plant, the sounds of gunshots were as natural to her as the sweet thrill of the whip-poor-will at twilight, but after being away, they registered differently.

She stepped across the familiar doorway, her eyes adjusting to the absence of anything but starlight. Her father was staying with her uncle, but she told him she wanted to see the house straight from the airport. She could've waited until morning, but for weeks, she'd imagined the worst. Maybe it was easier to see it this way, without the full glare of daylight.

"Here," he said, handing her a small flashlight. "Be careful, Pumpkin."

There was more smoke and water damage than anything, but the house didn't smell like smoke like she expected. The insurance company had hired someone to clean the soot from the walls, and pack up everything her mother had left behind in cardboard boxes. Eleanorah sat crossed-legged on the scorched carpet, where the piano used to be. Her mother had taken it with her before the fire, fleeing the scene before their family's collapse had anything to do with flames or smoke.

The first time Eleanorah sat at the piano, she was six. Her feet barely touched the pedals, so she had to scoot to the very edge of the wobbly, wooden bench. Before she was old enough to hold a pen and know its worth, she pressed the faded black and white keys into locks, turning knobs with music, opening hidden doorways now long forgotten.

"You have to learn the piano before you can learn any other instrument," her mother insisted and it was her mother who taught her math and science and God.

When she was fifteen, she told her a secret in a bolted bathroom in the nursery at church. "I'm leaving your father tomorrow," she announced with narrow eyes and set jaw, through barely parted lips. It was the first time she made good on her constant threat.

"Promise me you won't tell your brothers or your father," she warned. "I'm only telling you because I'll need your help."

'Don't tell your father, don't tell your father, don't tell your father,' Eleanorah had repeated the strain while plucking the notes of the piano, louder and louder. She gritted her teeth, using all of her weight to push the pedals to the floor, shaking the walls with sound. Her silence made her a traitor to her father. Yet her voice would betray her mother's confidence, and prove she had always been right about Eleanorah.

That she couldn't be trusted. Was a troublemaker. The black sheep of the family, after all. With every note, her body absorbed the electricity of the alarm she was trying to signal.

She spent that whole afternoon on the piano bench. Her fingers numb, she played until she thought there was no anger left. Until she was asked to please, please, stop. She could still recall her father's gentle face and the tune he whistled that day while puttering around the house. Oblivious to what was about to take place, she hated him for it, and herself, for not telling him.

Pay attention! She longed to yell through pursed lips. Do something, before it's too late!

***

The light is unstable, the wind blows it out, the lightning ignites it, it is never simply there, shining like the sun, but it is worth fighting for.

—Paulo Coelho

2

A continent of light

The memory of a slow spring awakening—forest rebirthed on a pale, robin-egg morning, contrasted with the groggy prolongation of winter in a city coated with gray, salty slush. Back on campus, Eleanorah felt herself pass between a world she once knew but no longer belonged, and one in which she could never fully exist.

She sloshed distractedly through the mud in a pair of red rain boots, late for her pharmacology class (again), secretly hoping she might fail. She was close—previously a straight A-student, she'd been white knuckling her way through nursing school for the last two years, barely scraping by with B minuses. After getting her first C in Biochemistry, she only had to get one more C to fail the entire program, an idea she toyed with hopefully, even while meticulously copying the names and classes of drugs on stacks of index cards.

"What would you do if you don't pass?" Margot walked beside her in a pair of fleece lined galoshes, her shoulder-length curls maintaining their perfect shape, despite the snow sticking to them.

"Move to Bolivia and teach English," Eleanorah answered more quickly than she intended, a warm blush on her cheeks.

She thought the only method of avoiding her family's delusions and disappointment were to plant two feet squarely in the realm of science and practicality. Proven recipes for alleviating the hurt, re-suscitating the drowned, and stopping the bleed. But her conviction was slipping.

"That sounds delightful!" Margot laughed.

"What would you do?"

"Hmm, maybe go back to Minnesota and work for my Dad's accounting firm for a while. Or travel!" Her eyes gleamed excitedly.

"Mmm," Eleanorah agreed wistfully, letting the possibility linger just long enough to entice.

***

The pungent scent of cigarettes and fermented breath, hers and his, lingered on her tongue. Eleanorah stumbled into her empty apartment, greedy for the warmth of his body underneath shrinking layers of winter clothes and another night of ignoring her home-work.

He kissed her, hard.

She wanted more. He picked her up in one swift motion and carried her into the small bedroom. She craved his skin on hers, the revolt of everything she was supposed to do and be growing with each inch of bare flesh revealed.

He set her down slowly, an unspoken question mark between them. She reached for his belt, undoing it deliberately. The answer of his weight on her moonlit body was heavy. It pressed against her, made her sink further toward the floor. Sweat collected between them, making it impossible to tell where he began or where she ended.

He tried to have her on the lower bunk, on the plastic mattress belonging to the college where she analyzed the anatomy of breasts and throbbing glans. He tried to have her against the wall with her legs wrapped around his abdomen, held up by his taut buttocks. While he tried to have her on her back, she pointed her toes in pirouettes, legs spread wide as an eagle's wings.

Outside, snow glittered wordlessly on recently shoveled sidewalks and drooping daffodils. Steam covered the window panes, dripping downward without resistance. Old radiators clanked on, hissing and rattling along with the groans of rustling bedsheets.

The ache was almost unbearable. And yet, she pulled him closer, didn't want it to end. The more it hurt, the tighter she grasped, curling her legs around his back, biting her lip, digging her nails into the blurry outline of his body. Embraced in the charcoal contours of his hips, she willingly became without form. Hot breath escaped her nostrils, billowing like smoke above them, hovering.

"Do you have any protection?" Benjamin gasped, finally. Eleanorah shook her head no, trying to hide the embarrassment at her lack of preparation. Together they'd broken campus curfews and contracts, split the legs of a coffee table under the pressure of their bodies, but until tonight, she'd managed to restrict the fullness of her desire.

The motion stopped as he eased himself out of her arms. Untangling her hair from his, he kissed her softly on the forehead. "I'll be right back!" He fit tight arms into the sleeves of her gray coat, not bothering to tie the laces of his leather boots.

The door creaked shut.

While he was gone, she bled on the comforter. All of her muscles relaxed. She reached her fingers toward the warm rush of wetness soaking her thighs. It poured out like lava, oozing in all the wrong places. Eleanorah shivered in the absent night, inhaling the smell of hemoglobin, and sweat, red ruby-stained sheets.

"Did it already happen?" She wondered.

"Is that all?"

***

Eleanorah shuffled the stacks of journal articles in front of her in the small office, trying to satiate the hollow aching with solutions. If only she could identify the source of the hurt. If only she could get close enough to plug the sinking and bleeding with her own hands.

She paused and looked out the window. A heavy spring rainstorm pounded on the roof. The small creek that ran through campus flooded with orange parking cones, discarded furniture, and other pieces of trash. To her surprise, she hadn't failed her pharmacology final, just barely earning her a C+ which counted for passing. Somehow, she'd made it through her senior year, and was graduating in just a few weeks. Both parents were coming to the ceremony, driving separately. Her brothers were coming too. Eleanorah smiled at the thought of them all being together, but the events of the past few months made it feel more like a dream.

She closed her eyes, trying instead to imagine what might be waiting for her beyond graduation. She needed to think of her future. Not Benjamin (a recent and welcome diversion), or her parents' failed marriage or the inevitable sale of the only home she'd ever known. But all she could see was goodbye.

"In Africa, AIDS has been described as an epidemic that is stalking the continent," she typed, determined to remember the reason she was here. "Though this disease crosses socioeconomic and racial barriers, its victims are not entirely random." She tried to focus again on her paper, but there were antidotes she could not pronounce, cocktails of liquid poison injected into blossoming viruses living inside shattered bodies.

She spelled them out in pairs: disease and cure. Mycobacterium tuberculosis and isoniazid. The combinations were stories from another reality, belonging to a world where children died from diarrhea and infected breast milk, where a mother's good intentions weren't enough to prevent the harm.

The room became unbearably quiet. The static of a tape recorder only added to her nerves. She clicked the button on and off again, squirming in her seat.

Finally, the door opened. A short, stout man entered, wearing a button-down shirt and thinly rimmed glasses. He took the seat across from her, arranging himself behind a borrowed desk.

Eleanorah clutched her notes, steadying her shaking hands. She cleared her throat. "I'm Eleanorah Baumgarten, a nursing student at the University," she said, reaching across the desk, introducing herself. "Is it okay if I record our interview?"

He clasped her hand and smiled generously, looking deeply into her eyes with flecks of ember still blazing, waiting.

Eleanorah primed herself for the somber statistics. For the narrative of poverty, warfare, and violence. She turned on the teleprompter and adjusted the microphone, bracing herself. "Pastor David, you're the pastor of an orphanage and school in Ndola, Zambia. Can you tell me about the impact of AIDS and HIV in your community?"

"Yes," he confirmed, his eyes brimming with compassion. "Almost all of the children in our home have been affected by this illness. The effect is devastating in our community. The children come to us because their parents, or their grandparents or their aunt or uncle have died from the infection. Small children are taking care of their younger brothers or sisters, and we see them taking on a great responsibility, beyond their years."

She scribbled notes in the margins of her research paper. She asked about death tolls. About access to health care. About rates of mortality and resources and scarcity. No rock was left unturned.

Silence stole seconds from the clock on the wall. The rain and rumbling lessened. Eleanorah took a deep breath and scooted to the edge of her chair, pen poised on paper, hesitating. Her next question had nothing to do with her final paper or the academic literature. But she needed to know.

"Tell me, Pastor, what is Africa really like?"

A knowing smile made its way across his kind face. His hands rested easily on the desk, holding each other. "Many people describe Africa as the 'Dark Continent,'" he proposed.

She nodded in agreement and looked at her notes, detailing the suffering. She'd seen the documentaries. Chronicled the tragedy.

"But Africa is not a dark continent. It is a continent of Light!" The room glowed with the conviction of his declaration.

Eleanorah shook her head, confusion replacing a glimmer of hope.

"You know," he said, studying her for a moment. "We could use someone with your hands. There's a group leaving from your university to visit us in a few weeks' time. One of the medical students had to back out at the last moment." His eyes sparkled mysteriously. "I believe there could be a space for you. Would you like to come to Zambia and see for yourself?"

***

Dust, the color of rust, spread out like a tide as far as she could see. A lazy, serpentine river carved a winding trail, its waters lighter than the noon sky. *Were its banks stained scarlet from that distant Khartoum? Did it carry the sorrows of mothers separated from sons and daughters?*

Witnessing the changing scenery from the windows of a small, pink van named Rosa, she collected as many polaroid images as she could, but they were only half-developed. She wanted to feel the dust beneath her fingernails, let the sweat wash away the guilt—for surviving, for having access to resources and treatment she'd never even need.

It was hard to believe that just 24 hours ago she'd walked across the stage, accepted her diploma, and finished packing up her apartment, while preparing for her last-minute trip to Zambia. Coming on this trip meant she could witness what she'd only read about, but the flight from Chicago to London and onto Lusaka was not enough time to make the transition from one place to the next. The other students leaned against windows, their heads bobbing against the seat or resting on each other. But Eleanorah was awake, her eyes a library of stories illustrated in real time.

By evening, they arrived in Ndola, the base from which they'd visit the orphanage and school Pastor David managed with his wife. The students were divided into smaller groups, hosted by friends of the Pastor in houses and small apartments spread out across the city. A woman named Ba Maurine greeted Eleanorah's group with robust arms, pulling them into her bosom, draped in a stained apron. She smelled of cooking oil and smiled with two gapped teeth in the front, like Eleanorah.

"*Mulishani, mulishani*, my daughters!" She hugged each of them, squeezing their bones and finding them coming up short. Before they could get their bearings, she eagerly served hot plates with chicken thighs and white balls of a starchy substance called *nshima* into their hands, ladling cooked greens on top.

Eleanorah ate hungrily, letting the juice from the chicken soak into the flavorless lumps that felt sticky and awkward in her mouth. As disorienting as it was to be on a new continent, she was relieved. For now, she didn't have to think about the strange dance of pulling Benjamin in, and pushing him away, giving into her instincts, and then immediately feeling guilty. She didn't have to think about starting work as a nurse, or the ruins of her home.

She was in Zambia now, far enough away to pretend she wouldn't have to go back.

***

Seated behind a makeshift desk in a crowded room with the other students, Eleanorah struggled to focus through the jet-lag. *I didn't come here to be stuck in another classroom,* she thought, irritated by the confinement. Her attention sharpened immediately when Pastor David entered the room.

"Welcome, my brothers, and sisters," he said, smiling. "Before we introduce you to our village, I wish to share some of our history." He took up a piece of chalk and began drawing. "The people of Zambia come from the Luba Kingdom to the north, the Tonga people, who are original to Zambia, and the Bantu, which means 'speaking people,'" he explained. "There are many more tribes in our country, and over seven officially recognized tribal languages.

"During colonial times, Africa was divided between France, Belgium, Germany, England, and Portugal. Zambia eventually became British territory. When Dr. Livingstone began his exploration of the Zambezi River, more white men followed. In our country, we have a saying, 'The British came with their Bibles. They covered our eyes, and took our land,'" he smiled ironically, looking at the faces staring at him, slightly uncomfortably.

He continued.

"When the white men came, they discovered our land was rich in minerals, including copper. The Copperbelt industrialized cities like Ndola and Kitwe, which became urban centers. In 1964, we gained our Independence from the British, and Northern Rhodesia became present-day Zambia. Our government has gone through many changes. We are still a young nation, but with the help of our brothers and sisters, we will learn to walk with our heads held high, proud of what we will become.

"Come," Pastor David said, directing them outside to the cool canopy of a wide, flat-topped baobab tree.

"Why won't you help me?" A man with a disheveled appearance stumbled toward them, his eyes unfocused and empty. "I'm a foolish man. Please, please help." He came nearer, his arms outstretched for balance, palms turned upward toward the sky.

Suddenly, children with missing clothes and shoes came out from under the protection of the shade tree, stretching their arms toward the man, shaking their fists, and yelling. Eleanorah moved aside as they clucked their tongues noisily, surrounding and herding him away from the rest of the group. Giving the students from Chicago one last glance, the man picked up his heels and hung his head, running into the periphery.

Eleanorah shuffled her feet nervously, recalling an old teaching from Sunday School, "It says more about the one who gives willingly than the one who receives out of genuine need." She didn't know what she had to give, but she was willing.

The atmosphere settled, and a low, melodic humming replaced the earlier disturbance. One by one, children dressed in green and white uniforms with clean faces paraded out of the school, lining up in front of the college students.

"We are so glad you are here because you are bringing us blessings, you are bringing us blessings," they sang, swaying together rhythmically.

The harmonies were rich and plentiful. Like grace, they filled the empty spaces, pouring over the parched ground, their voices bigger than their bodies. One by one, the children called the name of one of the students, inviting them forward to sing and clap and dance. They each received the same greeting: "We are so glad you are here because you are bringing us blessings."

First Laura, then Anthony, then Eleanorah. "We are so glad you are here because you are bringing us blessings." Tears glistened her cinnamon-colored eyes.

She wished more than anything it was true.

***

Roosters crowed before sunrise. The other girls stirred listlessly in their beds, still sleeping. It took Eleanorah several moments to remember where she was. The soft fabric of the mosquito netting brushed against her face and she smiled, feeling a thrill of wonder and adventure. She scooted to the edge of the mattress she shared with a girl named Clara and crept toward the bathroom, bringing her towel with her. The washroom was dim, with a small shower head next to the toilet and a drain in the cement floor. She stood naked under a stream of icy water, shivering.

And then, she thought of him.

His strong hands. And dark, curly hair. The one time he let it grow long.

How he kissed her nipples, her face. How he discovered that spot where she was ticklish, the only place that could make her shiver and wiggle and squirm when grazed by his touch. How when he snuck his hands under her shirt, gently running his fingers over that spot, low on her back, she couldn't help but squeal with delight and kiss him until he promised to stop.

The last time she saw Benjamin was right after she agreed to come to Zambia. The wind was blustery and cold, sweeping sassafras flowers off newly bloomed trees, scattering the sidewalk with patches of iridescent light. One of the blooms caught in his thick hair and she plucked it out, holding it in her hand before it blew away.

She'd shivered and he'd wrapped his arm around her waist.

"When will you be back?" he asked in the afterglow of the bar they'd just left. "You won't even notice I'm gone," she'd said, a little too sarcastically.

The arm around her waist went slack at his side. He stared at her for a moment before looking away. "Of course I'll notice."

A train shook above them. It screeched with the wind as it entered the station. "Red line to Howard," the recording announced indifferently.

"I guess I better be going," he said, searching her eyes one last time for an answer he couldn't find.

Eleanorah thought of his warm hands caressing her face, his strong legs tangled with hers. Their bodies pressed together like dried flowers in an unopened book. It was better not to open it.

Better not to disturb the memory. Better not to risk the whole thing crumbling in her hands, asking for more than it had to give.

She reached for the soap and stepped out from under the water's numbing effects, watching the goose bumps multiply on her skin. Tilting her head as far as it would go to avoid the chill, she rinsed small sections of her body. A shoulder here, a leg there, never fully immersing herself under the faucet. Wringing her hair to rid herself of regret, she wrapped herself in the towel, walking barefoot back to the room.

Ba Maurine padded down the hallway. "Hello, my daughter," she said, carrying a big pile of laundry hung out to dry on the balcony overnight. "Did you sleep well?"

"Yes, thank you. Very well," she answered with a lie. "Do you know what we'll be doing today?"

"Ba Rogers will come, and you will go with the others. This afternoon we will meet at the orphanage and eat there. The women and I are preparing a big meal." She smiled, looking at Eleanorah as if she could use a big meal.

Eleanorah's heart leapt. All she wanted to do was hold the little ones in her arms, letting them tug at her earrings and necklace. Hear them giggle unabashedly at the strangeness of her wispy red hair.

***

The rest of the morning unfolded lazily, the day unassuming. The van bumped down an unpaved road, crowded on both sides with scraggly bushes and flat-topped trees like before, but no children were running alongside them, no roadside stands selling trinkets or calling cards for outdated cell phones. Instead, a lone British Airways jet flew over them, a stark contrast to the reality in front of her. Ba Rogers turned, parking next to a few scattered vehicles, all showing signs of travel on dusty terrain.

When the engine turned off, a loud, high-pitched wailing and deep-throated, guttural noises startled Eleanorah's ears. She waited curiously, following the students as they piled out of the van together. Ba Margaret, Pastor David's wife, was there to greet them, wearing platform sandals and a dress shirt tucked into a *chitenge*—a large piece of patterned cloth traditionally wrapped around the waist. She looked dignified or indignant, Eleanorah couldn't tell which.

"A woman in the village has lost her son to AIDS. We've come to pay our respects before joining the children for lunch at the school," she explained.

Their expressions turned solemn. A pain in Eleanorah's gut brought a stinging sensation to the corners of her eyes. She was not prepared for this.

Before they could follow Ba Margaret, a woman with tears streaking her cheeks began shouting and waving her arms in their direction. Ba Margaret raised her voice, speaking in Bemba so they couldn't understand. The woman muttered angrily and let them pass, shaking her head.

"She is upset that we are not all wearing the chitenge cloth," Ba Margaret said, interpreting. "Some people are old-fashioned and too rooted in our Zambian traditions," she added, apologetically.

Eleanorah looked down at her bare legs and flip-flops, feeling exposed, and out of place. The whole group wore shorts and t-shirts, dressed for comfort under the blazing African sun. "Njeleleniko..." she whispered toward the woman's back, making an effort to express her remorse, but the syllables were puzzles with missing pieces on her tongue.

"Ye-e—e-e-e-egh! Ye-e—e-e-e-egh! Ye-e—e-e-e-egh!" The women shrieked. "May, baba-beeee! Mayi, baba-beeee!" The men echoed.

The sound was so powerful it shook the ground. Eleanorah wanted to cover her ears and block the siren song calling the dead home, voicing a grief she didn't know she was carrying. Ba Margaret stopped and laid a wreath next to a plain wooden cross, made from sticks. Like the hills next to it, there was no marker to distinguish one grave from another.

They were surrounded by them. Heaps of bare ground reaching toward the sky. Eleanorah looked down at her feet, studying the narrow footpath between mounds of red soil rising above the earth, covering bodies with names she would never learn. The enormity of it rearranged her insides.

Warriors. Kings. Diseased. *Los desaparecidos.* The earth reclaimed its own without discretion.

***

Eleanorah stood in a large classroom with wooden desks pushed against the walls, wearing a blue and red printed chitenge bound around her waist (purchased from a market in Kitwe a few days earlier), and a stethoscope around her neck. A line of children waited, weaving in and out of the room all the way to the acacia tree. She placed the new stethoscope, a gift from both of her parents, in her ears and positioned it gently on the chest of a small boy sitting on the makeshift examination table in front of her.

She leaned closer, listening for the heartbeat, barely audible over the noise of the room. Next, she moved the stethoscope to his exposed belly, round, and hollow. A sure sign of parasites.

"Can you stick out your tongue for me? Say 'ahhhhhh,'" Eleanorah prompted for what seemed like the hundredth time.

"Aaahhh." He followed her instructions, gazing at her sun-kissed hair with wonder.

She peered at his throat with her pen light and placed a thermometer underneath his tongue. "Close your mouth, please" she said, waiting for the beep."99.5°F," she dictated to Alice, one of the non-nursing students helping record all of the vital signs.

"How do you feel, Cephas?" She read his name off the chart in her hand. "Mumala?" she asked, pointing to his stomach.

He nodded.

"Umutwi?" She pointed to his head, looking at the circular white patches with missing hair, evidence of invading fungus.

He nodded again.

"We must try to get them through the line," a stern voice said, speaking quickly to the boy in Bemba.

"He has a fever," Eleanorah interjected.

The nurse, an older Zambian woman lifted him under his arms and set him down in the line heading out the door. "They all have fevers," she said, her voice softening. "We can give them one dose of Ibuprofen. If it's more serious, they will have to go to Ndola." She pointed a girl toward another line at the other end of the room, touching her arm where there was an open wound, saying a few more words in Bemba.

The ones with wounds like the girl's were treated separately, their sores cleaned and covered with white gauze and ointment to keep out the flies. The others were given medicine to expel the worms inflating their bellies and a nutritional supplement to take home and mix with water collected in jugs or barrels or buckets.

Voices in the clinic began ringing in her ears. The children filed by in fast-forward motion. Eleanorah placed a hand on the table to steady herself. The room was dark with bodies, swirling. The magnitude of suffering pulled her down, toward the uneven floor, spinning at her feet.

Something small and hard to see was tugging at her skirt. Eleanorah took a deep breath.

"Hello." She kneeled facing the girl, no older than four, maybe five. "My name is Ellie," she spoke slowly, pointing at her chest. "Can you tell me your name?"

Her gold-speckled eyes full of strength and weariness passed through Eleanorah as if she didn't exist. It was the girl she'd seen before in the village carrying a baby on her back, wearing a bright orange hat that was too big, and kept falling off her head. Today, there was no baby. Just the girl, hiding behind Eleanorah's chitenge.

"Can I listen to your tummy and your heart?" Eleanorah pointed to the table and her stethoscope.

The girl nodded, her unkempt hair sticking out in all directions, giving her face a fierce appearance.

Eleanorah gently scooped her into her arms and placed her on the folding table. Her pink dress was dirty and many sizes too large for her bony frame. It draped her in layers of gray and rust-colored dust that lodged itself under her fingernails, clinging to her shoulders.

Eleanorah went through the motions with a practiced, mechanical steadiness. She wanted to ask where her sister was, the baby she'd been carrying on her back, walking barefoot through the village alone. She wanted to ask about her parents, where she slept, and if she had enough food. She wanted to hold her in her arms, and never let go.

Instead, she listened. She pressed on her soft belly. She felt for fever, and pointed. Down the line. Bodies like objects, her hands like tools, probing, poking, prodding. How many children had they seen? How many had they not?

"Sister Eleanorah," a teacher named Judith called to her from the doorway. "We would like you to address the class tomorrow about some health talks," she began. "We will have students from the 5th and 6th grades. I have asked Pastor David for you to come in the morning. We will be waiting eagerly."

Eleanorah swallowed a protest, a fullness in her lower abdomen reminding her that she had not made the short walk to the outhouse all day, training herself to hold it. She couldn't hold it anymore.

"I'll be right back," she mumbled. Clutching at a handful of her chitenge, she scurried to the small shack with a tin roof, swiping at the flies. Inside, a dirty concrete floor surrounded an open hole in the ground. Lifting her skirt, she wrinkled her nose, trying to breathe without smelling the fumes. A sensation of relief replaced the pressure in her stomach.

"Shit," she said, cursing herself for being in such a hurry that she forgot to bring any toilet paper.

No toilet paper. No water. No soap.

She had some hand sanitizer in her bag. When she found it, she squeezed a half dollar size of gel onto her palm and rubbed her hands together, ignoring the brown streaks that appeared. The alcohol masked the pungent smell of urine and feces for a few seconds before it returned full force.

Bailing out a sinking ship with a teaspoon. Watering the desert with a backyard hose. *How could she give a health talk when no one in her audience had access to soap or running water? How could she tell them to wear shoes to keep the worms from burrowing into their exposed heels when they didn't have any?*

"Eleanorah, come on, we're ready to leave," Skylar, one of the student leaders, called. "You can leave the rest of the charts. Nurse Robyn will get them tomorrow. Let's go."

She ran down the dirt path, taking the only open seat left, next to Ba Maurine. Tears flowed in a steady, unstoppable stream. They plopped on the floor of the bus, turning instantly to mud. Tonight was their last evening together before heading back to Chicago. A feast awaited the students at one of the homes hosting them during their stay. One Eleanorah did not believe she deserved.

A gate swung open and several women bustled out of a darkened home, faintly glowing with candles in the windows.

"God willing, the lights return," Ba Maurine said, looking up at the crescent moon.

"If the good Lord's willing and the creek don't rise," Eleanorah remembered one of Mutti's sayings she repeated often while peeling the potatoes and stirring the gravy, taking short sips of black coffee in a blue marble mug. A rush of nostalgia for her grandmother's arms and incessant words washed over her. She would give anything to hear that constant chatter. The comfort in the disarray. The twinkle in her eye and her deep, belly laughter that shook all the folds of her skin, making her large, round face bigger than life.

But the creek always rose. It flooded and overflowed its banks. It brought down the trees her grandmother loved so much. It turned footpaths into rivers, destroying bridges.

It made it impossible to leave home or go back, once you left.

***

Their final morning together, Ba Maurine made an extra fuss over them at breakfast, boiling water for tea and coffee to sip with their cereal and bananas. She folded and refolded the chitenges around their waists, tucking in the fabric here, pulling it tight there. "Today is a special day," she told them, unpinning her hair, letting the short curls fall around her face.

Eleanorah stirred the cream into her coffee slowly. Her appetite was missing. A folder on the table held printouts from the Centers for Disease Control and the World Health Organization. Before leaving Chicago, she'd quickly gathered materials for the students about how to wash their hands and cover their mouths when they coughed. There were pictures and diagrams, reminders of all of the things the children in the village did not have.

Shoes. Toothpaste. Soap. It seemed so simple. The words and drawings, telling them exactly what to do, and for how long.

"I will see you at the church this afternoon." Ba Maurine cleared their plates, waving them toward the door.

"Thank you, breakfast was delicious," Eleanorah lied, the sour aftertaste coating her teeth. Ba Maurine beamed, and Eleanorah wondered how many more she would have to tell to get through the day.

Outside the city's borders, the van passed now familiar landmarks. The wide, flat tree by the clump of huts. The tall brush surrounding the lonely stall selling housewares and MTN cards. The larger than life anthills that became houses with people living inside a mixture of earth and cement. She immersed herself in the details so she wouldn't forget. The pattern of dirt on her skin and the way people spoke like rivers. Open mouths and wide, canyon smiles.

She combed the landscape for every curve and color, memorizing the shape of the women carrying avocados and sacks of cornmeal to market in large woven baskets on their heads. Their necks thick and sweaty, they moved with elegance, swishing their way through crowds. She watched the men, standing along the edges of roadways and sidewalks, hawking rolled-up paintings or peddling elephants and zebras carved from teak, mahogany, and ironwood.

Soon, all of the sights and sounds would be stories, recollections retold in fragments. They would shift like waves of light, become blurry, and faded. The more she tried to hold on, the more they slipped through her fingers.

"Good morning, Madame, you are welcome," the students greeted Eleanorah in unison, their voices like finely tuned instruments.

Ba Judith gave a signal and the students sat down the same way they stood, with one, fluid movement. "Thank you for coming, my sister. We are prepared for you," she said, pointing to the center of the classroom and stood to the side. Eleanorah's heart raced as she met their eyes.

"I wanted to share a few things with you before we left about how to take care of your health," she began. "Do you remember the clinic we had at the school yesterday?"

"Yes Madame, I was there!" "I was there also, Madame!" The students smiled, and nodded in agreement.

"Raise your hand before you speak!" Ba Judith rebuked.

Eleanorah cleared her throat. "Who can tell me something we must do after we use the outhouse and before we eat? The room was silent. Ba Judith rubbed her hands together. A hand shot into the air.

"Yes?"

"We must wash our hands, Madame."

"Very good!" Eleanorah smiled. "Washing our hands helps us stay healthy and keeps germs away that can cause us to be sick." She searched for simple words to communicate concepts like bacteria, disease, and sanitation. "Do you all know the alphabet?" she asked.

Laughter erupted and Eleanorah realized the silliness of her question.

"Okay, well when we wash, we should scrub the soap, and rub our hands together for as long as it takes to sing the alphabet through twice," she sang, demonstrating with cracked, dry hands. The students joined her, static electricity building between their palms.

Another hand shot into the air. A boy in the front row, who looked about fourteen, waited to be called on.

"Yes." Eleanorah nodded to him.

"Madam, if we work really hard in school, and we do our best, can we come to America?"

Ba Judith raised her eyebrows. The silence was alive. It bounced around the room like a ping pong ball, careening from corner to corner, moving faster and faster.

"Yes," she said, disguising the blatant untruth with a dose of encouragement. "If you work really hard and do well in school, you can go anywhere you want."

The boy grinned, sitting up a little taller.

Eleanorah turned her back and picked up a piece of chalk. "Human Immunodeficiency Virus. Acquired Immune Deficiency Syndrome." She wrote the names carefully in big letters on the faded blackboard, trying to decipher the code. Voices whispered names above unmarked graves, repeating the syllables and consonants belonging to their one life, over, and over again.

"Remember, remember," they plead.

She shook her head. The class waited expectantly, a soft light of persistent courage in their eyes.

Eleanorah wanted to scream with rage at the unfairness of it all. She wanted to shout and throw books at the wall, *the way her mother had at her.* She wanted to exorcise the grief woven into their DNA with hard facts and acronyms that would protect them from any more loss or pain.

She took the chalk and drew a shaky line down the middle, separating the board into columns of symptoms, and precautions. When she finally spoke, her voice was louder than she intended. It had an edge, a sharpness that made her sentences disjointed, and scattered. She cleared her throat again.

Ba Judith squeezed her shoulder gently and handed her a bottle of water.

Eleanorah stopped mid-sentence and took a long sip. She was giving answers to the wrong questions. Her lips felt cracked. She tasted a small amount of blood in the corner of her mouth. Faces blurred together, indistinguishable from the walls, the desks, the chairs.

"Are you okay?"

Her head jerked.

"Sister Eleanorah, are you okay?" Ba Judith repeated, more urgently this time.

She blinked, forcing her eyes to refocus. "Yeah, I'm okay. Thanks for the water. Everything got sort of fuzzy for a minute, but I'm better now."

Pastor David appeared in the doorway with uncanny timeliness. "Are you ready to go to the orphanage? We have a special surprise for you."

The students rose in unison, ignoring the abrupt ending to her presentation. "We will be joining you," Ba Judith explained.

They linked their arms through Eleanorah's, gathering on each side, holding her steady. "We will miss you, Madame," a student named Stephanie said, leaning her head on her shoulder.

Eleanorah pressed her cheek against her dark, coarse hair. "Me, too." It was the first honest thing she said all day.

***

Across from the school, the pale orange orphanage was almost the same hue as the ground in the early morning sun. Next to the house, under a shaded platform with a tin roof, a group of people were singing and dancing. Eleanorah recognized some of them from their evening dinners and some from the village.

A short man wearing all white held a microphone near the front, his voice ringing above the others. "Oh Jesus, you are Holy, Holy, Holy. God our Father, Abba, bless us, your children."

"Hallelujah!" "Yes, Lord!" The crowd raised their hands, nodding their heads in affirmation.

This must be the service Ba Maurine told us about, she thought.

She ached for the confidence of their belief. For the familiarity of her parents' faith. Its conviction and commitment, full of hope, and anticipation until it wasn't.

"We want to thank our brothers and sisters for sharing with us during these last few weeks," Pastor David said, quieting the crowd. "Thank you to our guests and partners from Chicago who gave us their support. Together we are making much progress and helping the lives of the children you see here today.

"Soon, you will return to your country, and families. Before you go, I want to tell you, you are Zambians now. When you go home, tell people about us. Share our story. You are our ambassadors." He looked across the room, slowly making eye contact with each student.

"Yet, this comes with a warning," he said, pausing. "Your words have the power to build or destroy. You can choose darkness or light. My brothers and sisters, I urge you, use your power to build." His eyes rested on Eleanorah's.

"I invite my brothers and sisters from Chicago to come and receive a gift to help you remember us. The flag of Zambia is very symbolic," he continued. "The red represents our struggle for freedom. The black, the people of Zambia. The orange symbolizes our mineral resources, and the copper belt that runs through the heart of our land. The eagle in the right-hand corner represents our ability to overcome difficulty.

"You are our ambassadors now. Go home and tell people about us."

Eleanorah stood in line to receive her flag with nervous determination; she wouldn't forget.

"I remember when we first met at the university," Pastor David said smiling, holding her hand steady.

"Me, too," she said, recalling an entire room, bathed in radiance. A continent of light, he had promised. She'd come all this way and still hadn't found it.

"Don't worry." He gazed thoughtfully toward the expanding horizon. "You will be back again someday." He picked a purple flower from his pocket and handed it to her, its delicate petals reflecting the smallest luminosity.

"For your book," he said.

***

Eleanorah reached for the newly purchased comforter fitfully, pulling it above her shoulders. Closing her eyes against the bright midday sun, she willed herself to sleep. There were just a few hours left before getting ready for another shift at Northwestern, a fact her body ironically resisted by refusing to rest.

Eleanorah rushed down the hallway, her tennis shoes squeaking against the freshly waxed floor as she pushed the heavy doors of the Emergency Room open. Halogen bulbs droned without apology, spilling bright light into sterile rooms. She kept her gaze straight ahead as she entered yet another hallway, sprinting toward the elevator that would take her to the third floor of the Intensive Care Unit.

Inside the elevator seconds, maybe hours passed.

She was late to work. Really late. It was five after nine and she was supposed to be at the hospital almost three hours ago. The elevator jerked to a stop. She took a deep breath and exited toward the nurses' station. In one of the rooms on her right, staff gathered around a critical patient, talking in hushed, grave tones. The curtains were wide open. The patient laid there, motionless.

Eleanorah kept walking.

"You're late," the charge nurse accused with a sharp tone. She pointed at the large clock hanging above their head. It tick-tocked in time

with the beeping monitors. The synchrony pulsed with a life divided by the second hand and cardiac strips of paper with p-waves and t-waves, measured in millimeters.

Down the hall, an alarm went off. She had no time to respond before a doctor grabbed her by the elbow, ushering her into a patient's room. With his other hand, he flipped through a navy blue chart making small grunts of displeasure. "What are the vital signs for this patient? Has he been seen by Dr. Roberts? When was the last time he received a dose of diuretic?"

Eleanorah's face went blank. She watched herself search frantically in her empty pockets for anything she might have written down that might explain who the patient was or what was going on. Her hands came up empty.

The alarm sounded again. This time it was right on top of her, loud, and piercing. She woke with a start, body full of adrenaline, ready to act.

"Just a dream. Just a dream," she repeated.

The vivid details flashed through her mind with so much clarity it was several moments before she believed it. The covers tangled. She felt for her alarm hidden underneath her pillow and hit the snooze button. Her bare feet stuck out from the end of the bed. Her toes were cold but sweat trickled down her forehead.

Gauging from the afternoon sun streaming through the window, she guessed it was just past four. The autumn light was more muted now, and shrinking at both ends, every day. Often, when she arrived home in the morning after a shift at the hospital, the sun was just beginning to rise. Before she closed the blinds, and crawled into bed, she could see shades of maroon and violet streak across the sky. It was a strange lullaby—the birds chirping and garbage trucks rolling by. Buses picking up children for school and neighbors starting their cars for work.

As the day began, hers came to a shaky finale.

She shivered and felt the tip of her nose. It was cold as ice. The radiator started whistling, right on cue. In a few minutes, it would bang and clatter like kitchen pots in the sink as steam poured into the small room next to her bedroom.

"These old Chicago apartments," she grumbled out loud to no one in particular, though she knew she was lucky to find this one so soon after coming back from Zambia.

The alarm went off a third time. She sighed and kicked off the covers, glancing at the miniature flag on her nightstand. She picked it up, remembering her promise, and Pastor David's, too.

The timed coffee pot sputtered to life and the familiar aroma of ground beans filled her nose. Some days, the smell transported her to the hills of Chiapas or the table nestled in the corner of a tiled kitchen with Maru, and Antonio sitting across from her. Today, it beckoned her down the red dirt roads with towering ant hills.

Instead, she padded barefoot into the kitchen, scrutinizing the black walnut and eastern redbuds spaced neatly along sidewalks. A few leaves clung stubbornly to their mostly vacant limbs in an inevitable battle against the pull of gravity. Piles of orange and brown scattered in the wind. Lifted temporarily along with debris from the street, they blew upward in a sudden gust. She watched them plunge downward just as swiftly, moved by an invisible force, over, and over again.

***

"Hey lady, how are you?" Margot's voice greeted her from behind the nurse's station.

Eleanorah returned her smile and checked the whiteboard that listed the assignments for the night shift.

"Don't worry, you have my patients tonight." Margot winked. "How's it feel to be off orientation?"

*Not good...*She wanted to admit. After graduation, she'd desperately wanted to work in the Neonatal Intensive Care Unit, the only place she really felt comfortable, cradling, and swaddling the little ones tightly against her chest. But the economy had crashed, flooding the field with more experienced nurses reluctantly leaving their retirement. Nobody wanted new grads, and if they did, they were lucky to take what they could get.

After months of interviews, Eleanorah was hired as a float pool nurse, the bottom of the totem pole. A 'floater,' meant every shift was in a different unit with a different set of bodies to care for. When she dreamed, she followed them from floor to floor, never sure where she was supposed to be or who she had checked on last.

"It's okay," Eleanorah said as sat down next to her, trying to put on a brave face. "It's still overwhelming, but I'm starting to get used to it."

"Are you still having nightmares?"

Eleanorah nodded without looking her in the eye. They came almost every night.

"It'll get better, I'm sure. I can't imagine having to be on a different floor all the time. I don't know how you do it." Margot shook her head sympathetically, brushing a stray curl out of her clear blue eyes.

"How's it going with you?" Eleanorah asked, picking up one of the charts from the pile in front of them, and flipping to the section with the doctor's orders.

"Great!" Margot enthused. "I love my co-workers and they've been really helpful. I wish you could work days, too!" She looked at Eleanorah hopefully.

Truthfully, Eleanorah was envious of more than just the day shift, even though she'd voluntarily turned it down for the higher paying night schedule. Margot emanated a confidence and surety Eleanorah longed for. When Margot didn't know the answer, she made one up and put her whole weight behind it, until she convinced herself and everyone else it was true. She bubbled with a vitality Eleanorah admired and resented with equal proportion.

Eleanorah scanned her patient list, avoiding her question. She was still struggling to flip between the night shifts and days off, which meant even when she wasn't working, she was often up at 3 a.m. watching reruns of sitcoms or whipping up her mother's recipes to pass the time. But the night shift paid more, significantly more enough to persist, for now.

"Anything else I should know?" Eleanorah folded several sheets of paper together with the names of the patients they shared, putting them in her pocket.

"Nope, that's it, lady! I'm off tomorrow. Do you wanna go grab a drink when you get up? I know a place that has a good coffee stout," she said jokingly.

Eleanorah managed a half smile. "I'm on for the next three nights, but maybe after?"

"Sounds good!"

Eleanorah waved her off and headed toward the supply room. The metal shelves reached the ceiling, each overflowing with bright blue bins. Each section labeled, and categorized precisely. Cardboard boxes of alcohol wipes, gauze, and saline flushes stacked on top of each other. Nothing amiss. Everything in order.

What they lacked in hope, they made up for in supplies.

She studied the excess and quickly lined her pockets with a handful of flushes, alcohol pads, and needle caps, filling her uniform before treading quietly down the beige hallway. Quickly unfolding the paper in her pocket, she reviewed her notes before gently knocking on the first patient's room.

"Hello, Mrs. Lykins?" She rapped on the open door again, drawing the striped curtain to the side. "I'm Eleanorah. I'll be your nurse for the night. How are you feeling?"

She greeted an old woman with permed gray hair, propped up with pillows under each elbow and left hip. Her skin sagged around her eyes. Her skeleton protruded from her body like scaffolding. But her lips were painted bright pink. "I've been better, dear," she said, smiling weakly.

Eleanorah unwrapped her stethoscope from around her neck and placed the two rubber ends in her ears. "May I?"

The woman nodded silently as Eleanorah listened to her lungs, first on the right side, then on the left. Next, she reached for the woman's wrist, pressing firmly with two fingers on the outside, by her thumb.

Suddenly, the wind rushed in, bringing the scent of pine needles and ripe hedge apples. Whippoorwills cooed. Blackberry brambles reached for legs and ankles, anything they could stick to.

Her grandfather stopped often, picking up a broken or fallen limb, inspecting it carefully.

"What are you looking for?" Eleanorah watched him press his ear to the bark, covered with moss, and ants. "Well," he said. "I'm listening."

"What do you mean, Grandpa?" She remembered the family tree in the office, and the strange whisperings they made when the wind blew.

"A chuisle mo chroí." Her grandfather's words sounded like a gurgling stream. "The beat of your heart travels through your whole body, like an echo," he explained, pausing to look at the cloudless October sky. Gently taking her index and middle finger, he placed them on her wrist until they vibrated. "Even when we can't hear it, we can feel it."

He pointed to her chest and placed a hand on his own. "The beat of your heart sings in harmony with mine and the trees and all that is," he said, motioning around them. Leaves rustled in soft agreement.

"Everything in life has its own special sound, like a note in a symphony."

Eleanorah frowned.

"But Grandpa, what happens if the tree dies? How can you hear its heartbeat if it gets chopped down or falls over? Isn't it dead?"

"Nothing ever really dies, my child," he said smiling. "Remember the butterflies? When one cycle ends, another begins. If we listen closely, even things that appear to be gone still sing to us."

Eleanorah removed her fingers, disconnecting from the vivid memory. The whiff of pine faded, replaced with filtered air. Her patient's pulse was strong, but rapid.

"Are you having any pain?" Eleanorah asked gently, looping her stethoscope back around her neck.

"Not so much pain as just general discomfort. Honestly, these beds are not made for princesses, are they?"

"No, definitely not. That doesn't mean you aren't one, though," Eleanorah said with a wink. "Do you mind telling me what day and month it is?"

"October." Mrs. Lykins squinted toward the whiteboard on the opposite wall. "Looks like it's Thursday, the 17th. It's hard to keep track, honestly, while all I'm doing is sitting in this bed."

"And the year?"

"Two thousand eleven. Do you think I'll get out of here in time for Thanksgiving? We're having it early this year on account of my grandson's in-laws being out of state, you know."

"I think that can be arranged. The word is we're planning to let you go tomorrow if you behave tonight," she said, patting her hand. "Last question. Can you tell me who the President is?"

"Mr. Barack Obama. I voted for him, but don't tell my husband," she whispered, smiling.

"Looks like you check out, Mrs. Lykins." Eleanorah grinned, hoping her lucidity would last through the night. "I'll be back to check on you before bed. Call me if you need anything, okay?"

A vision of her twisted on the floor flashed through her mind.

"Make sure you call me before you try to get out of bed so I can help." She reminded her, more sternly this time.

"I will," Mrs. Lykins said with an exasperated smile, waving her out the door. "Go check on your other patients. Surely they're worse off than me."

Eleanorah closed the curtain and sighed, briefly looking through her list before making a game plan.

"Are you okay?" A unit secretary in turquoise scrubs looked at her sideways from behind the desk. "You look kind of...pale." Her eyes narrowed as if scanning something and sensing a glitch.

Eleanorah nodded. "I'm alright. Just tired, maybe. It's my first night back, and I didn't sleep very well today" she smiled apologetically.

The woman tilted her head to the side knowingly. "Only ten more hours to go."

"Only ten more hours to go," Eleanorah confirmed, glancing at the clock above the nurse's station.

A pain in the middle of her shoulders tightened. It rounded inward as she tread down the hallway. Caved in a little when she stood outside each doorway, primed to knock, readying herself to do battle with the disease inside, waiting for her.

***

The gel felt cold and clinical against her exposed, fleshy abdomen. Every muscle was tense. The images on the screen shifted as the ultrasound glided across her belly. Gray shadows gave way to dark spaces. Clumps of white blended into surrounding crevices and hallowed spaces.

This was not how she imagined it would be.

The radiology technician looked at the screen and then back at Eleanorah, her face showing the tell-tale sign of bad news Eleanorah knew intimately. The forced neutral expression and thin lips. Ambivalent eyes that avoided direct contact with the patient wearing the gown lying on the table. The absence of small talk while the nurse or doctor examined the numbers on the machine with intense focus.

She shivered.

The technician offered a sympathetic smile. "Here you go," she said, handing her a paper towel from the dispenser on the white wall next to the sink.

"Thank you." Eleanorah wiped the gel from her belly and pulled the thin gown back over her anemic body.

"I'll have the images from the ultrasound to Dr. James by the end of the day. Someone from his office will call you to discuss the results, okay?"

Eleanorah reached for the crumpled, ceil blue scrubs folded on the chair next to the table. She tucked her newly cropped, chin-length hair behind her ears, and nodded. She did not want to appear desperate for immediate answers like her patients. She would remain composed. One by one, she put her legs and arms through her uniform and smoothed out the wrinkles. She clipped her badge onto the pocket by her chest and laced her shoes, trying to resist the urge to run.

The sun rose over Lake Michigan, creating a dense fog she couldn't see, but felt. The lights in the parking lot quivered as if trying to decide to turn on or off. Eleanorah sat in the cold car for several minutes before putting the key in the ignition, gripping the wheel with shaking hands.

The wind howled and moaned as it swept between towering buildings and narrow alleyways. Darkness licked the rolled-up windows of her car and windshield. In the distance, she heard the familiar wail of sirens, flashing red, and blue. Her heart drummed against her chest. Adrenaline coursed through her limbs ready to flee, or fight.

Instead, she froze.

***

There was blood on the floor. She noticed it right away by the smell, like metal. It pooled and smeared stubbornly as she bent down, intentionally straddling the maroon liquid between her blue and white tennis shoes, careful not to stain her uniform.

Blood is thicker than water, she dismayed. *It does not wash easily.*

Squatting, she tore off sheets of wipes to scrub the surface of the mistake she'd just made while drops of blood continued to ooze and leak from a small hole where the I.V. tubing had pierced through the plastic bag. She glanced up at the half-empty bag and wondered how long it had been dripping down the cold metal pole next to the patient, who was growing more translucent by the minute.

It couldn't have been more than ten minutes. I was just in here for the first set of vital signs. Her gloves smeared with red. The container of wipes read like a hazmat warning: "May cause cancer. Don't ingest. Wash immediately if contact with skin is made."

The thin layer of vinyl covering her hands offered laughable protection. This was life. This was death. She was not immune.

Eleanorah carefully pulled her gloves off inside out one at a time, and moved to the sink, waving her palm in front of the green sensor. The water from the faucet was lukewarm and turned on automatically, just like the soap dispenser, and paper towel machine. She waited for a few seconds until it was hot and scrubbed her hands rapidly, using several amounts of soap more than usual. Before they were dry, she put on another pair of gloves, and hurried to the patient's bedside.

"Mr. Arravos, I'm sorry to wake you. How are you feeling? Any trouble breathing? Any pain?"

He blinked, and glared. "I was fine before you came in the room."

"I'm sorry. I have to take your vital signs more often when you're getting a blood transfusion," she explained. "If there's a reaction we need to catch it quickly. There was a problem with the last bag. It was leaking, so I need to get another one and we'll try again, okay?"

He nodded and closed his eyes. The monitor above their heads traced his breath, blood pressure, and heart rate in a variety of colors. If any of the numbers went above or below the parameters set by the nurse, a red alarm would flash. It would beep in the room, at the nurse's station, and ring to the phone she carried in her pocket.

There were systems. Safety nets. Rules and practices to signal distress before it was too late. These were the things she could control. But, it was a battlefield even the most seasoned nurse sometimes miscalculated.

A warm, gushing sensation forced Eleanorah to quicken her pace down the hallway. Her pulse raced as she walked discreetly in the direction of the staff restroom. Squeezing her thighs together, she prayed she had enough time. The door closed behind her with a loud thud. She sat on the porcelain toilet, hunched over, and dizzy. Bright, red blood fell in an unending stream she couldn't stop. She listened as it hit the water, making plopping sounds, like rainfall.

The phone in her pocket rang. She jumped, inhaling sharply. "ICU, this is Eleanorah," she answered in a sing-song voice that was no longer voluntary.

"We're sending up another unit of blood now," a terse tone replied on the other end. "Please be more careful this time."

"Thank you," she said, but the sharp dial tone cut her off before she could finish.

Eleanorah quickly applied more padding to her underwear, in layers. *She was not a sieve. She was not weak.* She gritted her teeth and forced herself to get up, silently praying the blood wouldn't soak through her scrubs.

It had been months since the bleeding first began, constant, and steady. She bled when she was on her period and when she wasn't, without rhyme or reason. Sometimes she could sense it coming. More often, there was little time to react before red stains bloomed between her legs. The more she tried to hide it, the worse it got.

She pulled up her pants, retying the drawstring tightly into a neat bow, trying to regain her balance. For the third time in the last five minutes, she washed her dry, chapped hands, her skin split open around her knuckles, making the alcohol sting like salt in an open wound.

Walking down the hallway, she ran her fingers absentmindedly over the vials of medicine in her pocket. The small, glass bottles reminded her of the smooth river stones she used to collect, filling her pockets with as many as she could before coming in for dinner. Rock, paper, scissors. A game she played with her brothers. Now, she cheated the Angel of Death with pockets full of rocks every night.

Knocking gently, she paused briefly before opening the patient's door, out of habit. An older woman with white hair sat next to Mr. Arravos' bed, holding one of his hands. Her face was solemn but calm. Eleanorah noticed a second woman pacing up and down the room anxiously, her face flushed. The tension in the air told Eleanorah she was interrupting a heated conversation.

She smiled, apologetically. "This will feel cold," she warned as she moved to hang the new bag of blood. "Try not to move your arm or bend your elbow," she cautioned with a practiced, friendly sternness.

The woman in the chair stood to move out of her way. "I'm Susan, his mother," she explained.

"Eleanorah, nice to meet you. I'm taking care of him tonight. Can I get you anything?"

"No," she said, watching her son. "He's been craving a Coke all day but everyone keeps telling him he can't eat or drink."

"The doctors want to keep him NPO in case he needs to go to surgery," Eleanorah explained.

The bright yellow sign above his bed reiterated the order, "Nothing By Mouth," in bold, black lettering. Green mouth swabs and a mint-flavored paste lay on the bed tray next to a cup full of melting ice chips. That was all he was supposed to have. A little bit of white paste smeared on the green swab, two or three pieces of ice.

He pointed to his mask and tried to take it off.

"It's okay, I'll help," she said, lifting it slightly, making sure the majority of the air was still flowing over his ruddy nose.

"I don't...." He paused and swallowed. "I don't want to do this." His eyes moved across the room to the machines and bags of fluids hanging on poles.

Eleanorah fit the mask back over his nose and mouth snugly. "I know it's hard," she conceded. "Are you in any pain?"

He shook his head as she adjusted his pillow. "You're really doing better," she said encouragingly. "The medications are working and your vital signs have improved since you first came down." She looked at the monitors again.

"I don't care!" He pulled the mask off his face and glared toward the foot of the bed where the younger woman was still pacing.

"Dad, don't do that!" His daughter moved to the opposite side of the bed, reaching for the oxygen mask.

"It's okay, I've got it." Eleanorah smoothed his hair and gently put it back on, a gesture she'd repeated with countless belligerent patients.

"He told us he doesn't want any of this," the daughter said, looking at Eleanorah with tears in her eyes. "I told him he doesn't have a choice," she added quickly, returning to her father.

"I see." Eleanorah looked at all of the equipment and supplies keeping him alive. He was alive. Her only task was to help him survive the night.

"I'll give you a few minutes alone. He probably just needs some rest," she whispered as his eyes drooped closed.

"What is it?" The charge nurse, Michelle, peaked her head around the corner, reading the clues in Eleanorah's posture.

"His vitals are stabilizing, I think the blood is helping too." She shifted her weight from one foot to the next. "He says he doesn't want any more treatment. He told me he was done," she sighed.

Michelle clucked her tongue. "Okay. I'll go in and confirm. Better page Dr. Hale and the others to let them know."

Shouts echoed down the hallway. "Think of your grandson! Dad, please! We're not ready for you to go. Please don't go."

Eleanorah entered the room with Michelle and closed the door behind them, trying to contain the grief. The daughter's flustered body shook uncontrollably, but his mother stood next to the head of the bed, mechanically stroking his tangled hair. Her cropped white bob mirrored her skin and the alabaster paint on the walls.

Eleanorah was not ready to give up so easily. He could make it. *They could do this together.* It was almost morning.

"I spoke with your doctors. You realize you're doing much better now, right?" She provoked the question with care. "They think they'll be able to perform exploratory surgery first thing in the morning. They're hoping you'll be able to get out of here," she said, forcing a tone of optimism.

Mr. Arravos shook his head dully, eyes staring straight ahead. "I'm giving up." He shifted his gaze from the wall, looking at Eleanorah with clear, blue eyes. "I don't want this anymore. Take it off," he said, pointing at the wires crawling out from beneath his gown, pulling at the ones running down his skin like overgrown vines.

Unlike usual, there was no emotion in his voice, no crack to fill with the balminess of hope, no floating question mark to wrangle like a lasso, pulling him back toward life. Her heart beat faster, eyes frantically searching the room for a way to pour her life force into his, making up the difference.

Her bones knit together in a determined stance, pulling against gravity in a tug-of-war with despair. *This was supposed to be their battle. They were supposed to be on the same side.* Anger simmered to the surface, making her feel too hot in her layered uniform. If they gave up now, she would be the one placing her signature on the final line withdrawing care, inking her name next to his forever, dissolving herself of the blame, but not the outcome.

"I'll be right back." She walked hurriedly toward the vending machines just outside the waiting room. *A dying man deserves to enjoy a Coke,* she decided. "Fuck the rules," she said, blinking back tears.

She returned, placing the cold can on his bedside tray.

"Here," she said, scooting it closer and pulling a straw from her pocket, unwrapping it before putting on her gloves. "That should be easier." She bent it at an angle so he could reach it more easily.

He grasped the straw with puffy hands, taking a long sip through the small opening in his oxygen mask. He sighed, licking his lips. "Thank you," he said, resting his head back on the pillow and closing his eyes.

Slowly, she began disconnecting the wires to his heart, untangling them one by one. She turned off the medicine in the I.V. pumps, and then the monitor screen. She wiped the residue from the adhesive off his clammy skin, coiling the tubing neatly before discarding it. The sound made a hollow thud as it hit the bottom of an empty bin.

From experience, Eleanorah knew that sometimes Death came slowly, in predictable phases. But on rare occasions, it arrived unannounced like a POP! As if a valve had been released, and all of the air let out. Without warning it swept through like a winter wind, leaving only an insatiable ache.

It happened like this for Mr. Arravos, at 7:05 a.m. that morning.

In the middle of shift change, the monitor sent ominous tones to Eleanorah's phone. An eerie scream confirmed the loud ringing in her ear. By the time she ran across the hall, it was over.

He was gone.

Shrieks came from inside the room. Without warning, thick, co-agulated blood started seeping from his nostrils. Before Eleanorah could rush to wipe it away, more seeped out of his mouth. As if a dam had broken loose, it poured like a waterfall over the side of the bed rails and landed on Eleanorah's shoe, falling unapologetically onto the white tiled floor.

In the seconds it took Eleanorah to counteract the tidal wave of shock making its way through her body, something inside her gave way, too. That day, a portion of her followed him to the grave.

***

"Ellie, you're not okay," he said, putting down his fork with a bite of egg still clinging to the tines.

He paused, waiting for her to finish chewing her pancake while a waitress wearing a navy blue apron came, silently filling her white mug with more coffee.

Outside the plexiglass windows, a somnolent sun reflected branches with tiny red buds, waiting to unfurl. The shortest month of the year, for some reason, February always felt interminable. She forced a smile and a slight shrug of her shoulders. Avoiding his gaze, she watched her coffee turn a light brown with the addition of a small package of cream.

"What did the doctor say?" he prodded gently.

"That if the medication didn't work after a few months, to call him back and he'd refer me to a surgeon." What she didn't say was that things had been getting worse. That since that morning with Mr. Arravos, she'd barely been able to get out of bed in between her shifts at the hospital, an indication of her declining health, but something more.

"Has it been working?"

"No," she sighed, wanting to escape the whole conversation, along with the reasons she was there, eating breakfast with her father at an IHOP instead of back in Chicago, in her apartment, lying down.

The house was selling. Her Grandmother Esther, dying. She repeated the inevitable, hoping eventually she could accept it.

"Eleanorah," he said, his tone more firm this time. "You're not okay. None of us are okay. Your body is telling you that. Something is wrong and you need to listen. It's time to let go. You've been helping me and the children at the orphanage in Zambia and taking care of your patients. What about taking care of yourself? I think it's time to schedule the surgery."

"Dad..." Eleanorah looked down at her unfinished pancakes. "Can I ask you something? About you and Mom?"

"Sure, honey." His face softened.

"What happened? I mean, I know what happened. I was there. But, what really happened? How did it all turn out so...bad?"

"Well..." Her father leaned back, thoughtfully. "You know, I think it really began when the church started to splinter. Suddenly there were two sides of the pew—folks who grew up believing Zion was a real, physical place, and others starting to believe it was all just a metaphor. An idea, nothing more. Your mom and I decided to move here because we thought, if it wasn't real yet, *let's make it real.*"

She nodded. The only one who didn't move was Joshuah, her father's youngest brother. When the others received letters of silence, asking them to "cease, and desist" or lose their church membership, Joshuah did not. Instead, he was offered the position of Head Pastor, the same role her grandfather held before he was forced to leave.

The others had begged him not to accept.

"Can't you see, it's just another tactic in their aim to gain more power and control!" Her uncle Josiah fumed at his younger brother. "They're doing it on purpose. They're trying to split us up. They want our loyalties to be divided so that we turn on each other instead of them." But Joshuah wouldn't hear it. "We all know Father's ideas and dreams are hopelessly outdated," he said with a sneer. "All he can focus on is the past and his shop. It's time we all move on and grow up. You can go ahead and move to the middle of nowhere, waiting for God knows what. I'm staying here."

And he had. Eleanorah never knew him, only of him. He'd passed away several years ago, before there was time for reconciliation. He was too young. There was too much left unsaid.

Her father sighed, looking toward the windows advertising a 24/7 breakfast menu. "I think we were also running away from the conflict. We didn't know how to disagree so we chose to separate. We came here because we wanted a good life for you and your brothers, something even better than what we had growing up. A place to belong. Proof that all of this mattered," he said, waving his hands at the imaginary remnants of their life.

Eleanorah recalled the potluck dinners after church with countless cousins and aunts and uncles. Summer camps singing hymns by the campfire with her friends from Sunday school, sitting through hours of sermons she couldn't understand, wriggling in her seat or poking one of her brothers for a moment of relief.

It wasn't all bad. In the moment. But the aftertaste—what was left in the aftermath became impossible to endure.

"You know, I think your mother and I faced a lot of disappointment when our dream of Zion didn't come true the way we expected. We forgot what we were fighting for and started fighting each other," he said. "Home isn't a place or a person, Ellie. It's a choice. Love is a choice, a series of daily actions. I think we simply stopped choosing it."

Eleanorah looked out the window, willing herself not to cry. *If her parents stopped choosing each other, was she also a variable? A choice they could stop making?*

"What do we do now, Dad?"

How could they move forward without admitting total defeat? Her Mutti was still waiting for the end times, as were others, always coming up with new prophecies and timelines that confirmed the "Promised Land" was ever near. Mutti had built extra shelves in the pantry, and ones outside of it, too filling each level with different items from top to bottom in preparation—canned tomatoes from the garden, boxes of beans, diapers, and gas masks. She'd created a nest and fluffed her feathers, convinced the sky was falling and Independence would soon be the only safe place left.

"Is there any truth in all of the stories?"

"I don't know, Ellie. Honestly, I wish I did. I think what's still true for me is the hope we all felt. The courage it took to leave our past, and start something new. There's a lot of it I don't understand and probably wouldn't do over. But I'm glad we have you and your brothers," he said. "That wasn't a mistake. So that has to mean your mom and I weren't a mistake, either."

Eleanorah and her father drove to the house in quiet solitude. They sat in the living room facing the mantel, lighting the fire in the hearth one last time. A "For Sale" sign bent in the breeze at the bottom of the gravel driveway, warning a winter storm.

The couch sank low to the floor with the weight of their tired bodies. Ghosts and shadows surrounded them. Conversations with raised voices. Slamming cabinet doors. Sobs that shook and rattled the furniture. A smoke alarm going off, again, and again.

Her Father had used the insurance money from the fire and turned his mourning into carpentry—shiny faucets that no longer dripped. New windows in the warped frames. Light fixtures without the buzz. Colors selected for the strength of their character. Bright tones like yellow and green and coral, chosen for their ability to hide the wrinkles and uneven circles under their eyes.

"When your mom and I first moved in, I worked for weeks to even out this floor." He surveyed their home one last time. "I laid every board by hand. I wish I could have done more. I wish..." His voice quavered.

Eleanorah rested her head on his shoulder.

The air thickened with freezing rain. Crowds of unseen creatures burrowed deeper into the earth. A lone whippoorwill trilled a farewell song, *"I'm sorry, I'm sorry, please forgive me. Thank you, I love you."*

***

Her grandmother's swollen hand squeezed hers, letting Eleanorah know she could still hear. She watched the monitor record the level of electricity her grandma had left, the peaks and the waves dancing across the screen in neon green against a black background. The numbers told Eleanorah what she already knew.

"I love you, Grandma," she whispered in her ear.

She felt another squeeze of her hand.

"I love *you*," her grandma mouthed. Eleanorah stepped away and pulled the curtain closed behind her. She stood in front of the automatic doors of the Emergency Room, waiting for them to open. The air was cold, and still. It washed over her face like a brisk waterfall. *This was not a dream.*

Her grandfather came through the doors and stood next to her. Eleanorah wrapped her arm around his waist. Together, they stared at the empty parking lot. A handful of stars shimmered in the moonless sky. Tree branches swayed, as if sharing the latest news. A bird soared, unseen in the dark.

Eleanorah opened her palm. A thin, gold chain held the heart-shaped necklace her grandfather made, all those years ago. One of the nurses had given it to her before taking her grandmother for an x-ray. She hadn't been able to let go of it yet.

"Grandpa," she said, her voice barely audible. She swallowed the hard lump in her throat and tried again. "Grandpa, have you and Grandma talked about what you want for end-of-life care?"

A patient she'd recently taken care of reminded her so much of her grandmother, her body riddled with arthritis, fragile, tender. For an entire month, Eleanorah had listened to her moan with every gentle turn, the nurses taking care not to tangle the wires that extended like limbs from her shrinking body.

Her daughters were doctors and couldn't separate the two. They'd wanted everything done and more. The patient finally died on the operating table, chest exposed like a cadaver, all of the life already gone out of it.

He nodded his head solemnly. "The doctors told me she's in pretty bad shape. She told me when I brought her here, 'Joey, I'm scared if I go to the hospital, I won't ever leave.' I promised her I wouldn't let that happen."

"Grandpa," Eleanorah started again.

"I'll talk to the doctors, Ellie," he said, reading her mind before she could finish. "If it's her time to go, I want to let her go. I don't want her to suffer anymore."

"I know, me either. I'll stay as long as I need to, Grandpa," she promised. "Here." She gave him the necklace. "I wanted to keep it safe."

"You keep it." Her grandfather closed her palm and held her hand. "She would want you to have it," he said, his voice breaking like a wave, reaching the shore.

Eleanorah clasped it to her chest. It was time for her grandmother to fly. And maybe, she could too.

For three more days, her grandmother lay restfully in a hospital bed on the fourth floor. A red band hung loose on her arm, informing the staff not to do anything heroic in the fight against death. They could let this one go in peace.

Word spread. People from church came. All of the grandchildren came. Even the ex-daughter in-laws came, including Eleanorah's mother. They rotated in and out like a revolving door, so she was never alone. Whenever someone new arrived, her grandmother sensed it, opened her clear blue eyes, and smiled.

"Your grandma loves you all very much," her grandfather addressed the room full of people, looking at his bride with pride. "She loves unconditionally. Even the ones who have hurt her. She forgives them. Now, I haven't learned how to do that yet, but your grandmother has." He found a stray gray hair and gently brushed it from her forehead.

"Tell us the story, Grandpa," Eleanorah prodded. Ever since she was a little girl, she'd asked to hear the story of how they met, rehearsing the lines like an understudy, practicing in the wings of their love, waiting for her own to unfold.

"Ahhh," he said, smiling. "Okay, mo chuisle, just for you."

"Well, you know we met in high school," he began. "We were high school sweethearts. Your Grandma Esther was about fourteen and

I think I was sixteen. Now, she was jealous of a friend of hers who had gone after a boy she liked. She knew her friend liked me, so your grandma decided to get her back."

The room filled with giggles.

"The day we met, I was sitting on the window ledge with a few of my buddies around lunchtime. And your grandmother came right up to us, looked me in the eye, and said, 'Hello, Joseph.'

"That's it. Just those two words. 'Hello, Joseph,' and then she turned around and skipped away.

"Right about then, my stomach started doing flip-flops. I found out her name was Esther, and realized we were in choir class together. I'd never noticed her before. But after that day, I couldn't stop thinking about her. When we had a performance later that month, I asked her to go with me."

"What happened next? Did she say yes?" They waited on the edge of their seats.

"Well, yes, she did. But now my mother had told me, 'Joey, don't you pick her up without going inside, and meeting her father first.' So, I did. I went up to the door, rang the bell, and asked your Grandpa Peter if I could please take his daughter on a date.

"Most of you never met your great grandpa, but let me tell you, he was tall, and intimidating. His big belly blocked the whole door! I was so nervous. He looked me up and down for what felt like an eternity. He stared at me real good, and I stared right back. 'Best have her back straight after the concert, son!' he bellowed, and I thought the whole house might shake!"

Everyone laughed.

"It's a good thing you listened to your Mama!"

"I sure was scared, but it was worth it!" Her grandfather chuckled, squeezing his wife's hand. "We'll get you home as soon as we can, sweetheart," he promised, kissing her forehead.

The drive from the hospital to her grandparents' home took longer than usual. Or maybe Eleanorah drove it differently. The landscape greeted her in slow motion, rising and falling with the hills. There was a light dusting on the fields and rooftops, the same color as the sky. Was it afternoon, or maybe evening? The mirrored gray distorted all sense of time.

Inside, groups of two or three family members huddled together quietly. With everyone gathered, it was hard not to notice who wasn't. Eleanorah's uncle Joshuah—the prodigal son without a homecoming. An absence no one had really come to terms with, a phantom limb still felt, after all these years. When he died, his ashes were spread along the riverbanks of the White River where they fished for trout and played in the cold, clear water. It was the best they could do.

Eleanorah walked past the hospice nurse who sat at the red kitchen table in the spot her grandmother's wheelchair usually occupied. Next to him were packages of syringes and small glass vials. "These are the drugs you'll be able to give her so she's comfortable," Eleanorah overheard him explain, gently.

She waited impatiently by the front doors, opening them so the fireman pushing the stretcher had room to come inside. Her grandmother looked so small and frail next to their young, sturdy bodies. She lead them down the hallway with the framed pictures of the grandchildren on both sides. School and family photos with matching outfits and awkward teeth. Her grandmother loved every single version of them.

"It's okay, honey. You're home now. You're in your bedroom. You're home." Her grandfather kissed her on the ear and moved aside to let the paramedics pass.

There was no response that anyone could see. Perhaps a slight flutter of her grandmother's closed eyelids. Perhaps a slowing of her heartbeat. It's reasonable to assume that something changed, but there were no monitors or measurements to prove it.

Eleanorah helped lift her grandmother's body toward the head of the bed, fluffing the pillows, placing them underneath her backside and between her legs with the artificial knees. Many times Eleanorah had slept beside her, just like this. She remembered the softness of the pink satin sheets. The gentle snoring from her grandmother's small, button nose.

Her grandmother loved this room for the view, for the Christmas cactus that bloomed pink in winter. For the purple lilacs planted by the window, for the paintings of the Rocky Mountains she never truly left behind, hanging on the walls. Nothing escaped her eyes.

She noticed the foxes, the bluebirds, the deer. She watched the horses gallop, and the neighbors who came to catch catfish. She spent her days looking through the glass at the wild within. In the early mornings, when she first woke up beside Eleanorah's grandfather, she watched for the pairs of geese that flew over the sunrise, their wings reflected in ripples on the lake.

"I had a dream last night," Jeremiah spoke up, softly. "I saw Grandma laughing, and smiling and running."

Eleanorah reached for her grandmother's hand one last time and noticed the coolness of her skin. The pauses in her breath were longer. The pulse in her neck grew faint without struggle. Within minutes, she was gone. Like an invisible exhale you can't see or hear. Like the silence of light seeping beyond the closed door, finally free of weight, and gravity. It was then Eleanorah understood.

Even her death was an act of love.

***

The grass was thin and brown. The earth, hard. But Eleanorah was determined. Her fingers wrapped around the handle of a borrowed shovel, carving small holes into the ground with its sharp edges. The chain link fence by her apartment clanked in protest.

She could do this for her grandmother. It was almost spring. A cardboard box sat beside her with a tangled bundle of plants ordered from the seed catalog her grandmother had subscribed her to, as a gift. It was the last copy. Eleanorah knew because it came with the expiration date written in bold on the cover.

"Last chance to renew!" It stated on the pre-stamped card she was supposed to return in the mail for another year's supply of "Birds and Blooms." Holding it carefully, she'd dropped her bag from work next to the door, and taken it into the living room instead of immediately crawling in bed. When she closed her eyes, she was back in her grandmother's office.

The scent of white-out. A hint of hairspray and tea tree oil. The slow, rhythmic sound of typewriter keys. Light streaming in from the windows overlooking the lake. Laughter down the hall. The front door opening, and closing. The feel of a pair of scissors between her thumb and forefinger while she made collages of flowers from her grandmother's old gardening magazines.

"Will you always be you?" her grandmother had asked, the last holiday they were all together. It was a riddle she kept trying to solve, the way she tried to capture the movement of the branches in their family tree. The harder she tried to answer, to see, to make the pieces fit together, the more elusive it became.

She had not been herself in a very long time.

"In spring, lilacs are often shipped dormant, in bare-root form. The plants are not dead, only 'sleeping,'" the magazine explained. A seed needs darkness in order to grow. The box arrived in the mail several weeks later, filled with lilac roots, nothing more than barren twigs. Eleanorah buried each one with a prayer.

Grow, be safe, reach for the light.

***

Dark, green leaves cast shadows on the water. When the wind blew, it rippled over rocks, and bare feet. Eleanorah readjusted her posture, digging her elbows into the bank.

"We should do this more," Margot suggested from her chair nestled in the water, creating a slight current around her seat. She tipped it back with a daring grin. Eleanorah reached to catch her but Margot had already leaned forward again, laughing.

Eleanorah couldn't help but smile. The opening in the thick forest was their spot. Surrounded by pine trees and bluffs that rose from the water, they sat for hours looking at nothing in particular.

She started bringing Margot here last year, after they graduated nursing school to escape the city. Listening to the flow of the river, watching sunlight dance on its surface, counting all the water bugs gliding easily from point to point, never in a straight line, Eleanorah could stay this way forever. The river was not a clean, crisp mountain stream like the kind that ran through her veins, the kind she waded in up to her knees when she was just a kid, carefully stepping from stone to slippery stone. But it had its own calm. Its own sort of healing.

"I'm serious!" Margot splashed her playfully with the cool water. "Now that you've recovered, what do you think about taking a longer trip together? I've got some vacation saved up. We could go to Europe! Or South America! What do you think?"

Eleanorah recalled finally requesting a few days off to have the surgery after her grandmother died. The cold sensation of fluids in her arm. Warm blankets and a bright light over her head. The doctor curiously telling her later the fibroid he removed was the size of a "passion fruit."

Both of her parents and brothers had come to be with her, all together in the waiting room. A bouquet of flowers from Margot waited on her nightstand when she got home. It was the kind of support she didn't know she had permission to need.

"I think I'm lucky to have a friend like you." Eleanorah splashed her back. "Seriously, Mar. I wouldn't have made it through nursing school without you or gotten my job at Northwestern, for that matter. I know I haven't been in a good place for a long time but you've never given up on me. It means a lot."

"Okay, okay. So pay me back by going on a trip together!"

Eleanorah leaned forward over her knees, instinctively reaching for the place where her grandmother's necklace normally rested against her chest. It would be the first time she'd travel abroad "for fun," something her family would definitely disapprove. Traveling for educational purposes was allowed. Going on a mission trip with the hopes of converting lost souls was even encouraged. But traveling for leisure?

She could already hear their commentary, like pesky gnats buzzing around her. It was too expensive. Dangerous. Not something someone like her should be doing alone without the protection of the church or university, or a man.

Yet, she wanted it with her whole body. The aliveness she felt on top of the temple at Teotihuacán. Drums beating in time with her pulse. Whispers of the unseen and unknown, her fingers grazing ancient relics and mysteries her heart had yet to understand.

"Okay," she agreed tentatively, trying her best to ignore the humming of her family's anxious warnings.

"Let's go!"

***

"We'll take *il vino della casa*, red, *per favore*."

"No, white this time!" Margot giggled.

They were on their second or third liter of wine for the day, alternating between red and white every time their feet got too sore to keep walking. The current café overlooked the Ponte Vecchio, situated on the Arno River. Earlier, they'd walked across its stone path lined with flags fluttering the red fleur-de-lis, and shops selling miniature statues of The David, admiring the view. It was the oldest bridge in Florence, the only one spared by retreating Germans during the war, for its beauty.

"So..." Margot dipped fresh bread from the basket with checkered paper into a mix of olive oil and herbs, another daily staple. "Have you heard from Benjamin lately?" She raised her eyes flirtatiously.

Eleanorah blushed. "No, not in quite a while. We hung out before I went to Zambia last year but haven't seen each other since."

"What's the story there?" Margot took a sip of the cold, white wine, served in a clear carafe.

"I don't know," Eleanorah said.

She knew it was her fault they stopped seeing each other. A slow fade that required no effort at all, except the ceasing of all effort.

"I liked him, I think it was just too much with work, and being sick. And all the family drama. I think we had a physical connection more than anything else. It's almost easier to keep them separate, you know?"

"What do you mean?"

"Well, for example, Andrés and I never had sex but we had this really amazing friendship. I felt so comfortable, like I could be myself around him. I've actually been thinking about him a lot lately," she admitted.

"But with Benjamin, we had like, off-the-charts chemistry. But I think maybe I was keeping us from anything deeper. Like it's too much to have both, you know? An emotional and physical connection. It feels too, vulnerable or something."

Margot nodded. "I can see that. But don't you think that's the whole point? Learning how to share all of ourselves with someone?"

"Yeah, probably." Eleanorah rolled her eyes, and took another long drink from her glass. "What about you? How's your love life?"

"It's okay," Margot said. "I went on a few dates with this girl from the lacrosse team. Apparently, she was going on dates with other girls, too," she sighed. "I want to start settling down, you know? But I still haven't come out to my parents so I think that's part of it.

"When you fall in love, you fall in love with a person, not their gender, you know?" Margot's eyes watered. "I don't know why that's so hard for them to understand but I don't think they'll get it. I just keep imagining the look on my dad's face." Her voice broke.

"I'm sorry Mar, I can't imagine how hard that must be."

"It's okay, I'll figure it out. Besides, look where we are! We made it, baby! We're in Italy!" She cheered, clinking her glass with Eleanorah's.

"You're right! Who needs 'em when we have wine and pizza?" She laughed.

"Exactly!"

Eleanorah gazed at the wide plaza, the warmth from the sinking summer sun reflected in her eyes. "Thanks for bringing us here, Mar.

I haven't felt this good in a long time. I didn't realize how badly I needed it."

***

"Bonjour!"

"Bonjour!" she replied, surprised.

Waves crashed and the engine churned salt water into sea foam. A low hum propelled them forward across the Adriatic sea. She walked toward him and their seats in the back of the ferry, the waves causing everything to rock, ever so slightly. The motion magnified the sensation of floating, of being just a little bit off-balance, of zig-zagging into unexpected territory.

His eyes locked with hers.

The root. The trunk. The branch. *The tree.* How do we describe the separate within the whole?

Scientists and linguists have devoured the meaning out of words, dissecting our parts. Individual entities of limb and lymph, heart and soul, mind, and matter. As if tongue and speech can be divided in two, split down the middle like a fork in the road. Like the Devil from God.

There are things that we can't possibly know *but we do know.* Ordinary vocabulary fails to reach beyond the veil and unknown syllables fall at our feet like dew from the sky. *It is and it isn't,* an absence that points toward fullness. Beyond language, evading explanation, the Seers and Ancient Ones are wise enough not to name it. Even the word Mystery cannot contain it.

Let us try anyway.

Cartoonists draw light bulbs.

Scientists call it *coincidence*. Correlation does not mean causation. The carcinogen and the cancer. The cure and the poison. Evidence is a mask that shifts, depending on the wearer. Albert Einstein called it relativity. Perspective. The wave is also a particle. We are the Universe, entangled in subjective layers we can't pick apart. Schrödinger's cat exists, and yet it doesn't. The experiencer defines truth, hence, *there is no truth*.

Carl Jung defined it as *synchronicity*. The ability to assign meaning to that which appears meaningless. Moments of un-forgetting. Recognition. Serendipity. Chance encounters that shift your trajectory imperceptibly, eternally.

Buddhists call it karma. Kindness breeds kindness. Hatred marries violence. You deserve what you get, *even if you can't remember it*.

Christians have many words that speak around it. Depending on the particular denomination to which they prescribe, they call it Divine Grace. They call it Mercy. They say "It Was A Miracle." The infinite incarnate. Blood turned to wine.

Muslims don't speak it, they write it. It's the white space in-between their artful calligraphy. The glory of the angels. The way their noses touch the prayer mat in surrender, expectation, devotion. It's the adhan, the call to prayer echoed from rooftops, birds flying to the vibration of Holy.

For Eleanorah this knowing was a simple, one-word greeting.

"Bonjour!" The boy with moppy, blonde hair, and winter blue eyes said again, followed by a slew of words Eleanorah couldn't understand, making her pause in the aisle. She didn't know why she'd replied in the first place. It just came out before she knew what was happening.

Maybe it was all of the "Buongiornos!" she'd heard over the past ten days. The Italians had a musical quality to their conversation that was still ringing in her ears. She'd mimicked so many "Buongiornos!" it was an almost automatic response.

She listened again. But he wasn't speaking Italian. It was *French*. "I'm sorry, I only speak English," she said, studying him more closely, blinking the sleep from her eyes. He stared back. For a split second, Eleanorah had the uncanny feeling of looking into a mirror and seeing her reflection for the very first time.

He shifted his gaze to her t-shirt, visible under her dark, gray hoodie. There were French words she couldn't translate scrawled in cursive across her chest with a picture of a bicycle and a basket of flowers, below. She blushed and shrugged her shoulders. She'd gotten it as an impulse buy at a department store months ago, almost putting it back. It was overpriced, and whimsical. But she liked it anyway.

Had she known then?

"My name is Benoît and this is Lucas," the boy sitting next to him said, introducing them both.

Benoît was tall, confident, and lanky. He wore a newsboy cap, and a thin, dark mustache. His accent was heavy, but Eleanorah could make out the meaning.

In between the missing words, she traced the outline of the boy with the blonde hair's jaw, barely hidden beneath a day or two old beard. He grinned. She felt the color rising to her cheeks. Light pink. Rosé. Sweet, and subtle and brief. She looked away.

His smile grew wider.

There was something in his eyes, a familiarity she couldn't explain. She felt it the moment she saw him, even though she dismissed it immediately.

At the moment *it* was all around them. Full, yet spacious. No future, no past. Unasking. Unanswering. The boat swayed. It flickered, and then it was gone.

Lucas made space next to their backpacks and motioned for them to sit in the two empty seats next to them.

"From where are you traveling?" he asked.

"We just finished traveling through Italy, now we're on our way to Greece," Eleanorah explained, nervous at the sudden proximity of their arms, and legs.

"Ah, us too. Where have you traveled to in Italy?"

"Florence, Rome, and Bari, then onto Athens and Istanbul, before heading home," Margot said, listing their destinations cheerfully.

"No way!" Lucas' blue eyes brightened. "It's impossible," he said.

They had just missed each other in Rome and Bari. Like the girls, Benoît, and Lucas were also on their way to Athens, then Istanbul. Against all improbabilities, their paths had crossed in the middle of the ocean. Eleanorah noted the coincidence with an odd sensation as they waved goodnight, weaving back down the aisle to their seats.

"Maybe we'll see each other again," Lucas called after her, hope-fully.

***

"May I join you?"

Eleanorah and Margot sipped sangría with slivers of strawberries and one thick wedge of orange each. Before they could respond, an astute waiter placed an additional glass of water on the table. Beads of condensation fell, and formed again on the surface, dripping with light.

The stranger pulled out an extra chair and sat down. His long legs scrunched beneath the wobbly table but his body was relaxed and calm. He took a sip of cold water and pulled a wrinkled sheet of paper from his backpack, smoothing it out.

"You're staying at our hostel, right?" Margot asked. "In the top bunk across from mine, I think."

While they chatted, Eleanorah took in the view. Sunlight glistened on bright blue window frames and old pots filled with red bougainvilleas. A lazy, spotted cat dozed on a balcony below. She took another sip of her sangría, and bit into one of the fresh strawberries. From the restaurant's small plaza she could see the Parthenon, barely distinguishable from the white clouds, just above its ruined columns. It was a beauty, even in its current state.

They were more than halfway through their trip and the effects were potent. Each day they casually wandered neighborhoods and piazzas, with the main objective to follow their noses—which led them to oven-fresh bites of cream-filled cannoli and pizza with mozzarella and prosciutto, topped with handfuls of spicy arugula. In Greece they sampled thick, Turkish coffee, baked feta covered in sesame seeds drizzled with honey, and olives that melted the instant their teeth released that first, juicy bite.

It wasn't just the food. It was time. Time to wander. Time to sit and talk, surrounded by living history in motion.

Sacred temples and crumbling stone. Ancient gods with broken noses, maintaining their dignity in spite of the centuries passed. Conquered lands with shifting borders, and forgotten names. Death was all around but there were no graveclothes in sight. Rather, there was an urgency. A commitment to life in the wild gestures of hands, in the pleasure of buttered bread flaking at the mouth, the vibrant flutter of laundry drying in the wind.

It gave her time to survey her life, cautiously sorting through the rubble. Until now, it had never occurred to her to ask why she'd grown a fist-sized tumor in her womb, or why her body decided to betray her in this specific way. She'd taken the news in stride, like she'd taken the emergency phone call to meet her parents at the hospital when Micah was suicidal. Like she'd taken the news that Jeremiah was caught smoking pot, and put on probation at his new job. Like she'd taken the news that her parents couldn't afford to help her finish paying for college because her mother was using the money to leave her father, instead.

It all seemed absurd to her now. She sifted through the wreckage of their family, looking for something to hold onto, proof that it wasn't all bad, that it could have been prevented. That it didn't have to happen again.

Was there anything worth keeping?

"We're just passing through, traveling for a few weeks," Margot was telling the stranger.

"We just came from Italy and we'll spend a few days here before taking a boat to Milos and some of the other islands. Then we're headed to Istanbul for the weekend before flying home to Chicago."

"What about you?" Eleanorah rejoined the conversation, curiously taking in his demeanor.

The stranger was older, maybe in his late fifties or sixties. From what she could tell, he was traveling alone. So far, most of the other travelers they'd met in the hostels were their age or younger. Traveling in pairs or groups, they seemed to move in packs with their heavy, brightly colored backpacks strapped to their shoulders, sometimes carrying a smaller day pack in front.

The stranger studied them both and began writing on his wrinkled piece of paper. "I'm on a pilgrimage," he stated, matter-of-factly. "Walking from Rome to Jerusalem." He pulled a map out of his bag for a reference.

They leaned in closer.

"There are four sacred pilgrimages. Each one reveals a hidden secret or treasure. I'm on my third. You see the paper I'm writing on? It's translated into several languages. As I walk through different cities and villages, I ask the people to help me rewrite the text. Whenever I can, I show it to the local churches or places of worship. I ask them if I might take refuge in their sanctuaries. On this journey,

I'm trying to discover what connects the three main religions of the world: Christianity, Judaism, and Islam."

The worn words seemed to be clues, each one unlocking a key to Divine hospitality, and wisdom. The map and the lettering reminded her of *The Manual* from her grandfather's shop. Patterns and pilgrims. Tree rings and heartbeats.

"When will you return? Where did you begin?"

He took a sip of the beer in front of him. It sparkled amber, like his eyes.

"I'm not sure when I'll complete my journey. My wife is waiting for me in Holland. When I return I'm planning to leave my job to become a shepherd!"

He chuckled and Eleanorah and Margot joined him, laughing in unison at the pastoral image of the pilgrim drinking beer in front of them.

His eyes twinkled as he raised his bottle.

"Only you know what will make you happy. You only have one life to live, so why not go for it?"

Their glasses clinked merrily. A cool breeze floated among them. It gave them such a feeling of peace and hope they lingered a little while longer.

***

Back in Chicago, a crisp wind rattled fallen leaves. They lifted briefly, and then settled. Against sidewalks. Against curbs and drains and pairs of shoes. Eleanorah picked one up and held it against the gray light of the afternoon.

Another gust funneled down Michigan Avenue. She released it, watching as it dove and swirled into the traffic. Eleanorah wrapped her arms across her chest and tried not to shudder. Her refusal to dress in adequate layers had always identified her as not from here. Among other things.

She purposefully sat in the middle of the museum steps and waited, not too far from the street but not too close to the entrance, either. A calculated middle ground. The perfect vantage point from which to look unconcerned while the minutes passed.

Would he come? Her eyes scanned the crowd. They flitted and squinted at faces half-hidden by upturned collars and slouchy hats. It had been so long, and yet.

Memories paraded by, as real as the pedestrians scurrying in the cold. Flashbacks of jungle ruins, and caravan freedom. Red bandanas tied around necks and mouths. Coal-black eyes penetrating crowded marketplaces. Hoops of fire and ankles weighed down with seashells. The mist of the mountains. The heat of the cracked asphalt beneath their feet.

¿Realmente, me quieres?

Do you really love me?

Another gust blew loose strands of hair tucked behind her ear. It was getting long again. An unconscious barometer of vitality. Eleanorah brushed the hair from her eyes and watched, shivering again. No amount of clothing or courage could subdue the changing season.

"¡Hola, Eleanorah!" A confident, tenor voice shone through the sea of gray like a lighthouse. Goose bumps formed on her skin. She turned toward him instinctively.

It was Andrés.

Eleanorah had waited several months after a mutual friend mentioned he was staying in town before tentatively reaching out. His Father had suddenly passed away the year before and she regretted not saying anything. Regretted the brash ending that left no room for redress.

It was her father who gently coaxed her to make amends. "After all," he said. "Isn't love just one long story of forgiveness?"

"Disculpame por estar tarde," Andrés said with a smile, walking up the steps to where she sat.

I'm sorry for being late.

She stood up to take him in. His body, seamless with the city he was raised in, appeared out of step with Chicago's buffet of hard and hostile edges. He seemed shorter than she remembered, older but softer.

There were new wrinkles on his forehead, small grooves carved into mocha skin. He wore a suit and tie, but unlike the others, his head was bare and exposed to the elements. His face was shaved too, absent the dark beard she'd loved.

She smiled, wondering how she had changed, the details he must be noticing, too. It had been two years since their parting in Morelia. After too many months of holding the absence against him, he was finally here.

Isn't love just one long story of forgiveness?

He greeted her with a familiar gesture, memorized by the moonlight. The kind of movement written in the muscle, remembered by the heart. Intrinsic to how they were. Her heart skipped a beat, and she accidentally leaned in too far, stepping on his toes. He held out his arms to steady them both and touched his lips to her right cheek, tenderly.

"¿Cómo estás? ¿Qué hay de nuevo?" He pulled away gracefully.

"¡Bien, bien!" She smiled nervously.

Vaults of phrases and sentences long sealed knocked against heavy doors with forgotten codes. She ran down the abandoned hallways searching for clues for how to turn them loose. Each one she gathered was the wrong one. Incomplete, nonsensical.

"¿Me acompañas?" Andrés pointed in the direction of the park a few blocks away. Eleanorah nodded, following him down the steps onto the busy street. It was strange to hear the form of those words in a place neither of them belonged. Gone were the arches of the *acueductos*, the vibrant hues of colonial columns, the peeling orange of cement buildings, beautiful in their crumbling antiquity.

The map of their love was tethered to that city. There, she had only ever known him to fit like a glove. Moving with her movements, the first chair in her symphony, she trusted him completely with every turn of tempo and melody they played.

Here, under the cover of clouds and falling leaves, their hearts were refugees. His hands had once informed her, wrapped around her waist, turning her like a pirouette. Here, they fell at his sides. She realized with relief that the intoxication of young love, and revolution was simply, gone.

"I'm thinking of quitting my job," she admitted, switching to English, knowing he understood perfectly.

"¿Ah, de veras?" His brown eyes twinkled.

"Sí," she confirmed, if only for her own benefit. "I want to travel again. Maybe try out South America. My Spanish has gotten too rusty," she said, grinning.

"Well, that can be fixed," he said as they strolled unhurriedly, visitors to a landscape they could not stay.

***

"Are you sure this is what you want?" Her supervisor sat behind the desk, slumped in the chair.

Eleanorah licked her lips. The halogen halo cast a harsh glow. The truth was she'd been contemplating it for months, maybe longer. Since her trip with Margot, and the moment on the ferry with Lucas. Since her grandmother died, since leaving Africa, since standing on the steps of the Pyramid of the Sun with Andrés, and then saying goodbye.

She'd looked for other ways out...maybe she could enroll in a Master's program or join the Peace Corps. Her mother kept mentioning school nursing. These were all sensible choices. But none of them felt right.

When her vocal chords finally vibrated, they protested the drought.

"I'm sure. I have to at least try."

The woman nodded. Her lab coat crumpled as she reached for the letter sitting on the desk. *Resignation* it stated firmly, in 12 pt, Times New Roman.

Eleanorah looked down at her blood stained tennis shoes. She was breaking an unspoken pact. Fleeing the trenches in the middle of a never-ending war, deserting her colleagues mid-battle.

"What do you mean? How can you take that much time off?" A nurse with fine blonde hair snapped when Eleanorah told her the news. "You're an adult! You're supposed to work."

Eleanorah was supposed to do a lot of things she couldn't anymore. She knew they were protective of each others' weaknesses because they were their own. They pretended not to worry that death was contagious, that they were on the losing side of things, and that all of their fighting was sometimes in vain from the very beginning. But if Eleanorah's hands couldn't tell fear from love, how could she heal?

"What are your plans after the internship?" Her supervisor implored, looking for a hint she might return when it was finished.

"I don't exactly know yet."

She thought of the pilgrim in Greece. The *templos* in Mexico. The churning of water, and the steady gaze of his blue eyes. They were the moments she knew she was most alive. Times when her life had texture and space, brief passages when the questions didn't make her so afraid.

Eleanorah made her last rounds with a sense of urgency. There was no telling how long her courage might last. If she didn't leave now, there was a chance she never would. Methodically, so as not to make any missteps, she pushed the last dose of medicine through blue veins. She printed the final graph of vital signs, tucking them neatly into the heavy chart. Finally, she watched for evidence of a subtle shift in the light through her patients' windows, whispering a soft goodbye.

When there was nothing more to do, she gathered her things and waited until no one was looking. With each step, she quickened her pace until she was running, chasing the light down the hallway. She followed it through every crack of those heavy doors, pushing them open with all her might until finally, finally, she heard them close behind her with a loud, definitive click.

When Eleanorah looked up, she marveled at the first sunrise she'd seen in a very long time.

***

"Quito se llama, 'La luz de America,'" her driver explained.

Water trickled from the viscera of the mountain, like serous fluid seeping from open pores. Their car was wet from inside the tunnel, from diverted streams splashing through the darkness. Everything was emerald.

"How long will you be visiting Ecuador?" He turned on the windshield wipers.

"Two months," Eleanorah replied. "I'm here doing a public health internship," she explained. "I leave at the end of May."

"Ah, *muy bien*. They call this the route of *las cascadas*," he said, gesturing on all sides without taking his eyes off the road. Waterfalls appeared on either side, large, and small, carving shimmering channels through the mountains.

Out of the corner of her eye, she saw a billboard covered in graffiti. "Petrol unites communities," the original message proclaimed. It showed a group of dark-skinned people smiling with straight white teeth, their arms around each other, like a fútbol team. A can of black spray paint added another layer.

"Petrol=death," it stated simply.

"What do you know about the oil companies here?" she inquired curiously.

Vincente glanced at her cautiously in the rearview mirror. "A lot of the indigenous communities don't agree with what they are doing" he hesitated. "They cut down trees, building roads into virgin rainforests. They risk destroying the ecosystem, and scarring the land, but they do not care."

Eleanorah nodded. She saw the lines of detonation carved into raw mountains, liquid leaking from wounded stone. They passed ditches with broken limbs not yet set, mutilated debris discarded by the bulldozers purging anything and everything in their pathway.

"The oil companies are smart," Vincente continued. "They provide a lot of benefits the government can't afford to offer its own people. They promise to build schools and provide free health care if the communities agree to allow them access to their sacred land.

"But the people have no resources but the land itself," he said with a hint of bitterness. "They are bargaining with their lives."

Ours, too, she thought.

"Do you see that mountainside, to your left?" Vincente nodded out the window.

A silhouette protruded from a flat rock, a sheer cliff with a sinister face.

"They call that 'The Devil's Nose,'" he explained.

"What does it mean?"

"There was once a train built from Quito to Guayaquil, from the highlands to the lowlands. It ran through the heart of the Andes mountains. Some say it was the most difficult railroad to build in the entire world. They called it the 'Railroad in the Sky.'

"Two of our presidents were assassinated during its construction. Many people died. The government used the labor of Jamaican workers to blast a way through the crumbling rocks and cliffs.

"The Devil's Nose used to be named after the condors, magnificent birds that nested among the rocky terrain. When the men came with their tools and their dynamite, the great winged creatures fled, and never returned. Some of the men using the dynamite lost fingers, hands. Around two thousand, five hundred of them lost their lives. Our people say their souls were the price of trying to scale the face of the Devil.

"The government, on the other hand, said it was one of the greatest accomplishments for our country; its completion was celebrated in streets stained with anarchy. In the old days, the train was built to carry commerce to the coast, so our resources could be bought and sold in Europe, but nature took her revenge. She brought floods and chaos to the steel nails driven into Mother's flesh. Only part of the original track remains. Now, it is a train for tourists."

His face turned grave.

"Since before the revolution we have had our resources and our labor stolen from us. First, the Spaniards came. They made us slaves. They forced us to forget our traditions, our language, and our dignity.

"They call Ecuador the 'Light of America' because we were the first to regain our freedom on this continent. We drove out the monarchy, but we are still fighting. The light burns, and goes out. Money has power. For now, we are still powerless against its corruption. Our masters go by different names, but we are still enslaved."

A silence fell across them both. Steep curves gave way to gentler inclines. Fern bloomed from the ash. Resilient Tagua soaked volcanic spew into their roots and turned it into oxygen. First green like chlorophyll, then red like iron. The seeds they birthed were white, like ivory.

The car descended toward the border of what was left of Ecuador's primary rainforest. Their destination was Shell, located 45 minutes by bus from Baños to the West, and ten minutes by bus from Puyo to the East. An in-between place, it was an old oil town nestled at the edge of the deep green forest. An outpost. A hold-out.

The car slowed. Eleanorah strained to see the broken pavement, and torn-up debris where sidewalks used to be. The buildings were painted in faded pastels, yellow for the gas station, blue, and green for the houses, a light red for what looked like a corner store. The town wore the clothing of upheaval. Abandonment? No, that was too strong a word. There were signs of unfinished construction, the absence of machines making noise. The eerie feeling of disruption, resentment, of unkept promises.

"Estamos aquí señorita." Vincente parked in front of an iron gate, idling the car.

Eleanorah gripped her luggage a little tighter than she intended.

"Gracias, señor." She gave him a stack of folded dollars, the official currency of a country she knew so little about.

He bowed in a gesture of gratitude. "This is where I leave you, señorita." He set her bags by the gate. "They are expecting you inside."

The gate opened. A man with slicked-back hair wearing a white lab coat gestured to her, speaking in a slow, deliberate Spanish that made her grateful and embarrassed at the same time. He introduced himself as Fernando, an intern at Hospital Vozandes where she'd volunteered to work for the next two months.

"Esta casa es su casa." He dropped her bags in front of a small duplex with a wide, enclosed porch in the back. "This key is to your house, and this key will lock the entrance to the complex." He showed her the key ring. "Make sure you lock the gate behind you when you leave." Without further explanation he walked back toward the hospital, his gait slow, and lumbering.

Eleanorah took a deep breath. The air smelled like rain and bananas and iodine. Behind the complex, a mess of trees rose high, tangled, and ill-contained. She tried to separate them, isolating this tree from that, distinguishing one from the other. But there was too much life. It pulsed, and breathed, evading definition and sawblade simultaneously.

She turned the lock and felt along the wall for a light switch. Inside, it smelled too much like home—static, clean, sterile. She sighed, wistfully looking out the window.

Already feeling tired, she plopped her duffel bags next to the couch by the overstuffed chairs. Moving toward the bedroom, she picked up the books stacked neatly on her nightstand. A Bible and *Through Gates of Splendor*, a true story about the five missionaries who were murdered in the nearby jungle she'd been told about as a little girl. A tale of courage or caution?

The cover of the book showed a green wilderness against the backdrop of a textured, gray sky, deep, and layered with rain. The Waorani had spears. The missionaries, a gun. They used it once, firing a warning shot into the dense labyrinth.

"Are they savages?" Mutti asked when she learned of her granddaughter's travel to Ecuador.

Eleanorah's mouth gaped open. "What do you mean, Mutti?"

"I mean, do they have religion? Are they Christian?" Her Grandmother clarified with a blush on her cheeks.

Her Mutti didn't mean it, or maybe she did.

Surprisingly, the rest of her family had been more supportive. Her brothers told her she was brave. Her father made a special trip to Chicago to help her pack up her studio apartment in Logan Square. Her mother offered to store the boxes with all of her belongings in her new house near Independence, secretly hoping that when Eleanorah came back, she'd stay.

A cock crowed in harmony with distant church bells. Eleanorah counted the tolls. They rang in quick succession. The night was encroaching.

Her eyelids fluttered. Exhaustion that existed long before she had the excuse of travel fatigue made her body droop. "We are all sinners," she was told, over and over.

Are we all savages? she wondered.

Questions circled the craggy surface of the Devil's Nose. Their wingspan wide, both shadow and light. When she rested her head on the pillow, the sound of church bells and dynamite boomeranged through her sleep.

***

A one-engine plane circled the lush landscape. It purred like a giant, sleeping cat as the pilot glided above a small landing strip. Flanked on either side by burning grass, the cleared land bore the scars of machete blades. It was a three-day journey by foot from here to anywhere with electricity or roads or medical care, the pilot told them. Assuming one didn't lose their way.

The plane swooped a little lower. Eleanorah's stomach dropped as the air gave way below them. The plane was painted red, like the humerus in her anatomy coloring book. The limbs of the jungle were green, like pulmonary arteries.

What color represents lungs full of carbon dioxide? What lines fall off the page every time we clear-cut the mountains? When we dissect valleys and forests? she wondered.

The heart of the jungle is the heart of us, but we don't see it that way.

"We bleed money," say the politicians. "We need stronger Wi-Fi signals," say the plump children addicted to the mirrors in their hands. "We drink oil," say the mouths of the masses." She found herself tripping on the crosswires of politics and religion, and capitalism. The more she tried to untangle it, the more enmeshed she became.

The jungle opened itself to their descent, making just enough room for small rubber tires to find gravity, and then stillness. Figures emerged from the thatched huts scattered nearby, running toward the familiar splash of color falling from the sky. Beyond the toy-sized window of the airplane, the green threatened to consume them.

The door opened, and they were immediately greeted with hands, arms, and cheers. The pilot was well-liked. Eleanorah could tell by his gentle effect and kind smile. The people, dressed in a mixture of traditional and Western clothes, were at ease and treated him like a friend.

One of the women smiled at Eleanorah, picking her out from the small group. Her hair was straight and black, her cheeks round and weathered by the sun. Eleanorah smiled back, delighted when she confidently grasped her by the elbow, guiding her toward a large, open-air building. In the corner, an old, toothless man sat in a wooden chair under the protection of the banana leaf roof. His earlobes hung low toward his shoulders, stretched by years, and what some might call vulgarity. But his smile was wide.

Eleanorah absorbed her surroundings as more people arrived, dressed in white skirts and mostly bare chests. Smears of red paint, the color of *achiote,* made a cross on their forehead, chin, and cheeks. A deep, fast-moving melody sprang from their mouths and hips as they circled the group of foreigners, carrying pointed spears with gold, orange, and brown feathers.

"The dog and pony show," Eleanorah overheard a seasoned expatriate describe the interaction with the Waorani and travelers like her with an exaggerated eye roll.

A shimmer of shame ran down the back of her neck.

She shifted uncomfortably while someone placed a small headband over her hair, frizzed by the humidity, smearing her face with pigment from fingertips dipped in brown and crimson, like the earth. When a wayward strand of hair fell over her face, the stranger with the painted fingers gently adjusted it again, his expression full of warmth and mirth.

"They are singing to thank the gods for the good weather and sunshine and for bringing us to them," the pilot with bronze skin and short, army-length hair explained. "Do you see the man sitting over there?" He looked over his shoulder discreetly.

Eleanorah followed his gaze to the old man she'd noticed before.

"His name is Dewey. He's one of the men who speared the missionaries," he whispered.

Eleanorah searched his timeworn face for a sign of anything but innocence, scrutinizing his posture, the wrinkles of his forehead, the sagging skin on his arms, and legs. What residue of evil was left, if any?

"He's the last survivor from that day," the pilot continued. "They say now he makes amends by praying for the safety of every pilot in every plane that flies overhead."

She smiled. Of course. The missionaries were pilots. The prayers of the sinner. The prayers of the saints. If there is a God, he (she?) bends their ear to them in the same way.

If we are capable of murder, we are capable of mercy.

***

If we are capable of hurting, we are capable of healing.

The woman's eyes were vacant. Placeholders. Her silence suggested a throat box without a song. The physicians spoke around her, carefully avoiding the exposed electrical wires protruding from her heart. A touch may soothe, or shock.

"¿Qué tiene, señora?"

Dressed in starched lab coats, the medical interns swathed wide angles of caution from the top of the stretcher to the bottom of her feet, practicing the Pythagorean theorem with their footsteps. If $a^2 + b^2 = c^2$, the answers were there. A velcro cloth squeezed her arm, tentatively measuring what they could without breaking the skin, keeping her inside, away from herself, away from them.

Eleanorah stood in the bright room while the darkness gathered. Heat rose slowly, like steam from bodies after a cold shower. The small jungle hospital echoed with confusion. "What are we supposed to do?" they asked in hushed tones, consulting their thick textbooks full of disease. "What could possibly be wrong?" they gossiped.

Eleanorah grazed the tips of her fingers like ice, intuitively recognizing the familiar dullness of her pupils. It was a heart defect. The same one she once carried in her own chest. A passageway where there was supposed to be none. Fluid leaking between the chambers. The blue mixing with the red.

Glaciers with an eruption inside.

A gift. A curse. Something that shouldn't be. With time, the opening in Eleanorah's heart had grown smaller and closed in on itself. Compartmentalized. Eventually, her fingers stopped tingling when the wind blew through the narrow valleys of her skin. Instead, she learned how to protect her heart by redrawing the lines and walls it needed to survive.

"It was a miracle!" the doctors exclaimed, but her heart remembered.

The young mother in the hospital bed remained silent.

Eleanorah held her soft, weightless hand in both of hers.

"Está bien," she whispered. A spark of static electricity passed between them, re-awakening dormant muscle in long forgotten chambers. "Estamos bien," she repeated.

"We're okay." This time, her voice above a whisper.

***

She stirred languidly, just in time to watch the fog clear from the palm leaves. Shuffling barefoot onto the balcony, she looked across the banks of the mighty Napo River below. Pairs of eyes as deep as a cavern stared back. She'd longed to escape the hospital hallways and gated community but the resort, situated on the opposite side of the village, felt like more of the same.

"¡Buenos días!"

Eleanorah jumped at the hard knock at her door.

"Are you ready, señorita?"

A man wearing a simple staff shirt stood in her doorway. Long hair hung down around kind eyes. Thick rubber boots covered his ankles and shins and soft belly calves.

"My name is José," he said, offering a sturdy hand.

"Eleanorah," she said, smiling nervously.

"We are ready for you, señorita. Come this way," he said hurriedly. "We must begin before the heat of the day."

She nodded, stepping into the black boots he provided, pulling them up to her knees. *Maybe this was her chance to go back to the very beginning.* The thick rubber soles were heavy, clunking and squishing as she walked. Behind the pristine lodges, another man waited in a white pick-up truck. He sat in the driver's seat, turning the engine when he saw them approach.

"We have to stop by my house," José explained. "For my machete." He opened the car door and waited.

Eleanorah looked at the two men and then back toward her room. She hesitated, trying to calculate the risk. Voices of caution filled her head, urgent whispers of warning, some warranted, some, not.

"Just don't walk anywhere by yourself," her dad gently suggested before she left, not understanding the impossibility of this task, or that he'd never ask the same of her brothers.

"You're going alone? Are you crazy?" Her co-workers said with raised eyebrows, as if she had a certain death wish, not an insatiable curiosity to experience the immense variety of all life had to offer.

"You're a woman. Do you know the risks?" they admonished.

Rape, murder, robbery. She rehearsed the implied checklist of what could happen to someone for existing outside of the perceived protection of certain (but not all) men.

The truth was that one in four women in the world were sexually harassed. Likely more. Most by those they knew.

The logic didn't compute. As long as you weren't alone, you were safe. A lion will protect a gazelle from other lions, it promised. But how could you tell one lion from the next? How could the predator protect its prey? The system was rigged.

And she was not a gazelle.

Yet, the jungle was unforgiving to the presence of trespassers. It did not favor intrusion. It did not trust curiosity. Many betrayals were committed under the flawed premise of discovery, development.

Nature had its own defenses.

Weeks before her planned excursion, two Australian women were captured near Cuyabeno, just up the river. They were tourists with a guide like her, visiting a nature reserve dense with primary rainforest, and pink river dolphins. A rebel group from Columbia held them overnight, told them to hide in the bushes when the helicopters came searching.

The headlines said they were safe now. Shaken, but safe. Rescued by 100 or more soldiers from the Ecuadorian army. Sent back to the capital. Notice of the good news given to their families.

Eleanorah quickly searched José's eyes for signs of malice and ducked her head inside the truck, her whole body alert with fear, and exhilaration.

The pick-up stopped in front of a small hut. José ran inside and came out with a curved, steel blade, glinting in the sun. He placed it in the back, and they continued, bumping along a narrow, unpaved road, passing over several small creeks, and a building painted in bright colors. "This is the school." José pointed out the window. "The children come from all over to go to classes. Some of them get up very early in the morning to walk for an hour or more," he said matter of factly.

They stopped at a clearing at the bottom of a gentle incline. José jumped out and hooked the machete onto his belt next to a hand-held radio. "Carlos will bring our supplies for lunch." He opened the door for her to join him. "I have some *limonada* for us to drink if you are thirsty." He waved goodbye to the driver, slowly disappearing into the arms and legs of the jungle.

Sweat dripped from Eleanorah's forehead. Static came through the small speaker on the radio. José fiddled with the knob until it clicked off and the static stopped. She tried to move some words around in her mouth but they got stuck, overwhelmed by the possibility of this moment, good or bad.

Beyond the small opening, the trail was dense. Leaves stirred under the soles of their rubber boots. Insects crawled lazily over decaying trunks, feeding on plenty. Vines twisted toward the narrow sky. Creatures rested in the comfort of day, sinewy muscles relaxed, and ripe passion fruit burst forth in ecstasy at the falling.

Eleanorah caressed the smooth bark of a toppled tree, the circular grooves mirroring her fingerprints and the pattern of orbit across the sky. Her feet, like roots, tethered by gravity. How tall, how high could she grow?

"Here, *tengalo*." José handed her a small, pliable piece of timber. "Put it in your mouth, and chew for a minute. Like this," he said, peeling the rough bark from the smooth interior.

She obeyed. Within seconds, her whole mouth went numb.

"This is nature's anesthetic."

Eleanorah spit out the remnants and let the feeling return to her cheeks and tongue with a smile.

"Take a sip of limonada." He laughed, pouring some onto the ground before handing her the jug. "Por Pacha Mama," he said with a wink.

"In Lak'ech Ala K'in," she whispered, remembering that ancient prayer of connection. Return to the earth what is hers. Return to the earth. She gladly took the jug, pouring her own offering of thanksgiving before letting the sweet nectar coat her throat.

***

"So…" Aberdeen took a bite of hamburger. "What are your plans after you leave Shell?"

Eleanorah sipped *jugo de naranja* from a tall glass, straining the pulp between the spaces in her teeth. She bit into a soggy bun and let the juice run down her chin before wiping it with a napkin. Hot yuca fries and grilled chicken covered in mayonnaise between two soft pieces of bread. This was her favorite meal in Ecuador and she had it at least once a week.

The food in Ecuador was lacking the spice she'd grown to crave, the life infusing, subtle burn of chipotles, poblanos, or serranos. Her tastebuds routinely protested the bland, brothy soups, parceled with left-over chunks of meat. One time, she found a suspiciously kidney-shaped glob in the thin liquid, and lost her appetite for a full day.

Pollo a la plancha redeemed it all.

Aberdeen dipped one of her fries in the pale *ají*, studying Eleanorah with the sharp inquisition of a protective older sister.

"I don't know, actually." Eleanorah took another bite, swallowing thoughtfully.

Her internship had always been more of a bridge than a final destination. Instead of working in the field like she had hoped, she'd been confined to the same clinical practices and disease centered care she left behind in Chicago. Working alongside the missionaries at the hospital only confirmed what she already suspected—she was participating in a system that disempowered patients and medical providers alike.

But the time she'd spent outside the gated expat community—visiting with the Waorani in the jungle, meeting fellow backpackers in Baños on her days off, and taking a solo trip to the highlands of Riobamba, gave her the experiences she was hoping for. A taste of kinship with others seeking answers to questions they hadn't fully formed yet, either.

Her thoughts drifted unwillingly to the boy on the ferry. "You are welcome to France!" he enthused when they said goodbye at the port in Patras, two years ago. The way he leaned in, his backpack shifting to one side as he placed a soft kiss on her left cheek. The way he looked at her was...

"You should come to Ghana." Aberdeen paused eating and gave her a serious look.

Eleanorah met Aberdeen halfway through her internship at a spaghetti dinner hosted by a family of American missionaries. Aberdeen was from Northern Ireland and lived close to the sea. She was employed by HCJB to work on clean water development in rural communities and had been in Ecuador for about a year. After a few weeks, an unlikely friendship had formed between them, built on the common ground of two people living on the fringe of a place neither of them belong.

Eleanorah stuck a yuca fry in her mouth to delay answering.

Africa was a place she knew well enough to avoid. It was magnetizing. It riddled her cells with tension and grief and quiet contentment. She was afraid that if she went back, she'd never leave.

"I'm going to be there for two years working on a new project," Aberdeen continued. "You should visit."

Her straight, blonde hair fell to the side of her angular face, framed by a pair of square glasses. It was more of a statement than a question.

Eleanorah considered her proposal a second time. A sharp ache filled her whole body, an unnamable longing threatening to overcome everything else. It was a concoction she didn't want to drink again. Not now. Not anytime soon.

"I'll think about it." She lied, making a firm resolution that Ghana would be the last place she'd go.

What then shall we choose? Weight or lightness?

—Milan Kundera

3

Vole (love)

E merald pastures rolled by, green and pristine. The train me-
andered through wide open countryside sparsely dotted with
steeples and old stone houses. Through the blur, Eleanorah picked
out the details—a solitary cow and a blooming flower garden, bright
purple and blue hydrangeas, a figure leaning out of an open-shut-
tered window. In the distance, she could smell the bright, summer
seaside.

Saudade.

She turned the word over and let it touch the roof of her mouth,
whispering. The closest English translation stated that this word was
a sort of nostalgia for someone or something. It spoke of longing
for what once was. But Eleanorah disagreed. For her, it was a deep
yearning for something or someone still held captive by the future.

The wheels slowed. In a sing-song cadence she was still getting
used to, a male voice informed the passengers of their next scheduled
stop. She scanned the small platform, looking for the name of the
town she'd written down the day before, *Bayeux.* This wasn't it. She
looked at her watch, calculating how much longer until she'd arrive.

There's always a moment, she thought, squirming in her seat. The moment you know that whatever happens next, your life will never be the same.

She held her breath, wiping clammy hands on her shorts, pretty sure the refined lady with the red lipstick reading *Le Journal* seated across from her might raise an eyebrow or two at the sweaty girl sitting awkwardly on her hands until she couldn't feel them tingling anymore underneath the weight of the body she was afraid might float away.

Maybe this whole thing was a mistake.

It started out innocently enough, with a wish for a "Bonne Année!" in her inbox, and a shy invitation to visit France. She'd kept in touch with Lucas periodically since first meeting, a few sentences exchanged online here and there, then longer ones. After Andrés, he was the first person she'd told about wanting to quit her job. "You must," he'd said so confidently, she knew it was true.

Together, they'd counted down the months, then weeks, and days before she went to Ecuador. The day she told him she'd bought a one-way ticket to Paris, his enthusiasm mirrored her own. She'd wanted to visit "La Ville Lumière" since reading Hemingway's *A Moveable Feast* in college but she couldn't pretend that was the only reason.

Eleanorah forced a slow exhale and held the small heart fastened around her neck between her thumb and forefinger for luck. The train made another stop. She shifted nervously and peered out the window. It was time to get off.

The station at Bayeux was crowded. She had no idea where she was, only that it had taken her two and a half hours from Paris to get there. She reached for the new mustard-colored backpack above her head, looping it through her shoulders and tightening the straps around her hips.

And then, she saw him.

They moved toward each other in slow motion, finding their way around people boarding or exiting the train without shifting their gaze. His whole face beamed, a beacon she did not realize she was searching for. A stranger but for those eyes, winter blue.

"I think after two years, I have to say to you, thanks," he said, referring to the first time they met on the ferry.

He'd asked to borrow some chapstick.

"I have just showered," he had said, standing on the deck of the ferry waiting for the first burst of light. "I promise I don't have any microbes."

At the time, Eleanorah tried her best to swallow a laugh as the sea-salt wind whipped through their hair. Biting the corner of her mouth, she'd focused on digging through her bag, looking for the item he'd politely asked to borrow. She was probably falling for him then. She certainly was now.

Lucas guided her through the crowds, toward the exit. They crossed a small, stone-paved street catty-corner from the square and sat down.

"My friend is arriving soon. I thought we might visit the coast a bit, share a picnic?"

"That sounds amazing!" She smiled with relief, relishing the idea of letting someone else choose what happened next.

"Do you have plans for the rest of the summer yet?" His eyes sparkled. "Will you stay in France?"

"I don't know, yet." Eleanorah gazed at the other passengers milling about the square, greeted by friends and relatives, coming and going. "I'd like to spend more time in Paris, after that, maybe travel down the coast, toward Spain. I'm honestly not sure," she admitted.

He took a cigarette from an open pack in the middle of the table. "Do you want one?"

"Non..." She hesitated, shaking her head to confirm. "Non, merci."

"The best plan is to have no plan!" He laughed, blowing the smoke away from the table. "Sometimes in life it's good to lose control." He took another drag and winked before stubbing out the butt of his cigarette.

Eleanorah leaned back and took him in. He was demure, reserved. Gregarious, but within certain limits. Confident, yet composed. Her stomach churned. She wondered what kind of control they'd lose together.

***

The day was sunny and clear. Overgrown grass covered the rocky coast, waving gently in the breeze. They walked solemnly through the cemetery, bodies of heroes buried below their feet. Down the hill, waves lapped at the memory of fallen soldiers—thousands lost in a long moment without peace, the outlines of their twisted figures a figment of the imagination on a quiet day, meant for falling in love.

"Do you want more time?" He paused near the entrance to the museum.

Flags fluttered. Colors of red, white, and blue in different patterns of patrimony, side by side. Her hair tangled in the wind. She paused, swaying between the devastation of the past, and the uncertain possibilities in front of her.

"I'm okay. We can go."

"Are you sure? There is no hurry."

She looked at the coast one last time. "I'm sure." She turned to follow him to the car where his friend Yann was already waiting.

"Are we ready for a picnic?" He held up a box of wine and grinned.

Her stomach growled loudly, a common pattern, no matter where she was.

"I think that means to say, yes!" Lucas laughed.

"D'accord, on y va!" Yann plopped into the back seat.

They drove slowly down a two-lane road, past small farms with crumbling walls, and newly planted, wet fields. Eleanorah scanned the signs for something she might recognize. They pointed in all directions, each representing a new adventure.

"Have you already seen Le Mont-Saint-Michel?" Lucas asked, driving toward a roundabout.

"Hmm-mm." Eleanorah had heard about it but hadn't realized it was so close.

He turned up the radio. The Beatles' youthful voices singing "Michelle" came through the speakers. Lucas sang the chorus loud and off-key while Yann joined in heartily from the backseat. Eleanorah hummed along shyly, her cheeks now bright pink.

"Okay, let's see what we can do." Lucas turned the wheel sharply and circled the roundabout twice before veering off to the left.

Eleanorah held on as she slid toward him. The laughter she normally kept on reserve bubbled up so easily, the sound of it caught her by complete surprise.

"Sometimes in life it's good to lose control," he said with a smile, winking again before straightening out the car, straight as an arrow.

***

A gentle wind brushed brisk air across exposed shoulders and ankles. Two weeks after saying goodbye to Lucas, she was settling into a work-exchange near Saint-Malo, instead of returning to Paris like she planned. She'd stayed near the coast, craving the quiet, fresh air. And she wanted to be nearer to him.

Fat, somnolent flies rested on the open contents of pickle jars and remnants of pâté on crumbs of toast. Half-filled glasses were topped off with white or red wine from a spigot. Eleanorah leaned back and took a sip, letting the stickiness drip down her fingers, gripping the stem. She was just a few hours from where Lucas dropped her off at the train station in Bayeux.

"I think, maybe we have known each other before," he said. Alone for the first time, they'd stood together on the train platform savoring the silence.

"I have the feeling you know me better than some of my friends I've had for ten years, always meeting together in a bar, talking about things that don't matter," he spoke with a seriousness she hadn't seen before.

The train came. He helped lift her backpack onto her shoulders before checking the ticket one last time. There was a pause. She wanted to but didn't say, "Me, too."

The doors opened and the sing-song voice played over the speakers. He held out his arms, placing one hand on each of her shoulders. "See you soon?"

She nodded. The doors closed. Eleanorah hurried inside and slipped her bag off her shoulders, still warm with his touch. With some effort, she lifted it above her head, gave it one more push, and sat down, facing him.

"See you soon," she whispered and waved goodbye.

"Where have you gone?" A teasing, sharply accented voice broke her reverie. Hans looked at her with a knowing glance.

Eleanorah blushed. His beard was dark and speckled with gray. When he smiled, it twitched below his mouth in a way that made her laugh. He sat across from her at a long table situated in the front yard, a cluster of old cottages behind them. In the last week, they'd spent their mornings and afternoons inside the small chalets tearing down walls and cleaning decades' worth of dirt from every surface imaginable.

But the evenings, the evenings were for amusement and drinking and conversation.

Hans was the younger half of a couple from Hannover. From her estimation, he was just shy of fifty. His wife, Alfreida, was several years his senior, and a bit more plump. Her blonde hair had streaks of white and she wore it pulled back into a tight bun. But when she spoke, her words were exuberant and carefree; she had the youthfulness of a woman who had never known motherhood.

"It's okay to leave it for a while." Hans gestured at the dirty table Eleanorah had moved to clear. "You're so pragmatic! There's no hurry, you know," he said with a tease.

She set the stack of plates back on the table, glad he couldn't see her sheepish expression in the fading light. She could tell he was watching her with bemusement, waiting for her to tidy and clean and pursue the next activity on the agenda. It was hard to be still. The agitation of her mind demanded an outlet like a pent-up tantrum. It needed a flight path to escape, a runway to chase. Without it, she felt trapped.

Alfreida poured the remnants of the last bottle of red into Eleanorah's glass. She shifted in her seat, reminding herself there was nowhere else to be.

For some reason, from the moment she'd arrived, Hans and Alfreida had taken her under their wing. She knew they felt a fair amount of disdain for the owners Paul and Cynthia and was certain they found the girls from Australia and Alaska absolutely annoying because they had told her so. They were not shy about the eye rolls exchanged or the impatient tone that translated into any language.

Yet, they liked her. They made fun of her stumbling French accent, correcting her kindly. The first weekend they were at the cottages together, they invited her (and no one else) to go to the beach with them in their stylish, black convertible with the top rolled down. The day was sunny and bright and she'd done her best not to think about her drive with Lucas and Yann or the field of wildflowers where they'd shared a picnic, hours before the train station goodbye.

In the mornings, before everyone else got up, Eleanorah sat with them, watching Hans heat milk in a small pan on the stove, making it foam before pouring it into their French pressed coffee. When it was their turn to prepare a meal for the whole group, Alfreida asked Eleanorah to help and taught her the recipe for homemade gazpacho. With big hands, she wielded the kitchen knife deftly, demonstrating the delicate way to slice tomatoes and cucumbers before tossing them into the blender with a generous portion of olive oil.

The more Eleanorah learned, the more enamored she became. They told her about taking a sabbatical and leaving academia for something a bit more liberating. There were papers to author and tenure to preserve but they'd said, 'screw it,' packed everything that would fit into their convertible, and drove to France anyway.

Their story and lives were purposefully messy, even in their fifties.

There were some side projects they were working on but nothing was settled. Nothing was certain. Just a tender hope growing into the tenacious belief that a turn-around was possible. At any age. Anywhere. Anyhow.

"Do you think we're crazy?" she asked one night when the smoke was thick from the crackling campfire.

Alfreida parted her lips for a long while before she spoke.

"There is a photograph of when I was very, very young. Perhaps only three or four. I found it the other day when we were packing our things to leave. It's a picture of me following a parade of people away from my family, away from home. I remember this moment, being intrigued by the costumes and the music, feeling the pull of the unknown, even at this young age," she said nostalgically.

Hans grinned and pointed toward the sky. "If you ever feel lost, just look at the moon. You'll know you're in the right place."

Eleanorah looked up toward the white, crescent moon. For a moment, she almost believed him.

***

Her computer rang. The sound made her heart skip. A photo popped onto the screen, waiting for an answer, a connection. She clicked the green button, eager for the signal to come through.

"Salut, Eleanorah!" His face, like sunshine, warmed her body leaning against the cool exterior of the stone cottage.

"How are you?"

"Très bien, merci." She smiled shyly, trying not to beam too much or too brightly.

"I see you are outside, enjoying the good weather? Have you done something nice for the weekend?"

"Uh...Oui! We all went into town for Bastille Day. The fireworks were beautiful!" Eleanorah remembered the small hill where they gathered to watch bursts of light above the town at nightfall. Behind them, a walled castle overlooked narrow boulevards lined with blue and white hydrangeas mixed with red dahlias.

"What about you, did you do anything fun to celebrate La Fête?"

A shadow passed across his face. "No." He hesitated. "My girlfriend had a race along the sea in Lorient so I went to watch. We stayed in after." He moved the computer and disappeared from the screen. There was shuffling in the background. "Sorry, the battery is dying, I'm looking for a plug." His voice sounded far away as if coming from another room.

She held her breath. *Girlfriend.*

"How long will you stay *à la maison?*" He returned, facing the camera again.

"I don't know," she admitted. The truth was she had been waiting on him. She tried to freeze her expression into a neutral one while the meaning of the word girlfriend sank into her body.

"Will you be free next weekend?"

"I think so."

Eleanorah furrowed her brow, reaching for a plan or excuse for not being available. She could go back to Paris or pick another region of France to explore, or move south toward Spain. But she didn't have any details yet.

"Great!"

There was that smile again. All earlobes and shooting stars. The one she couldn't believe was directed at her. The one that offered no hint of a girlfriend waiting on the couch for him to come back into the living room so they could resume the movie.

"If you like, you can join me for another festival. It's in my hometown, in Loudéac. What do you think? We could meet in Rennes on Friday, and then go together on Saturday and Sunday. If you think you can put up with me for that long?" He looked at her hopefully, a slight flirtation in his voice.

She blushed. What was the harm? He had a girlfriend, so they were just friends. Nothing had happened. Nothing was going to happen.

She knew it wasn't true the instant she said, "Yes."

***

She lay on the bench and looked up at the clear blue sky, knees pointed up so she could fit within the space allotted for sitting, her head resting against her backpack like a makeshift pillow. A small red phone was on her stomach, the one he gave her the last time they saw each other, at the first festival in Bayeux.

"It's an extra," he said, slipping the charger into one of her outside pockets.

She checked it again to make sure the volume was turned up. "50 km away!" was the last text she'd received, about twenty minutes ago. There were other messages, too. Ones that once she discovered by accident, she guiltily deciphered them as best she could.

It was clear they were old texts between Lucas and his girlfriend Camille. From what she could make out, there was one where she told him she'd baked his favorite cookies, and he'd called her "ma cherie." Other messages where it looked like they'd had a fight, and he was going to stay with a friend for the night.

Her French wasn't very good and so a lot of the words she'd had to look up in her pocket dictionary, but some of the meaning was still cryptic. Phrases and expressions crafted within the context of two lovers. A secret language meant just for them.

Eleanorah knew was the intruder. She was the one who didn't belong and had no right to feel what she did. It was reckless and foolish to hope that there might be any affection left over for her.

The phone vibrated on her belly. "Hello?"

"Salut! C'est Lucas!" He laughed. "I have arrived in Rennes. Can you meet me by the harbor?"

Eleanorah pressed the phone against her ear.

"Meet you by the árbol?" She looked around at all of the trees, trying to figure out which one he might mean.

"The harbor," he repeated slowly. "By the sheeps."

She turned her head and looked toward the water. "The ships...Okay, I understand! I'm in the park but I'm coming now." She hung up and put the phone back in her wrinkled shorts pocket, wishing more than anything there was a mirror nearby.

Halfway up the hill by the docks, she saw him. He wore a pale blue, button-down shirt rolled up at the sleeves and tucked into a pair of crisp, light tan corduroy pants. A few wisps of honey hair fell across his forehead.

He was alone.

***

Lucas poured thick, rust-colored wine from an open bottle. A ripe, fleshy melon sat in front of her. It served as a bowl, an offering. Eleanorah slurped the sweet liquid, carving out bites of the pale cantaloupe with a small, delicate spoon.

"One of our specialties," he said, smiling.

Loudéac was small, with just a handful of stone buildings. Its roof lines sloped toward brightly painted shutters that opened and closed, latching in the center. Few cars passed and most of the people seemed to know each other, waving greetings across the narrow streets, embracing briefly with a kiss on both cheeks. The town was lost in time, or maybe it wasn't lost at all. Maybe it had seen enough of the past, and decided not to catapult toward the future.

"So, where will you go next? Have you thought of Ireland?" His eyebrows raised curiously.

Eleanorah thought of her Grandfather Joseph's family with an ache. The stories from that side weren't passed down, so she'd had to make up her own. Part of her was afraid of discovering if the reality matched her fantasies as a little girl.

"I really like it here so far," she said. "It reminds me of home, in a way. The farms, and the countryside. It feels familiar, like where I grew up. Except for the ocean! We didn't have that."

"But...my visa only allows me to stay in The Schengen Zone for three months at a time, and that's basically all of Europe, so I don't know. I think I'll travel south and explore a little. Maybe visit

Barcelona or Seville?" She shrugged. She couldn't bear to think of what would happen at the end of the summer, yet.

"You don't wish to stay in Brittany?"

"I do! It's really lovely here."

"It is the best of France!" His eyes sparkled.

"I'm sure! But I haven't found another host nearby. I think it will be nice to see some other parts of the country, no?" she addressed the unspoken question between them.

"Maybe you should trust your instincts, see what happens. I've been meaning to ask you, by the way. You keep saying you're from Chicago but that's not true, is it? Where is it you said to me earlier...." He tilted his head slightly. "It has a funny name, Independence?"

"Yeah," she admitted sheepishly. "I guess it's just easier, everyone knows where Chicago is so I don't have to explain anything."

"But home is home!" He laughed, gulping the last swill of wine. "Speaking of, I have a surprise for you," he said, stacking their plates on the table. "Let's go, I'll pay inside."

She followed him down the hill toward the square, approaching a makeshift stage with a band playing what sounded like Celtic music. A large circle of people were laughing and dancing in a circle, their hands intertwined by their pinkies, first going in one direction, then the other. Lucas scanned the crowd, nervously smoothing his shirt and tucking it in again. An older gentleman with kind eyes and glasses made his way toward them. He greeted Lucas in French, embracing.

"This guy is my dad!" he explained.

The man smiled. "Enchanté."

"Enchantée," she repeated, leaning in for the customary kiss. Even in the dark, she could see the resemblance. It was in his eyes, the spark of subdued fire, still burning bright.

"Shall we dance?" Lucas motioned toward the front of the crowd.

Eleanorah accepted his hand and waved goodbye to his father, shaking her head at the unexpected introduction. The circle opened for them, and then closed again. In an instant they were part of the pattern—left, left, kick! Right, right, kick! Their arms circled up and down, intertwined at the smallest knuckle. There wasn't time to be nervous. Or think about how she'd just met one of his parents. Or wonder again where his girlfriend was.

***

Moonlight rippled across the water and their flushed faces, full and promising. Eleanorah hugged her knees to her chest, the grassy hill a soft cushion, enfolding her. Lucas sat next to her by the small lake, his shirt loosened, hair ruffled.

"You know, from when you told me you were quitting your job, some months ago, I have been following your travels. Your time in Ecuador, and all your adventures. I told my friends about the American girl who was traveling the world. They were very impressed!" He laughed.

"Thank you!" She blushed. "Have you thought any more about your association? The one you told me about starting with your friend Benoît?"

"Yes. I remember when I traveled with my Mom to Togo. It was a humanitarian sort of project. It left a deep impression. That's why we started our eco-travel association. We wanted to show a more green-friendly way to travel, by train instead of airplane, for example, doing eco projects along the way."

"What happened?"

He shrugged. "Life, I guess. I am not brave like you to quit my job! But I know some things have to change. I keep thinking about how I'm turning thirty in just a few years. I want my life to be mine, not for my parents or my friends. Or my job's."

She nodded. "It's still hard for me, even though I feel like I'm learning so much about the kind of life I want to live. I'm not totally there yet. I have this idea for a tattoo I want, a map of the world, here." She pointed at her bare feet. "Like a souvenir to remind me of all the places I've been. That no matter where I am, I carry them with me."

"I love the idea!" He gazed at the stars, thoughtfully. "I love where I am from, my home, my country. I feel very passionate about it, very proud! But...I don't want the same daily life my parents have. Always taking care of the kids or grandkids. Working their whole life, waiting until they are retired to live for them."

"I think..." Eleanorah waited for her thoughts to catch up to her. "I think it's good to know what we don't want. For example, I know I don't want to go back to nursing, at least not for a long time. But, at a certain point, we have to figure out what we *do* want. Otherwise, what will change?"

"You are right." He looked at her affectionately. "Thank you for the talks. I feel I can be myself with you, share. You know you can ask me anything. I'm an open book," he urged gently.

Eleanorah leaned back on her elbows. "I know," she said, hesitating. "*Poco a poco...*"

"It takes time." He nodded.

They stared at the open sky in silence. There were questions whose answers she was not yet ready to hear.

***

White and gray buildings mirrored an un-brightened sky. The streets were surprisingly quiet, giving the city a lazy, absent feeling. Back in Paris, she lacked the buoyancy she felt with Lucas by her side. Her legs ached, and the weight of her belongings put pressure on her hips and shoulders. When Lucas offered to join her for a daytrip, she declined. She wanted to be here alone, especially today. Maybe to prove she wasn't just here because of him.

Eleanorah strolled toward the Seine at a slow, contemplative pace. The sinking sun cast a soft glow on matte buildings that now seemed pink, and purple and honeydew. People sat in pairs around tables large enough for a drink and an ashtray, their legs crossed nonchalantly. A cigarette in one hand, they gestured playfully with the other. There was an ease. A gaiety that maintained a certain elegance in the quality of the milieu.

Raindrops sprinkled the hard surface of the Seine's concrete banks, making small, dark watermarks. She sat by the bank, unwrapping a piece of crunchy baguette folded inside thin butcher paper, watching the raindrops fall into the river. It was her third day in Paris, and the drizzle hadn't let up.

This city wears the rain like a woman dressed in black, carrying a bright red umbrella, she thought.

Stepping off the train from Loudéac, the city had assaulted her nose with the scent of dried urine, fresh bread, and a subtle layer of grime, a sharp contrast to the open air skies of the Brittany countryside. Paris was not for everyone, and it didn't pretend to be.

But it was growing on her.

She finished the last piece of bread and pulled a small card from her backpack.

"Twenty-four years ago, I was twenty-four, and I had you," she opened the birthday card her mother gifted her months in advance, tracing her finger over the familiar cursive handwriting. "After twenty-two hours of hard labor," she whispered, finishing her mother's retelling of her birth.

"Your first breath was an act of freedom," her mother repeated, often. *Defiance* was another word she used.

Eleanorah had been carrying the small envelope in her backpack until today, promising not to open it ahead of time. Inside, her mother tucked a picture of her holding her as a newborn. Back then, she was a young woman with a bright, gap-toothed smile, thick glasses, and wavy hair, cut just above the shoulders. She wore flowy, floral dresses with wide sleeves. Eleanorah wondered at the lifetime (hers) between them.

She closed her eyes against the evening shower, falling heavier now. A tear fell onto the concrete. She missed her. Whether she wanted to admit it or not. Eleanorah wiped her face, letting the salt mix with the rain, carefully tucking the card back into her bag.

***

After wandering down the cobblestone rues and avenues of Paris for too many days, Eleanorah moved back toward the coastline, traveling south. Beyond the border between France and Spain, Basque country maintained its rigor, claiming loyalty to itself alone. It was a quality she admired, yet failed to live up to.

A waiter dressed in a white shirt and black bow tie brought her a glass of dark red wine. The plaza was full of tables like hers, people sitting in groups of two or three, drinking, and laughing, eating *pintxos*, with their fingers. Beyond the plaza, a cool sea breeze played with the waves, rolling, and swooshing over the top of the water.

"Gracias."

Eleanorah acknowledged the waiter with a smile and returned to the journal in front of her. The words were angry, confused. Made the emptiness undeniable, unraveling all her fears.

They hadn't made firm plans for meeting again—Lucas had to work, maintain his daily rhythms and schedule. But she missed him. And at the same time, was angry at him for it. For not being hers.

She pulled a thin cigarette from the new pack of Lucky Strikes she bought, just before crossing the border. The blue, pocket-sized lighter sparked. She inhaled. It was her second cigarette of the day, not that she was counting. The smoke was comforting, like something she had been fighting for so long, finally allowed to fill her lungs. She exhaled slowly, watching as it hung in the air.

As soon as the train crossed the imaginary line between the two countries, her tongue had loosened. All of the tripwires in her mouth detonated, and the words poured out. On the page in front of her, to strangers on the street, in gurgles and babbles and sonnets of relief.

San Sebastián welcomed her without hesitation. It was loud and raucous in every way that France was charming and politely, albeit smugly, reserved. In its presence, she felt the temperature of her blood rising. The corset of refinement and rules unfastened at the gathering. Here, she was allowed to fall apart. To suck on the tar of desire, and disappear, for a little while.

She would cross the border again, return to France for as long as she could. She would find a way back to him. But for now, this small act of rebellion gave her a sense of control, of exercising a little power in the face of a hopeless yearning.

She pulled the small red phone out of her pocket, wondering if his girlfriend knew about it—about their connection. Lucas had called, like he said he would, but Eleanorah had missed it. "We have to stay in touch, and keep traveling our whole lives," he said earnestly in a voicemail. She hadn't had the courage to call him back yet.

Eleanorah considered her options.

She'd purchased a small tent after spending the night riding the bus in Biarritz until the route ran out and she found herself wandering through a suburban neighborhood, well after midnight. It was then she realized that if disaster struck, she would not know how to ask for help. Did not know how she would explain a robbery or, worse.

At least now if the hostels and local hosts were all full, she had a backup. A small consolation, but it was something. With her tent, she could go back to Dax for the festival alone and try to meet some fellow travelers.

Or, she could ask him to come.

Her heart sped up, just thinking of it. So far, he'd always been the one to initiate contact. It was easier that way, less risky than her admitting her growing need to be near him. If he reached out first, she could carry less of the blame, avoid taking responsibility for her part in whatever it was they were doing.

But she was tired of being cautious. Of worrying about his girl-friend finding out, or what she may or may not know. *Besides, they hadn't done anything*, she reminded herself with shaky fingers pressing small keys.

"I'm going to Dax for the festival next weekend," she typed slowly. "Would you like to join me?" She hurriedly put the phone back in her pocket and took out another cigarette, steadying her breath, waiting for his answer.

***

"I love you. Or, I think I could love you," he said, following her through the dwindling crowd, his words slurred.

Eleanorah marched angrily ahead of him around the empty glass bottles and paper plates discarded by thousands of people too merrily inebriated to care, red noses, and cheeks looking just like theirs. "You're drunk," she retorted.

"That's true," he agreed sheepishly, ignoring the fact that she was, too. "What happens in Dax, stays in Dax. But Elle, I feel differently about you," he added as justification for what had just happened, moments before.

Lucas had driven all day to get there, meeting her back in France just across the border from San Sebastián for the festival. She wasn't sure what they were celebrating, but it didn't matter. He had come.

She'd greeted him with an Abbaye De Lille and crumbled up homemade chocolate chip cookies, gifts she'd kept in her shoulder bag, waiting. By the time they found each other in the throng of people wearing white with hints of red catching in the sunlight, the cold beer and whole cookies were no more. There was a look of confusion on his face for a split second when he received the warm beer and crumbs. But then he smiled, accepting them graciously.

She'd loved him a thousand times over in that instant.

A tall, thick girl with short blonde hair caught up to them and put her arm around Lucas, murmuring something in his ear with a heavy German accent. Minutes earlier, Eleanorah had watched them kiss by the stage. She was also not his girlfriend.

A flash of heat appeared on Eleanorah's cheeks. His friend Benoît, who'd driven down with him, noticed, and handed her a plastic cup of water. She took it, grateful for the distraction.

"Is there something going on between you and Lucas?" He teased, affirming an observation rather than asking a question.

"No. We're just friends," she asserted with a firmness she didn't mean. "Ah. I thought, maybe there was something more," he said, playfully nudging her with his elbow.

As far as she knew, Benoît was the only one who suspected there was anything between them. That's why he'd tagged along. Dax was squarely outside Lucas' stomping grounds, but he had made an effort to see her that might have elicited questions from Camille had he come alone.

"No. I have to go." She handed back the cup, still full. "Will you tell him? I'm going back to my tent to sleep. I'll see you in the morning."

Eleanorah quickly turned and walked in the opposite direction before Lucas could protest. Hot tears streaked her face like war paint. She let them fall, let them say what she couldn't, let them be enough truth for both of them, for now.

***

Eleanorah woke with a start. *Was it already morning?* She reached for her phone to check the time.

"We have had no luck to find each other again tonight, see you in the morning!" It was a text from Lucas, sent several hours after she snuck away.

"I think I love you. Or, I could love you," she replayed those uncertain, stumbling words of half-declaration. They weren't enough to stand or hold onto. They wouldn't break a fall or catch a misstep. Yet, she found herself leaning into them as much as she dared, feeling their impermanence. The fragility, and shiftiness. Testing the texture and wearing it like a new silk robe. Sheer and beautiful, thin and cold.

It was light outside. The night—fitful and furtive, had passed. There was no chance of sleep now. She rummaged carelessly through her backpack. She needed to brush her teeth. That was certain. There was just enough water left to swish the suds around and spit out some of the sweet, stale taste of the ferment still in her mouth.

It would have to do.

The dew was gone. The ground, patchy under her feet. Except for the birds and a few cars crossing the vacant bridge up the hill, the revelry was on hold.

The phone vibrated inside her pocket. Another message from Lucas. "Good morning! I hope you have slept well through the night? Would you like to meet on the bridge for a coffee?"

She eyed the bridge. It was just past eleven. People were beginning to mill about, exiting their tents. She smiled, in spite of herself, her anger from the night before quickly fading. He had that infuriating effect on her. *What effect did she have on him?*

"Bonjour! I've slept well, merci. I can meet you on the bridge. In 15 minutes?"

"See you soon!" He confirmed.

She saw him first, gazing out over the water, leaning against the stone wall. His hair was messy and uncombed. Hands in his pockets, he wore the same shorts and tennis shoes as the night before with the addition of a clean t-shirt.

"Hey," she said, walking up to him softly.

He turned, an embarrassed grin on his face. "Have you slept well?" he asked hopefully.

"Not really." She looked at him with raised eyebrows and a series of silent questions.

"I'm sorry. About last night...I am not proud." He gazed at the river, meandering slowly.

She stared at the sea of Quechua tents on the other side, pitched like small, colorful dots in an impressionist painting, waiting for an explanation. "I guess I don't understand. What about your girl-friend?" The words came out more accusatory than she meant.

"It's complicated." He looked away, purposefully avoiding her probing look.

Eleanorah deserved more. She knew it. And yet she did not yet know how to distinguish potential from substance. Fantasy from reality. She tilted her chin toward the sky, waiting for the clouds to clear, wishing the powder blue didn't match his eyes so precisely.

"What do you say we get outta here?" she suggested. "Have you been to San Sebastián? They have the best pintxos." She smiled, excited by the idea of showing him around for a change.

***

Eleanorah picked at the label on her bottle of La Casera, absent-mindedly scraping the wet paper from the glue, scanning the crowd for handsome men of the burly type. Here, they were in ample supply. The basement of the surf shop, turned into an art gallery, was full of photographs of men in wetsuits, slick like seal skin, balancing precariously in the Spanish sea. From what it looked like, many of them were here tonight, their sculpted muscles protruding easily beneath their tight, short-sleeved t-shirts.

Maybe one of them could become a healthy distraction from Lucas.

The gallery was open to the public and offered an unlimited amount of free beers and lemonade in buckets of ice-cold water. Eleanorah was on her third of the latter, hoping to avoid another night of confessions they couldn't take back.

They'd arrived with Benoît that afternoon, wandering around the city in search of the best pintxos, and "non-touristic" sites. But they were tourists, exploring territory that didn't belong to either of them. Children in a forest, building forts of leaves and sticks, and calling it home.

Lucas walked toward her with a goofy smile, as if she was the only one in the room. "Pour toi, mademoiselle," said with a curtsy, handing her a bag of crisps from the car.

She giggled, ruffling his hair in a gesture of playful tenderness. He made her laugh a lot, she realized. Maybe it was the energy in the room, the pulsing music or the feeling that they were on more equal footing now that they weren't in France, that made her less cautious of the space between them.

"I think you're someone I could have a deep relationship with." He looked at her intently, his voice suddenly deep and serious. "Let me know what happens when you come back to France. You're someone I could change my plans for."

Eleanorah looked at him, bewildered. The air in the room suddenly felt hot, suffocating. She nodded her head toward the exit, away from the noise of a language neither of them had yet mastered.

He followed. A cool breeze rearranged the creases in their clothes. She let it clear her head, waiting several moments before she spoke.

"What do you mean you could change your plans for me?" She paced up and down the narrow alleyway. "Lucas, that sounds serious."

"I'm not a serious guy." He laughed uneasily, fumbling in his pocket for a pack of cigarettes, offering her one. The lighter flicked, his hand cupped around the end, first hers, then his. She took a deep breath, inhaling the savory smoke.

"Look, I feel a deep connection to you." He shrugged as if it were inevitable. "I don't know what else to say."

They moved down the alley away from the doorway and sat on a small curb, watching waiters and waitresses scurrying to keep up with the flow of alcohol and the bite-sized sandwiches drizzled with sauce, and delicate olives. Above the noise of the bars, music came from the harbor. Another Basque festival in full force; the atmosphere drunk on waning summer possibility.

Her shoulder brushed against his. The exhale of smoke wafted upward. She let her body relax into him and the pulse of her rushing emotions. He noticed.

"Do you think I'm someone you could be interested by?" he asked shyly, leaning forward to kiss her on the cheek.

"Mmhmm." She turned her face so their noses were touching.

He pulled her close, his hand on the back of her neck, the warm breath of surrender. "What are you going to do about it?" His eyes were yearning, timid.

"Elle...I have a friend coming to meet us from Paris. He can't know, I don't want him to know about us," he spoke softly.

Eleanorah recoiled immediately. Her eyes flashing with lightning. He reached for her hand, touching her arm lightly.

"No." She stood up and folded her arms across her chest. "We can't do this. I cannot do this with you while you still have a girl-friend. No more secrets. It's not fair."

"Okay." He slumped toward the ground, head in his hands. "I understand."

She wanted so badly to take it back. To pick him up. To be the reason his whole face glowed, no matter the time of day or night.

"Eleanorah..." He stood and pulled her close again. "Je t'apprécie beaucoup. Je ne regrette rien."

"No. I don't want you to...I don't have any regrets." She blinked back tears, falling into his embrace for a moment.

"You've understood!" he exclaimed. "I've said it like I would a friend," he whispered, kissing her lightly on the forehead.

She pulled away and stared straight out in front of them. It was over. There was nothing to do or say now.

"Hey, I was looking for you guys!" Benoît strode over, taking in the scene. "Woah, *qu'est-ce qui ne va pas*? Qui est mort?" He joked. "Who died?"

Mort. Morir. Morose. The patterns were in the words if only she could isolate the root, trace them back to each other, and re-orchestrate the events that led them here.

"Nous," Lucas replied, a slight ache in his voice. He touched her hand.

She ignored it. Penitence for letting things get so out of hand. For wanting them to get out of hand. For wanting to hold his hand.

"I'm hungry, do you guys want to find some food?" Benoît mediated their standoff.

"I've got to get something from the car. You guys go ahead, and I'll meet you." Lucas glanced at her wistfully.

She looked away.

A time out. She needed a time-out. Eleanorah linked her arm through the crook of Benoît's elbow as they walked through the dark alley and didn't let go until they made it to the front of the line at a *resto* serving kebabs.

"What kind of sauce do you want?" he asked.

"What's the best?"

"La sauce blanche. Do you want me to order for you?"

"No, I can do it. Thanks, though." Eleanorah stepped up to the counter. Steam from the roasting shawarma enveloped the man leaning on his elbows, notepad in hand. "Bonsoir, Monsieur. Je voudrais le kebab avec la sauce blanche s'il vous plaît," she stuttered slowly, but the man nodded and wrote her order on the paper.

Benoît added his order and pulled out his wallet to pay. "Pour toi, mademoiselle." He bowed with a slight curtsy and handed her a white paper bag that smelled like Heaven.

Eleanorah winced at the repeated gesture, wondering if this whole thing was just a farce.

"You know you deserve better." He took a big bite of his gyro. "I don't understand," he said, finishing chewing. "Lucas is a good guy. I've known him for a long time. I don't know why he's acting like this."

She lowered her eyes, ashamed her feelings were so transparent. "We should probably go back. It's getting late."

He studied her for a long moment. "Okay," he conceded. "Let's go."

They walked toward the car and found Lucas sitting inside with the window rolled down, clearly on the phone with Camille.

Eleanorah slowed to a stop.

"I think it's better if I head back toward the harbor," she said, pivoting toward the crowd, gathering for another fireworks display. "I'll see you in the morning." She picked up speed, running down the hill in the opposite direction, kicking the trash in her way, deliberately sending a water bottle flying through the air.

"Wow, you have some power!" Lucas jogged ahead of her to pick it up and set it on top of an overflowing trash can. "Is it okay if I walk with you?" His flip-flops flapped against the asphalt next to her, keeping pace.

"Don't you have someone more important to talk to?" She glowered.

"I think, what's more important is enjoying my last night with you. Do you want to sit here for a little bit and watch the fireworks?" He pointed to a grassy spot overlooking the sea.

She nodded reluctantly. The ground was warm, and their knees almost touched. No matter how far apart she tried to keep him, the distance always closed.

"I want to tell you about my girlfriend," he began.

Eleanorah forced her exhale to be measured, inaudible. "Okay. I'm listening."

"We met six years ago, in college. At first, we were just roommates, sharing an apartment, paying the bills together. We were just kids, but we fell in love." His voice faltered.

He pulled a wrinkled piece of paper out of his wallet and unfolded it, handing it to Eleanorah.

She looked at it and held her breath, making out a small form, about 10 weeks along.

"Four years ago, we lost a baby. It wasn't expected. We weren't trying but once she found out, she was so happy. Before we told anyone, it was gone."

She wrapped her arm around him, nestling her head against his shoulder. "I'm so sorry."

"I don't want, I don't need your pity," he said, shrugging away.

"I know. But it's not pity." She tightened her embrace.

He paused, relaxing into her in the silence. "She's said she'll commit suicide if I leave. I could never, I'd never forgive myself if anything happened to her. I couldn't go on." His words came like a rush, stumbling, and falling.

"It's a locked relationship. We're not in love anymore, but we're still tethered." He took the picture of the ultrasound, gently tucking it back into his wallet. "When I travel, *when I'm with you,* I can escape. When I go back, I have to take care of her. It's like living a dual life."

She cradled him, caressing his face in her hand, feeling the stubble of the hair on his cheek against hers. A lump in her throat made it difficult to speak. It was worse than she had imagined.

"I think you have to go to Africa." He straightened back up again, reading her mind. "You're not going to find the life-changing experiences you want while you're here in Europe. I don't want you to wait for me."

"I know." She blinked back tears. "I'm just scared. I'm not ready to leave yet. Time feels like it's going by so fast, and I don't know what's next.

"I only have a few weeks left on my visa. I know I can't stay here. It's just Africa is like...this void, like a portal for me. I'm afraid it's going to suck me in, and I'll never be able to get out again. It's like this force calling me, pulling me toward it, and I don't know why."

"I think I know what you mean." He cupped her face so their eyes met.

Even in the dark, the constellations were clear. She leaned forward, pressing her lips into his. The firmness of his response made her heart leap before her feet noticed the absence of gravity.

Fall, or fly?

***

"Have you heard from the boy yet?" Poppy asked, raising her glass and her eyebrows.

Eleanorah took a slow sip of walnut wine. It was dark, homemade, and sweet like maple syrup. The recipe was a closely guarded secret Poppy refused to disclose, even as she refilled the glasses of everyone around the dinner table.

Poppy and her husband Janez owned a large château with a U-shaped design. It had a brick courtyard filled with chairs to lounge in the sun and overgrown rose bushes. Nestled near the Pyrenees, every sunset was streaked with a velvet, violet hue.

Eleanorah arrived on their doorstep for another work exchange assignment or rather, Poppy plucked her from the train station near Toulouse hungover, and smelling like an ashtray. Her eyes were puffy from crying and she'd caught a cold from the lack of sleep after the festivities in Dax and San Sebastián. Lucas had to go back to work and his girlfriend. Eleanorah had to...she wasn't sure yet.

Poppy was sure of a lot of things and told her all about them while they drove through acres of August sunflowers. Poppy was from Wales and moved to South Africa in her early twenties, she explained. Her husband Janez, was several years older, from Belgium.

"He was an actor and I worked in television." She paused for dramatic effect. "I saw him across the room for the first time and I just knew—that's the man I'm going to marry. I called my mother that day and told her the same. Janez asked me on a date within a month. We had a young family but had to leave when the children were still in school, during the apartheid. So we decided to move to France, and start over," she said.

"Forty years later, here we are."

The first few weeks as their guest, Eleanorah watched how Poppy told the same jokes, and Janez chuckled every time, like a rhyme. How Poppy doted on him, and how he set the table with exact precision while she finished cooking. She listened to the sarcasm between them that led to more laughter; she watched the spark in their eyes ignite when the other one entered the room.

She wanted their love, their history.

Eleanorah set her glass back on the table and took another delicious bite of quiche lorraine. It melted in her mouth with so much flavor she thought she might die. The Boy. That was how Poppy referred to Lucas. She was not impressed by Eleanorah's story of how they met, or how they'd reunited off and on all summer.

"The only vegetarian we've met who'll eat bacon." Poppy teased her, leaving the unanswered question lingering, for now.

Eleanorah wasn't the only traveler Poppy and Janez had taken in. There was also Daphne from Holland, who'd shown up just a few days after Eleanorah, driving alone in a beat-up van with a sticky sliding door. They liked each other immediately. She caught her gaze now from across the table and rolled her eyes playfully.

Daphne was strong. She went into the garden they were tasked with pruning with the big hoe. Like an orthopedic surgeon, she hammered and yanked and put things back into their place. She forged a path. Eleanorah's approach was slightly softer. She preferred to sit with a bucket and pull out all of the small weeds between the cracks one by one. She wanted to leave the dirt intact, not ruffle too many feathers or accidentally remove the flowers that had yet to bloom.

Being at Poppy and Janez's with Daphne was the first time Eleanorah had felt settled since she'd broken her lease in Chicago and hastily put everything she owned in cardboard boxes, now stacked in her mother's garage. Leaving her brick apartment in Logan Square was the first time she'd acknowledged that maybe Chicago wasn't home, either. Maybe it wasn't the place or the life she wanted to come back to.

***

"Do you see him over there?" she asked. "I'm pretty sure I left him close to the ditch in the grass, on the corner right around here." Daphne squatted on her heels, peering closely at the ground.

They were looking for Henry the hedgehog. Wide scarves wrapped around their shoulders to shield against a slight chill, Eleanorah and Daphne walked down gravel lanes that led to country roads and rescued forest animals. Henry was just one in their recent collection. Together they shooed bloated bullfrogs out of dried-up potholes and gently walked wayward turtles to the side of the road, cajoling the scared critters to safety.

They had a special way of communicating with each other and the creatures they passed on their walks, too. They playfully "baaa-ed" at the sheep when they took the shortcut up the side of the mountain so they could pass the bedraggled herd on their way to the village *marché*. Not leaving anyone out, they waved at the cows lazily sitting in circles next to the barn, reaching out their hands to touch the damp noses of the horses who came to the edge of the barbed-wire fence on the other side of the road. But whenever they passed the large, barking Doberman that lived next to the old stone church, Daphne got scared.

Eleanorah found it adorable. She walked ahead, growling and baring her teeth, hissing like a protective lioness. Meanwhile, Daphne practiced karate kicks and gave it plenty of space. Whether from the kung-fu-like moves, the lion-like noises, or sheer confusion, the dog stayed in place, letting them pass in peace.

On their daily walks to Carrefour to buy more cheese and wine and chocolate, they wound through orchards and fields of wildflowers, dreaming. The path to town was lined with Queen Anne's Lace and uphill climbs. They sweat (eventually unwrapping the warm fabric from their necks and stuffing it into backpacks), they laughed, and paused to look at the view while practicing their French.

"Je cherche un bon homme." Eleanorah giggled out loud, picking a small sunflower, and placing it in her windswept hair.

"J'ai un chat noir!" Daphne tried with enthusiasm.

On these walks, Eleanorah learned that in some countries, burnout was a diagnosable, psychological condition. Not just an incessant carousel of worries in her head. There were real causes, and maybe, solutions.

"I think I could do a lot of other things," Daphne mused. "It could be nice to milk cows, or maybe go to New Zealand, and take care of the animals."

"I think that sounds lovely," Eleanorah agreed.

She could see it clearly—green pastureland, pails full of thick cream, and dirt on their noses. Maybe they could start a farm in

France together, shearing sheep or planting apple trees. Maybe they wouldn't have to go back to where they were from.

In return, Eleanorah told Daphne about her ongoing night-mares—patients falling out of bed in the middle of the night, practicing CPR in her sleep, and waking up to the sound of cracking ribs. Post Traumatic Stress Disorder. It was the first time she put those words together, and said them out loud.

Somehow, word must've gotten out that they were friends of small things. One day, they came home from an afternoon prome-nade to find an entire army of ants invading their box of sugar cubes on the counter next to the sink. They laughed and panicked and finally decided to leave them outside on a plate under the acorn tree to have their fill.

And then there was the mole. Oh, the mole. Poppy and Janez were determined to kill that fella. He was their favorite villain, a daily topic of complaint. The hills he created were unseemly in their budding rose garden. He dug tunnels of escape, and left mounds of evidence everywhere.

Whenever the subject of THE EVIL MOLE WHO MUST BE FOUND AND DESTROYED came up during dinner, Eleanorah and Daphne crossed their fingers under the table. They nodded solemnly in agreement, secretly hoping THE CASE OF THE MYS-TERIOUS MOLE would remain unsolved, and that Meow, the cat, would stay lazy and sun-soaked forever.

Eleanorah was worried she might give in to the temptation to stay that way, too. It was almost too easy at Poppy's. Too comfortable. She knew it couldn't last, but didn't want it to end.

"What are we supposed to tell people when we go back home?" she asked Daphne, giving up on their search for Henry. "Everyone's going to want to know what I'm doing with my life, and I honestly have no idea."

"What do you mean?" Daphne smiled mischievously, weaving her way back to the château. "Just tell them you're living it!"

***

"Coucou, comment ça va?" Lucas grinned on the other side of the screen. "You are symbolizing sunshine for me, each time we meet, there are festivals, and barbecues!" He joked.

"I'm okay," she said, returning his smile, wanting to tell him all about Poppy and Daphne and the evasive mole, proof she could be happy here. Maybe even build something.

"Have you thought anymore about going camping?" she asked, hopefully. They'd been talking about it since Dax, trying to manage one last time to see each other before her visa expired.

"I'm sorry, Elle." His tone turned serious. "I'm scared I won't be able to see you again before you leave. I won't be able to take the time off like we wished."

"I understand." She tried to hide her disappointment, embarrassed that she'd let herself believe they could continue what they'd barely begun. It wasn't his fault. He had obligations she didn't—constrained by time, and space, and...*her*.

She said goodbye to Lucas with as much dignity as she could muster, closing the window. As an act of defiance or resignation, she opened the one that had the work exchange in Ghana she'd been staring at for days. "Volunteer in Teiman, 40 minutes from Accra, and help empower youth through education." She re-read the description, clicking through photos of other volunteers and students in maroon and white uniforms with a makeshift school in the background.

A warmth flooded her body when she looked at their bright smiles. She searched through her worn journal for Aberdeen's contact info and sent a short email. "I'm coming to Accra in a few weeks. I'd love to see you!"

Eleanorah took one last walk with Daphne through the gardens surrounding the stone farmhouses. Tiptoeing in the twilight, they watched the sky for a meteor shower that was supposed to pass overhead. Squishy mud evened out the raised tread on the bottom of their hiking boots as they waded through the night, illuminated by headlamps strapped to their foreheads.

"Whenever you're stressed, just look at the sky!" Daphne pointed at the stars, putting her arm around Eleanorah's shoulder.

Without trying, they found Henry the hedgehog huddled next to the road, motionless on their way back. Cold as an unfinished poem, all the life had left. Plumb gone out.

"Let's bury him by the garden shed," Daphne suggested.

Together, they carried his round body like a belief they once shared. Delicately, tenderly, they laid him to rest beneath an open night sky. Tears fell down their cheeks. It was an ending, but maybe, more.

They clutched that maybe to their chests and never said goodbye.

***

She was still waiting on her visa from Ghana, but that didn't entirely explain why Eleanorah had ended up in Aix-en-Provence or what led her to visit an old brick mill on the outskirts of town, now a museum. Camp des Milles.

The night before, sleeping in her pitched tent outside a stranger's home, she'd dreamed about Mutti. Mutti looked for catastrophe and saw it coming. So many reasons for it to come. And she wanted to be ready. Prepared. Safe in the shelter of her home. Rooms full of food and furniture and fear.

"What shelters can become a prison," she'd told Eleanorah in the dream, her face streaked with tears.

"Can what holds us captive also set us free?" Eleanorah's mother had timidly walked toward them both with an outstretched hand she couldn't quite reach.

Eleanorah wondered what it all meant as she placed her purse through the scanner, waiting for permission from the officer staring at the screen in front of him. "Bonne visite, Madame," he said. "Allez-y!"

The entrance to the old mill was accessible through a small, one-room checkpoint, surrounded by barbed wire and high fences. A shiver of recognition passed through her body. She cautiously made her way through the vacant yard with old railroad tracks that used to lead to Paris, now empty. Deserted. Like the eyes in the photograph at the concentration camp she'd seen as a child. Black, and white. Emaciated. How she wanted to feed and clothe them. Hollow bodies with a spirit, yet.

"Why are the men wearing striped pajamas?" she had asked her mother.

She didn't know then that the uniforms divided the prisoners by the color of the triangle sewn on the outside. Red for communists, pink for homosexuals, purple for Jehovah's Witnesses, yellow for Jews.

Her memory recalled that first exposure to human cruelty with surprising clarity. She was nine. It was a warm day in May. An entire wall of a museum, covered by an enlarged photo of skeletons. Skeletons with people still inside of them.

Her Grandpa Filibert and Mutti had returned to Germany for a year as missionaries, hoping to gather more saints to the safety of Independence before the end times. Excited for the chance to travel, her mother had organized a special family trip to visit while they were there. "I want you to see a world beyond this town," she said, with hopeful resignation.

Eleanorah remembered her two older brothers walking solemnly through the abandoned work camp with their father while she trailed behind with her mom, looking at the photos. Even as a child, she could feel the ominous presence of thousands of lives lost, could imagine what happened when the guns in the towers pointed downward, could interpret the black signs with skeletons and white crossbones, warning visitors away from the trenches that held death like a blanket, like an oath.

"What do those words mean?" she asked her Papa Filibert, pointing to a sign at the entrance of the camp called Sachsenhausen, a name she couldn't pronounce back then. He stood beside her and squinted into the sun.

"Arbeit macht frei," he said, reading the German phrase with a Texan accent. "Work makes you free."

She remembered wondering if that's why her Papa Filibert liked to talk about work so much. If that's why he had holes in his slippers so you could see his big toe poking through. He was too busy working to buy new shoes.

"I'm smarter than the average bear, you know."

That was his favorite joke. He would bend down, shake his fist in her face for emphasis, and then laugh. Afterward, he would tell her the story of how he never finished the sixth grade because his parents, German immigrants from Odessa, Russia, needed his help on the family beet farm. About how they were told to forget their past, and who they used to be in order to become something new.

He'd remind her about how he used to work in the oil fields, learned everything he could, and then finally started his own construction company. Explain how he had gotten everything in life through hard work and determination. But her papa didn't seem very free. And neither had the people wearing striped pajamas in the photograph.

Eleanorah looked around the old, musty mill.

Inside, it seemed ordinary. Like it could have been any old forgotten place, left behind by the forward march of progress. It could have been a granary, set in an open field in the Midwest. Could have been a sewing factory or stockyards.

There was nothing significant about its architecture or appearance. The only clues suggesting its nefarious use were etched into the walls of its empty halls—outlines of portraits, small phrases in German or French, messages, and caricatures—symbols of hope drawn in the darkest of nights.

Artists and professors. Fathers and sons. Here, sleeping in the barren barracks among mortar and exposed wooden beams. Here, they painted murals in deserted kilns. There, one of the kilns was turned into a theater, a testimony to the resilience of the human spirit and the need for laughter, even in prison.

The museum displayed timelines and more photographs, lessons for schoolchildren who might visit on a field trip. The reasons for catastrophe were neatly arranged and categorized like small, pretty beads on a necklace, strewn together to make sense of the unthinkable. A chronology of chaos. An organized horror, pieced together posthumously.

She scurried breathlessly down the stairs to the first floor. Away from the telling of something that couldn't have happened. Away from a recollection that couldn't be true. Away from an eerie silence, begging for relief.

Other images returned—building sandcastles in the playground outside her grandparents' small apartment in Neuruppin, and watching the neighbor kids kick them over with glee. Sleeping on the floor with her brothers in the only bedroom next to their parents, who slept on the air mattress next to her grandparents' bed. Checkpoint Charlie and drinking flavored iced tea on the small balcony overlooking a quiet road. Peach, and strawberry.

She remembered posing next to pieces of the Berlin Wall that were left standing, covered in graffiti. Ugly, concrete barriers, trying to keep out or hold in. There was another photograph of her family next to a fence with white crosses, each one with a name representing someone who'd died during the occupation.

Her nine-year-old heart had broken in pieces from the terror of it.

Eleanorah blinked. She had been standing still for a very, very long time. She looked at the picture on the wall in front of her. The enthusiasm of the people captured in the photo was three-dimensional. The fury of it, the excitement was palpable. But when she looked closer, something was off.

Everyone's arm was raised in a salute known for Nazi Germany. They were supporting the regime, pledging allegiance. All except for one man. He stood with his arms folded across his chest, an expression of skepticism on his young face.

The title above the photo offered an exhortation. "Between passivity and resistance: everyone has a choice. To do nothing is to be complicit. What would you do tomorrow, if...?"

Panic flooded her chest. Red crayon scribbles. Bloated bellies and barefoot children. Blood on the white ceramic tile. The boom of the ammunition plant and red flares in the night, tracing bullets.

It all swirled together until she couldn't breathe. She turned and ran, searching for the exit, a way out. "Please, God, let there be a way out," she begged.

***

Leaves rustled, readying themselves for an inevitable descent. Eleanorah dipped her toes into the cold water, her back turned to the wide, open plaza. A strong breeze blew a renegade tangle of hair across her face. "Le Mistral," she whispered. It was coming. Not yet, but soon.

Church bells rang in the distance. A street musician closed his eyes, singing the music of his homeland. The trees were beginning to turn, and the evenings were crisp when she walked at night. Even now, she wore a light rain jacket, the only one she had.

She watched the plaza slowly begin to empty, ruminating on her conversation with Jeremiah earlier that morning. "I think you need to come home," he'd said in a no-nonsense older brother tone he hadn't used in years.

Eleanorah had averted her eyes from the screen, blowing smoke sideways while they chatted. "And where am I supposed to go? To live with Mom or you, and your girlfriend?" She raised her eyebrows, knowing neither one was an option. His pursed lips told her it was getting harder to hide her exhaustion and the nagging uncertainty that followed wherever she went.

Since leaving Poppy's, she'd made a mad dash through as many places as she could. Each day, a bus or train or metro. A breakfast of quiche or pain au chocolat, and cheap coffee and cigarettes. In the evening, an apéritif alone at a café or Tabac, resting sore feet.

Like a forlorn lover, she'd photographed acres of sunflowers against the backdrop of the Pyrenees, their heavy petals drooping toward the horizon, faces chasing the sun. She'd walked to the edge of the unfinished bridge in Avignon and stared into the swirling current of the Rhône, visited the centuries-old Palais de Papes, running her hand along its cool, damp walls, listening.

"Honestly, it doesn't matter, Ellie," he sighed. "Don't you ever miss being around people who know you? Or knowing what you're going to do tomorrow and the day after that?"

"No," she retorted. "That's exactly why I left in the first place."

She could tell the last remark hurt more than she intended.

"Look, I know you don't understand why I'm doing all this. I mean, *I* don't totally understand it, so how could you? All I know is it's not time to come home, yet. But I love you, and I'm glad you're in my life. Thanks for being my protective older brother."

Jeremiah rolled his eyes. "Just be careful, Sis. And don't forget you have a safety net of people who love you to come home to whenever you're ready."

"Thank you." She blew a kiss and quickly ended the call before he could see the tears threatening to fall down her chapped cheeks.

Eleanorah watched as the sun sank below the old harbor. A Moroccan who lived in one of the high rises close to the coast was preparing a meal for them, oysters or mussels, she couldn't remember which. He was tall and handsome and kind. She'd stayed with him for the last few days, exploring the city while he worked at an office downtown.

"Did you know Morocco was the first country to recognize the independence of America from Great Britain?" he asked one night when they were sharing a cigarette on the balcony.

She didn't know. Connections lost, revealed. History seen through a different lens, a prism of possibilities.

She reached for the butterfly, her fingers gently tugging at the thin gold strand it dangled from, tucked safely beneath her jacket. It was her last night in Marseilles, her final stop in France. Jeremiah's questions were hard to ignore because they were ones she'd been secretly wondering, too. Afraid to speak them out loud.

More than anything, she wanted a big house with a stone porch and a Maple tree in the front yard. A place of her own to invite friends over for a cup of coffee or tea. A yoga studio where she knew all of the instructors by name. A library card.

Someone to share it with who was fully hers.

Eleanorah pulled a lighter out of her pocket. It was time to move on. She had to move on. She ran her thumb against the metal and heard the familiar clicking sound before the spark ignited and she tasted that first, gritty inhale. The sun disappeared from the horizon. In its wake, a fiery burst of crimson streaked across the Heavens, like the night of the explosion, reminding her of home.

"You know you should stop smoking," Jeremiah had warned her before they hung up.

She never told him she agreed.

***

"Each time we meet, we see how each other is with talks, long talks. I'm sure our relation is strong enough to survive two continents. Keep me informed of your travels. I'm breathing through you..."

She re-folded the note Lucas gave her at the train station in Dax after staying up all night talking. It was signed, "Your friend, Lucas." She still wasn't sure what to make of it, of him. *Of them.*

She put it back in her pocket.

If he was breathing through her, he took hers away. She had not realized her own retreat, the shrinking of her appetite. How her center of gravity had shifted into someone else's body. Not that he'd asked for it. The opposite, in fact.

"You don't have to put me in a box," he'd reminded her, gently. "We're not that common," he insisted. "The connection we have is..." He shrugged his slight shoulders, searching her eyes for the words neither one of them needed to say out loud. "Maybe we don't have to be categorized," he protested, even as she tried to tie a neat bow around the lid.

Boxes could be carried. Contained. Made into fortresses. Separated from each other by four walls. Organized and labeled. Kept safe, apart from the uncertainty of life.

Bob Marley's voice filtered up to the second floor from the hostel lobby. She'd finally processed all the paperwork she needed to go to Ghana, but wasn't ready yet, needed a pit stop on the way. A distraction from her heartbreak before it would inevitably break again. It was in Marseilles that she decided to come to Morocco, even though she'd been cautioned against it.

Immediately transported into another universe, her arrival was chaotic yet cathartic. A place to reset and gather her senses before meeting Aberdeen and volunteering in Teiman. The irony of going to the last place she wanted to be was not lost on her. She should've known when she swore under her breath not to come, the Universe would double down on its request.

Her gaze shifted to the group downstairs. She watched one of the hostel staff greet the other travelers with ease, laughing and joking in more than one language. He was handsome, self-assured. For a brief second, he looked up and caught her gaze.

Eleanorah looked away, absentmindedly rolling up her sleeves up to scratch at her arms. They were covered in hives. Red, swollen, itchy. She was pretty sure they were caused by bed bugs from the bunk she'd slept in the night before in one of the shared rooms, a common nuisance to travelers staying in less-than-reputable establishments. She'd been lucky to avoid them. So far.

She sighed. The desert heat radiated from the outside in, permeating the long-sleeved shirt and cotton pants she wore in an attempt to dress more modestly, as advised by other solo women who'd visited Morocco. During the day, she swam through the souks slowly, limbs heavy and deliberate. Nothing could be hurried. The pace of life decreased to what felt like a standstill, as if there was a risk of short-circuiting if approached too quickly. The sultry warmth lessened at night, lifting high above the white and blue painted buildings, drifting beyond the walls of the *medina* where it met the sea, only to return the next day.

Her senses did not mind. Lost in the tented market of Essaouira, she eagerly imbibed the earth-toned fabrics draped over wooden ladders—bolts of coral, copper, and sapphire. Each stall was a world of color, at once foreign and familiar. In the evenings, the entire city became bathed in warm light, vividly illuminating the orange and pink minarets dotting the skyline.

Men on mopeds weighed down with items for sale wove through traffic alongside cyclists and donkeys and women selling bottled water and fresh fruit. Palm trees waved in the wind, and children ran down dirt streets dressed in long, colorful *djellabas*. It was Africa, but it wasn't.

Morocco was a fusion of many things. French and Arabic. Red sand deserts with outlets to the ocean. Muslim heritage with a hint of moral flexibility. Cuisine that dripped with juice down both hands. The sweet aroma of saffron.

Of all the things that surprised and delighted her about this small country, the food was at the top of her list. Clay pots set on top of steaming vegetables, and meat slowly cooked until it fell apart in your mouth, blooming with flavor. Couscous with the simplest of ingredients, each spoonful a hearty yet light offering. Assorted olives, rose-seasoned pastries that flaked at the mouth, tea infused with whole plants of mint, and more sugar than her mother's sweet tea.

It was bringing her back to life.

She leaned over the balcony again, debating whether or not to join the travelers below or make one more round through the town center on her own before dusk. The boy with brown eyes looked up again, beckoning. Hunger swelled. A combination of desire, and anarchy. Tired bones aching for embrace.

She answered with her descent.

***

"Don't go," he said, wrapping his arms around her bare shoulders, still slick from the argan oil gingerly kneaded into sore muscles. His fingers clasped hers, interlaced. The weight was an anchor, a safety she longed for yet knew was temporary.

She closed her eyes. Soft elbows and knees braided together in the satin sheets. It was okay to rest. To let her body pause from a state of deprivation, withholding nothing.

She would leave, that was certain.

The ticket was already purchased before the exhilarating rides on his moped, the lazy afternoons spent on a fisherman's boat watching the seagulls, the mornings of thick coffee and hot showers together, letting all the dust from her travels run down the drain. The date of her departure was planned before she knew that someone else's limbs could initiate her into such a state of blissful satisfaction, surrendered.

"Stay," that word she so wished for, uttered from someone else's mouth, lips.

It was tempting.

"Don't be like Jonah!" Micah had warned with a laugh when Eleanorah called him from the hostel, sheepishly admitting she was thinking of cancelling her trip to Ghana. Jonah, the man who ran away from a place he had no desire to go. Jonah who, disobeying God, was swallowed whole by a whale. Jonah, who spent three days in the bowels of a fish before he was given a second chance. Spit up on shore, trembling, humbled, humiliated.

Her brother was mostly joking. Unlike their mother, they'd taken to quoting passages of scripture to lighten the mood. Yet, there was a truth in her brother's playful admonition she couldn't shake.

"Don't cry," the boy murmured, brushing her cheek dry with his thumb, returning her to the shelter of tangled covers.

Eleanorah curled into his arms, avoiding the inevitable. She closed her eyes, forgetting the identity of the person next to her. Replacing it intentionally with another.

The next morning, she waited until he was awake before kissing him softly on the forehead and gathering her things. "Thank you," she whispered, her faded mustard colored backpack cinched carefully around her waist.

All the natural movements of the soul are controlled by laws analogous to those of physical gravity. Grace is the only exception. Grace fills empty spaces, but it can only enter where there is a void to receive it, and it is grace itself which makes this void.

—Simone Weil

4

Hope is not yet finished

The night was black, like her dress, camouflaging bare white legs, hiding her hunger and fear. Inside the taxi, muted sounds filtered through. Police car sirens. Shop owners in dimly lit stalls, advertising their wares through shouts and loud, busted-out speakers.

"This is Madina," a voice explained from the front seat.

She rolled the window down, halfway. When she entered a country at night, the first thing she noticed was not the way it looked but the way it smelled. She could feel it the moment she stepped off the plane, a particular lightness or heaviness to the air. There was a tone, a resonance that carried hidden messages. Words to unravel, secrets to be revealed, or remain a mystery. Each place had a signature perfume, a unique fragrance that the spell of light could never break.

Ghana smelled like burnt rubber, dried fish, and packages of powdered Nestle cocoa. It smelled like boiling pans of palm oil and thick dust that turned to clay when the rains came. It smelled like sweat and coconut milk and vats of hot dye used to make *kente* cloth.

"This is Oyarifa." The young man in the front seat pointed to a small sign illuminated by their headlights. "It's next to Teiman, where you'll be staying with your host family, Pastor Adofo, and Auntie Yaaba. They're waiting up for you."

When he turned to speak, his eyes were lost in the midnight. All she could see were his teeth. White and straight in the palpable darkness. The paved road turned into a dirt one with wide, open-mouthed puddles waiting to be fed. After what seemed like too many miles, they parked next to a concrete house.

Eleanorah smoothed her hair, making an effort to exhale all of the perfumes she'd previously worn—dried lavender, and vegetables stewing in clay pots. The waft of Spanish wine that greeted nostrils just before the glass grazed soft, open lips. The memories convinced her she was alive.

But it didn't make up for the loss. That was sharp, penetrating. There were breadcrumbs scattered across continents, but she wasn't sure where they led, or where her body was in relation to her heart.

"I'm not suggesting that what you're doing is wrong, or asking you to come home," Micah insisted on their last long-distance call. "All I'm saying is that I think you should start evaluating the whys. I want you to be in a place where everything's not up in the air. I always hated Alice in Wonderland. In the end, all that happened was that she had a lot of bizarre experiences until she finally made it home. Why did it have to take all that?"

Micah's worry ran up and down Eleanorah's body, looking for a way in. But she couldn't feel it. Or, she felt too much. She didn't know how to stop. If Micah's doubts mirrored her parents' or even her own, he was the only one brave enough to voice them out loud. At least this time Eleanorah believed her wandering held some kind of purpose. As much as she had resisted coming to Ghana, there was a sense of relief now that she was here.

A porch light shone on an empty clothesline. A baby cried in the distance. The light of the full moon cast shadows on hills of pale, red soil, almost translucent. She stopped and listened to the crickets sing.

The young man took her backpack and motioned for her to follow. She walked tepidly toward a door on the side of the house, not wanting to disturb the nearby neighbors with their lights turned off. A man in a white dressing gown and sandals stood outside in the entryway.

"Akwaaba." He smiled and extended his arms. "This is your home. Welcome to the land of the Asante. You are very welcome here," he said, clasping both hands over hers.

Her body filled with warmth. She remembered the purple flower in her journal. A dark continent full of light.

She couldn't explain or even trust it, yet.

***

The smell of grease and coal heat came in through the crack in the doorway. She rolled over, blinking her eyes open. They were dry, unwilling to focus. She closed them again, feeling the hardness of the cool floor, and the weight of her body pressed through the thin, foam mattress.

Ghana.

A knock on the door forced her to sit up.

"Sister Eleanorah, good morning. Your breakfast is ready, please."
It was a male voice she didn't recognize.

"I'm coming," she answered.

A tall, young man entered. His arms were like rope, like the kind
that used to hold the tire swing she played on as a child. Tight.
Knotted. Sturdy. Bound to something outside itself. A thick scar ran
down the side of his right jawline.

"My name is Kofi," he said, bowing slightly, handing her a plate
of thick, spongy bread, and fried eggs. His expression was shy with
the underpinnings of a warrior.

"Nice to meet you, Kofi."

He bowed again and backed toward the door. "After breakfast,
you can wash. I will accompany you to the school today."

"Thank you."

Another knock came.

"Sister Eleanorah, the washroom is open. You can bathe now," a
girl's voice informed her, opening the door.

"Thank you!" She swallowed the last bite of soft bread soaked
with runny eggs and wished desperately for a coffee. Privacy was
something else she would have to do without.

Amma, whom she'd met briefly last night, followed her into the
washroom, heaving a bucket full of cold water. She was younger
than Kofi, maybe twelve or thirteen. Dressed in a maroon and white
school uniform, Eleanorah noticed small scars up and down her legs.
Her head was shaved but had grown out long enough that coarse,
thick curls were starting to form again.

"Do you need anything more?" she asked.

"No, thank you." Eleanorah smiled, making a mental note to learn where the water came from so she could fill her own bucket. The door to a small, windowless room closed. Her eyes adjusted to the lack of light. Piece by piece, she slowly stripped off clothing already coated in fine dust. It mixed with the dampness of the concrete floor, making a gritty paste under her bare feet.

The bucket was heavy, slopping over when she carried it closer to the drain. A smaller, plastic one floated on top. She filled it and poured this over her head first, gasping and shaking as it ran down her bare neck and back.

Goosebumps appeared on her arms, and she wiggled her naked body in protest, repeating the process several times before taking the bar of soap and running it up and down her buttery skin, chasing the cold away with the heat of her body. The big bucket was almost empty now. She poured the remainder over her, shivering one last time before reaching for her towel and clean clothes.

Kofi waited outside on the small cement porch crowded with at least ten pairs of shoes. Big flip flops and small sandals, dress shoes, and ballet flats. Eleanorah found her pair of worn Birkenstocks and slipped them on.

"The tro-tro man is ready for us." He nodded down the narrow footpath that ran like a small creek between the houses.

What is a tro-tro? she wondered but didn't have time to ask.

"Obruni! Obruni!" A woman hanging clothes on the line stopped to watch them stroll by. "Obruni, ete sen? Obruni!" she shouted, her echoes drowned out by the sound of a loud running motor.

"After you." Kofi motioned her inside, ducking his head behind her.

The bench seats were tattered, the van mostly empty. It reminded her of the Mexican *combis*. A woman wearing a blue and green brightly patterned dress sat in the first row next to three children dressed in school uniforms. A large basket of clear, plastic bags rested in her lap. Kofi reached to tap her on the shoulder, purchasing two of the waters with four *pesewas*.

He gave Eleanorah a bag and bit the corner off his, squeezing the water into his mouth with both hands. Eleanorah followed suit. It was smooth, and refreshing. It dripped down her chin to her thin blouse, already drenched in sweat.

The tro-tro beeped its horn impatiently. Dust flew behind them. Goat herders and children on bicycles moved to the side as they bumped past. By the time they reached the village center, the tro-tro was full of elbows and knees and soft folds of skin pressed against each other, creating its own damp heat. Eleanorah and Kofi shimmied out, past the cramped bodies. The dust rose to meet their footsteps, undeterred by gravity.

A few older men sat in makeshift chairs under an abbreviated shade provided by tin roof overhangs. Women cooked and pinned laundry on lines that stretched from house to house. Some carried baskets or bowls of water on their heads, others stood behind scattered stalls in the shadows, their eyes waiting.

They all noticed Eleanorah.

"We are almost here," Kofi said, pointing in the distance to a walled complex, painted red and green. It was on the edge of a large

open field that smelled putrid, like rotten fish and sulfur. The area
surrounding it was grassless. Thick, crimson billows of dust formed
in the air at the slightest hint of a breeze. She scrunched up her nose
and took short, shallow breaths, hesitating to cross.

Could it be different this time?

Once on the other side, she was greeted by students of all ages with
hair shaved close to their heads, running from one class to another,
borrowing chalk or erasers, or shooing a flock of baby chicks out
of their way. White letters screeched across blackboards. Tongues
capable of speaking several languages twisted themselves into gram-
matically correct British English while goats bleated.

Teachers held large canes in their hands, flexible, and far reaching.
Voices raised, they snapped and smacked the sticks against small
wrists. In an uncovered hallway, two women cooked near what appeared to be an outhouse—a closet-sized building leaning to the
side, covered in tin, buzzing with flies.

The soft tone of a young man's voice floated above it all. "Good
morning, Sissssster Eleanorah." His chin trembled with a stutter.

For the first time, she noticed just how young he was. A few years
younger than her, even. Maybe twenty-one or twenty-two? He had
a scar just below his jawline, too, but his smile spread out around
him in beams. Little ones ran to him, wrapping themselves around
his legs, giggling while he stopped to pat their heads or lift them high
and swing them around.

Pastor Kwado David Afia. The one who picked her up from the
airport and dropped her off last night. He was the real reason she
was there.

She heard about him from Aberdeen, who was less surprised than Eleanorah when she told her she'd finally decided to come to Ghana. "There's a young guy who started a non-profit, not far from Accra. He came and spoke at our church. They were asking for volunteers. I think you'd like him. You should check it out," she encouraged, long before Eleanorah found herself staring at the work-exchange page, refreshing it daily to see if anything had changed.

The name of the organization was The Anidaso Nsae Foundation. Its mission was to provide school fees and free healthcare to as many children in the village as possible. "What does it mean in Twi?" she asked Pastor Kwado.

"Ah. It means, hope is not yet finished," he said, without stuttering.

***

Eleanorah spotted her among the crowded tro-tro station immediately. "How are you?" Aberdeen enveloped her in a tight embrace she didn't realize she needed so badly.

Seeing a familiar face made all of the emotions she hadn't expressed swell to the surface. *How are you* was a question she didn't know how to answer yet.

Thankfully, Aberdeen didn't wait for a response but hooked her arm through Eleanorah's as they navigated toward the edges of the market. "I made lunch, I hope that's okay! Just some tea and sandwiches. I thought you might want some comfort food, or maybe you're getting used to all the *fufu* and *banku*?" She laughed.

"That's not so bad, but what's up with the sponge-y bread here?" Eleanorah wrinkled her nose, thinking of her daily portion of thick slices with fried eggs.

"Yeah, it's definitely not like the biscuits from back home, eh? I live just through here." Aberdeen guided her down a narrow side street toward a modest apartment behind a metal gate. Nearer to downtown Accra, it was clear this neighborhood was full of ex-pats—a relief after being the only foreigner in the village for the last three weeks since her arrival.

Aberdeen let them in and poured a cup of tea. "Would you like cream or sugar?"

"Yes, both please!" Seeing her apartment made Eleanorah miss the creature comforts she'd willingly given up to feel a greater sense of gravity to her movements. Somehow, going without running water or access to Wi-Fi, or a way to wash her clothes (except by hand), felt like penance for her summer in France. Not that it'd been extravagant, but now even the nights she'd camped in her small tent alone—a fresh baguette and wedge of cheese for dinner—felt far away, almost dreamlike. Seeing Aberdeen here instead of Ecuador, where they first met, made her realize just how far she'd come.

"So." Aberdeen set two brightly painted mugs on the table, her voice lilting with a long Irish pause. "How are you really doing?" Her green eyes glinted with the same maternal affection and "Don't bullshit me" clarity as the last time.

Eleanorah held the blue teacup carefully, taking a rare moment to reflect. Her heart was full—maybe it was finally feeling needed again, but her hands still felt empty at her sides.

"I'm...okay." Eleanorah exhaled slowly. "To be honest, I don't think I've been alone long enough to really process it all yet. Living with the host family is lovely, and I adore the students at Nkrumah Academy. But the schedule is really full, so by the time I get home for dinner, I barely have time to make lesson plans for the next day!"

Aberdeen smiled. "What do you think of the Pastor?"

"PK?" She used the nickname she'd given him after a few days of working together, wanting to respect his title without the formality. "He's inspiring...even intimidating, maybe?" She thought of his radiant smile that matched his eyes, and the determined set of his jaw when he spoke about his hopes for the children. His passion and dedication were all-encompassing. Part of her envied it, in a way.

"Mmm." Aberdeen nodded. "I felt the same when he came to speak at our church. He's so young and maybe even a little bit intense?"

"Yeah," Eleanorah agreed. "But in the best way."

"And what does your family think about all of this?" Aberdeen gestured outside the window. "First you were in Ecuador...then France? And now Ghana. It's a bit of a whirlwind, no?"

"Yeah..." Eleanorah took a long sip and leaned back in her chair. "Can I ask you something personal?" She shifted slightly.

"By all means!"

"How long has your family been in Northern Ireland?"

"Farther than we can count, I suspect," she said wistfully. "The borders have changed over centuries, but the land is the same. Doesn't your family have a tinge of Irish as well? I mean, I always guessed by the color of your hair." She glanced at Eleanorah's high bun, held in place with a colorful headband tucked behind her ears.

"Yeah." Eleanorah blushed. "I'm the only one with this color hair, though. I don't look anything like the rest of my family, which is a good thing here, I guess. I'm used to not blending in. My grandfather's side was originally from around Londonderry, I think, but I don't know any of the details about when they came or why they left." She shrugged.

"My grandfather says he was the only one in his family with red hair, too, but I haven't been able to find any photos of him that aren't in black and white before it turned gray." Her voice tripped with longing.

"Sometimes I wonder if I'm doing all of this, trying to resolve something deeper—a loss or many losses that happened before I was even born. All I have is a vague family history of moving from one place to the next, always hoping for something better, and never quite grasping it." A tear fell down her cheek. "It all feels a bit rootless sometimes, you know?"

"That's a lot to carry." Aberdeen offered her a handkerchief. "I can see why this is so important to you, finding a place to belong, making sense of your legacy," she said. "But have you ever considered that you might be rooted in love? Maybe instead of looking for a physical place, you can let love be the place you call home?"

***

"HI! HI! HI!!" Her voice was unmistakable, a single word with a thousand expressions.

Eleanorah laughed at the little arms chugging in the distance, propelling chubby legs forward unreservedly. Like clockwork, she set her bag with school books and drawings and plastic sachets of water down on the dusty path between Nkrumah Academy and PK's house and stood still, watching the limbs come flying toward her. As soon as Mary got close, Eleanorah crouched down and held her in her arms, pressed close to her chest.

It was quickly becoming the favorite part of her day. No matter how challenging it was to teach computer sciences to twenty children with just one computer, or how often her English lessons were interrupted by flocks of chickens or stray goats wandering through the open courtyard, one thing was constant. Every afternoon on her walk home through the village, Mary would be waiting for her.

One didn't meet Mary. She met you. Confidently stepping through the open doorway of PK's two-room house the first week Eleanorah arrived, Mary immediately made her presence known by tapping her hand on Eleanorah's knee repeatedly while Eleanorah sat in a lean-y plastic chair writing emails to potential sponsors, telling them about the school.

After teaching at the school all morning, Eleanorah spent afternoons with PK in his two-room house doing administrative work—updating the NGO's website, responding to volunteer inquiries, or applying for funding. Usually, she'd have dinner with her host family, brainstorming lesson plans on the walk home, and prepping for the next day's classes before bed.

It didn't leave her much time for thinking about what was next or missing Lucas, a gift she was willing to receive in exchange for standing out like a sore thumb everywhere she went. Every morning, she heard the now familiar call of "Obruni, Obruni!" by the large woman selling canned goods and phone credits from her roadside stand. "Foreigner, foreigner, how are you?" She asked from her place in the shade as Eleanorah passed by.

"Foreigner, foreigner, where are you going?" "Foreigner, foreigner, good afternoon!" The phrase was echoed by the men herding goats and sharp-horned cattle across wide, dusty roads lined with shacks with fresh pineapples and coconuts. All of Eleanorah's comings and goings were inspected carefully, and overtly. Eyes looked her up and down when she bought a bag of rice for dinner and some bananas for breakfast. They openly stared at her moles, brown, and red against pink flesh and matching hair, swinging down her back.

What they didn't know was that she was watching them, too. When she felt the hard gaze of their eyes while riding the tro-tro into the capital city, or running through the village, she just stared right back, taking in all of the foreignness. Pretending she wasn't the one who stood out.

She stared at chiseled biceps underneath dusty t-shirts with brand names like Prada and Dolce & Gabbana. She noticed the leanness of the men, envied the way their shiny bodies reflected the sun instead of absorbing it, like hers. She watched the women carrying babies bundled in boldly colored cloth, their heads bobbing gently, legs sprawled against their mothers' backs, hips wide. She admired the way they could sleep, bound tightly to the warmth of the woman carrying them, impervious to the noise and interminable heat.

"Bye bye foreigner, bye bye!" The village children called daily, suddenly running beneath sagging clotheslines or emerging around the corners of brightly painted houses to grab her hand, and encircle her in a grubby hug. Her skin seemed foreign to her in those moments, too, lost in a sea of black, enveloped in their arms.

But none of them were as special as Mary. A soiled, gray dress barely covered her body, the same one she wore every day. Mary rested her head on her shoulder, and Eleanorah felt the top of her skull for the receding bump of a rough and tumble fall that left her tired and cranky for days.

"Ete sen?" Eleanorah searched intently for the tell-tale signs of emotion she was still learning to discern. It was hard to believe Mary was only four. Her eyes were ageless, storybooks of unspoken words. They were reservoirs of life containing deserts and waterfalls and moonlight that didn't wait for the sun to set before it shone, right along beside it.

Mary shimmied out of her arms and ran excitedly toward PK's house. Eleanorah followed, picking her way around the small concrete buildings, ducking beneath low-hanging electrical wires, past circles of women washing laundry, following her tiny, pudgy body. It was for Mary that she stayed at his house every afternoon until late evening, writing what her students were teaching her. Trying her best to translate it into something that would help others see, too.

How unfair it was. How hopeful. How devastating and maddening and yet still worth fighting for. Worth loving until your whole heart broke into so many pieces, there was no chance of ever putting it back together again.

Capturing their stories, infusing them with details and aliveness, made her hands feel less useless, gave them a purpose they desperately needed to stave the hurting.

***

Three-thirty. Time for her afternoon cigarette. Eleanorah snuck past the bedroom door cracked open with her host family asleep on the cool floor, avoiding the afternoon heat. Smoking was taboo here, a discreet activity that, if found out, garnered loud comments from strangers and heads shaking in shame. Another reminder that she wasn't in France anymore—neither invisible nor anonymous.

Nearby, a rooster crowed loudly, arrogantly, as if it were his duty to pierce the silence, to bring life to the thick, sultry stillness. Down the road, a truck carrying polyurethane tanks filled with water lumbered by, groaning as it sank and rose from the deeply rutted holes yesterday's rain left behind. A storm was coming. She noted a subtle change in the breeze. Heat gave way to a cool humidity, and dense, gray clouds began to collide with fervor. She gazed skyward, judging her luck. How much time until the rain would start?

She thought of Lucas, somewhere under the same Heavens. He had a way of soothing her restlessness. An ability to lighten her mood and ease her fear without making her feel ashamed for being afraid in the first place. She didn't realize how much she'd been relying on it, this whole time.

The night before, she'd dreamed they were sitting on the porch together at the house she grew up in, facing the big Elm tree and the wide pasture beyond. A storm was coming then, too. The sky was pea-green with streaks of yellow and soot. The wind picked up, and a tornado came raging toward them. She could see it in the distance, a big, vertical, tunnel of fury.

In the dream she ran into the house and hid in a closet next to an old vacuum cleaner, waiting for him to come inside. Where it was safe. Together. And then she woke up, the dream unfinished.

Did he come?

She flicked the ash from her cigarette a little too harshly, exposing the leaves of the tobacco, neatly rolled and compacted inside the paper. Re-lighting the butt, she noticed a small boy on a pink bicycle, his bald head staring in her direction, motionless for a few brief seconds. She waved and smiled, wishing for the possibility of going unseen, if only briefly.

Eleanorah bent down and tightened her laces, deciding to take a chance on the weather. There was something about running that made her feel powerful. In control. Free. It was something she could do anywhere. She started running in high school at night, up and down those old, country roads. She kept doing it in college, jogging miles of shoreline along Lake Michigan to stay sane.

Here, her route was fairly direct. From Pastor Adofo's house by the cul-de-sac left, away from the hills that rose to her back, and then straight, past the school, all the way to the village center where taxis and tro-tros idled, waiting for passengers. She leapt off the last step and set a comfortable pace, cognizant of the heaviness in her lungs from hidden encounters with London cigarettes, bought for two cedis a pack.

The clouds parted, and the afternoon softened. Baby goats lay in the grass, worn out from a full day playing King of the Hill. Most of the roadside shacks were empty, their owners retreating until evening. Even the mates were loitering without their usual loud cries, hawking each destination with unique calls and trills.

Eleanorah reveled in the quiet, finding a place to stretch next to the big tree at the edge of the village. No rain. She let it sink into her cells.

No storm today. It was just a dream. She was safe, for now.

So was he, she hoped.

***

The field next to the school was a whirlwind of dust and flying feet. On one side, women sat peeling cassava, stacking large, fibrous roots on top of each other to take to market. In another corner, the same pool of murky water and floating trash permeated the air with a factory-grade stench. A fickle breeze brought both relief and repulsion.

It was almost Harmattan, the dry season from November to March, when a strong wind of the same name blew dust from the Sahara across Northwestern Africa on its way to the Amazon rainforest. There, its barrenness cultivated life. Green, dense, fertile. *The lungs of the earth.* She wondered at the possibility of it. How two vastly different places could be so interconnected.

There was nothing fertile about the thick dust here. Students ran across its wide expanse, undeterred by the cloud or smell, chasing a beat-up soccer ball up and down, aiming at make-shift goals. Two big rocks on one end, a building, and a tree on the other.

Most of them were only wearing one shoe. Their bodies slightly off-balance, they jogged back and forth, hips and joints accommodating for the difference in height. They shared shoes, she realized, so they could all play the game. After distributing the shoes as equally as possible, they put one laced-up tennis shoe or cleat on the dominant foot, kicking the ball powerfully and swiftly, while their remaining foot, caked in dirt, lagged behind.

Hope is not yet finished, she thought, realizing it could be an action, not just a belief.

Izaak sat next to her, holding Mary in his lap. A newly arrived volunteer from Düsseldorf, he played trombone in a ska band, used words like "pedagogy," and pronounced it "maths" instead of "math." He was a balm of belly laughs and wide-legged fabric that billowed in the wind, letting everything around him breathe just a little bit easier. On a gap year, he'd just been in Burkina Faso and was intending to return after a few weeks or months in Ghana (yet to be decided). Until then, he was staying with her at Pastor Adofo's house in his own bedroom across the hall.

He reminded her of Hans and Alfreida, pure practicality with a sense of expansive curiosity, surpassing her own. While she taught English and computer classes, he taught math and political science. They instantly became friends, spending their whole day together, from breakfast in the morning to walking or taking the tro-tro home at night, both struggling to eat the overly proportioned heap of fried rice doled out by Auntie Yaaba.

"Auf geht's, Ghana! Yeah, let's goooooo!" He waved his hands, cheering for both teams in German and English whenever they scored a goal.

Eleanorah watched their lopsided running with brewing irritation.

"Why don't we give the kids new shoes instead of sending them our old, used-up ones?" Eleanorah pointed to the field. "This whole system is so messed up. Aren't we sending them a message that they aren't worthy of the same quality we have?"

Almost Harmattan meant almost Christmas back home. It meant big box stores overflowing with toys and shoes and impossible things her students would never see or touch. How many times had she prepared a care package full of toiletries or dollar store items wrapped in glaring green or red paper for kids just like these, dropping it off at the collection bin without a second thought?

The Madina market was full of donated items from the West, sold for retail. Worn rubber and thin fabric. Outdated electronics and plastic. So much plastic.

Izaak paused and readjusted Mary, now asleep against his chest. He shook his head thoughtfully. "Yeah, but the real question is, why can't they afford to buy their own shoes? And why are we here teaching for free instead of paying local teachers a decent salary?" He shrugged his thin shoulders casually, as if he'd already made peace with their implications.

But why did it have to be this way? And how could she extricate herself from the equation?

Good intentions with bad results. Bad intentions with worse results. Militant missionaries. Fabricated history. Mounds of unmarked graves. The wires crossed and fused. Sparked as they separated and then came together again. Ripe for an explosion.

***

Fever pitched. Malaria. The words swirled inside her parasite-ridden blood.

She groaned and stretched across the sweat-soaked mattress. She was in a different room now. Shared with a girl from Belgium named Béatrice, the two of them paired together to accommodate space in Auntie Yaaba's already overflowing house. Like the big sister she'd never had, Béatrice gave Eleanorah straight talk. Tough love. She pinpointed her self-doubt, and with the flick of her wrist plucked it from her heart, painlessly. Béatrice with her beautiful, curly brown hair, and wide, pink-lipped smile. The way they parted when she laughed was so contagious.

Izaak was in her old bedroom, across the hall. Izaak. Fraternal. Funny. Exquisitely himself.

And then there was PK. Her mind grazed over the length of his arms, the swish of his long dressing gowns, the swerve of the taxi he was still learning how to drive. He was the glue that held them all together, brought them here, and made them feel like they belonged to each other. He'd even gifted them with a set of matching clothes, cut and custom tailored from bold-patterned fabric.

Like a chosen family. She smiled briefly before closing her eyes, shaking with chills.

Her father was stoking the fire. He added another log and it sparked red, orange. Her Mother was in the kitchen, humming along to her favorite opera singer, Andrea Bocelli. The house smelled of campfire, and roasted turkey. It was Thanksgiving, she remembered. The aunts and uncles and grandparents would be coming over soon. The table needed setting. Her Mother needed help with the pies. But something was wrong. The fire was coming out of the stove, into the living room. Her Mother was yelling but her voice sounded far away.

It was hot, too hot.

There were children running up and down drainage ditches like they were sidewalks. They scampered on beat-up cardboard and rotting planks that covered open sewage and thousands of plastic sachets with the words "pure drinking water" printed on them in bright blue. Full-grown men washed in streams of garbage. Exposed, they bent and reached into the sewers, rinsing polluted water over their naked bodies shining, like glory.

Eleanorah's own body was black and blue. Her lips, swollen. Bloody. Her throat an empty ravine of silent screams. She watched, paralyzed, as the smoke engulfed her house and family until everything was gone.

***

The imprint of an invisible hand on the flesh of someone you love. The stinging red outline, the sharp pain. She had been the recipient more than once.

"Shut up! No. You, shut up!" The teacher in the next room, Charles, raised his voice. He handed his cane, a long thin piece of wood, to a young girl, and brought the students forward, one by one. "Hit them like this! Harder, harder! Kill him!" he instructed, crooning with glee.

The bamboo stick made a whacking noise. Her shoulders stiffened, close to her ears. Fever from the malaria made her lightheaded. The chalk between her thumb and forefinger quivered against the board. Izaak was home today, sicker than she was. Béatrice was helping PK with a different project. She looked around, realizing she was alone.

The cane made another "WHACK!"

The chalk between her fingers broke.

Adam, her brightest student who sat near the front, jumped up and ran to get more. Eleanorah waited. And tried not to listen. But beyond the awkward silence, there was laughter. The kind that's filled with relief, and shame, and nerves sending fight or flight impulses up and down spinal cords bent in submission.

The teacher laughed, too. He smacked the cane on a broken-down desk that tilted to the side and held three or four or five students, depending on the day. One of them, a robust boy of about twelve, repaired these desks after school. His name was Elekam. He was one of the bullies who chased the other students around the school with sticks yelling, "I will beat you, I will beat you!"

Using a large rock, she had watched him patiently bend the contorted nails into a straightforward shape, forcing the bench back together. He labored with precision, and patience. In these moments when the school emptied itself of chaos, his face softened in focused determination.

Adam returned with fresh chalk.

"Madame," he said with a slight bow, spilling it into the palm of her sweaty hand, hurrying back to his tilt-y seat.

She forced a smile and returned to the board. But the echo of the bamboo cane bouncing off the body of another student distracted her from writing pairs of helping verbs. She peered through the crack between the two walls separating their classrooms.

It was Linda. Linda, who fell asleep in most of her classes because she spent long nights helping her mother sell phone credits and cigarettes and baby formula to families instead of studying for her exams. She must've nodded off again.

But now she was out of her seat, head lowered before the man responsible for the sharp, whacking noises and nervous laughter. A smirk revealed itself beneath his black beard. He raised the cane again.

Eleanorah watched, frozen.

The room grew silent. All of the baby goats stopped bleating. The laughter evaporated. The chickens scurried and took their clucking noises with them. The children in the nursery swallowed their tears before the wail left their mouths.

All she could hear, the only noise that mattered, was the swift whip of air before the belt struck soft flesh with a resounding

"CRACK!" The invisible imprint of her mother's hands smarted with heat and sharp, stinging pain.

The chalk dropped to the floor.

Suddenly, she was around the corner, standing in front of the young teacher with thick hands, still gripping the cane. "Please stop," she begged. "Please, please stop. Can't you discipline them in another way? They're just children!"

Tears flowed freely now, whetting her words. "How would you like it if I came over here, and caned YOU?" She stared at him like arrows drawn, ready to fly, latent lethargy ignited by hellfire.

A surprised look crossed his face. For a moment, he stared back, unmoving. Adrenaline from adrenal glands beat its way into her heart. Every muscle tensed. Blood scurried with raised pressure to the edges of fingertips and toes and ears, ringing. Fists clenched, and her jaw set itself straight, ready to fight.

He turned to the students. "Do you know why we use the cane in school?" His voice was punctuated with a low growl.

Hands flew into the air.

"So that we do what you say!"

"To help us pay attention!"

"So we can learn our lesson!"

"Because we are bad students and need to be punished!"

He faced Eleanorah again with a sly, triumphant smile.

As soon as the adrenaline came, it went. Everything moved in slow motion, including her limbs, which fumbled through the air as if it were thick, opaque. Darkness coiled, wrapping itself around, and around.

She felt it take the breath out of her, but not the fire. Not this time. It flickered in her eyes, refusing to be doused.

She thought of Mary and Daniel and Adam. Of Evans and Diana and Rebecca. Of all of the children she now loved and scooped up into her arms, close, close.

She knew the beat of their hearts. The stutter in their speech. The pitch of their laughter. The size of their shoes, two sizes too small for their dirty feet. She knew which pathway led to their home. Who had a natural talent for drawing or spelling or acting. Which ones needed her sternness, and how to make Wegina smile, so briefly you'd miss it if you looked away for even a fraction of a second. But it was there.

They were hers. Fragile, wholly. Infinitesimally. Somehow.

"Madame?" Mary, now dressed in a clean school uniform, reached for her hand. Eleanorah scooped her up, not caring that she was supposed to be in a different class.

"Mary." She kissed her on the forehead, remembering why she was here.

"What is the difference between having a voice and being silenced?" She took a deep breath and faced her students.

Twenty-six pairs of brown eyes stared, unblinking.

She tried again. "How does it feel, in your body?"

Slowly, hands began to lift. One at a time.

"Silence feels like alone, Madame."

"Silence feels like afraid."

"It feels like clothes that are too tight and no longer fit."

The chalk scraped, collecting words on the blackboard.

"Okay..." She searched for beacons. Homing devices. Lighthouses built within the cliffs and contours of their irises.

"What emotions do you associate with speaking up?"

"Madame, Madame!" Arms stretched, and wiggled, reaching for the sky beyond the slatted tin roof.

"It feels like strength."

"It feels like courage."

"It feels like love."

More words on the board.

"Okay, if you could write to another classroom, maybe in America or Germany, and tell them about your school, what would you want them to know? What do you need? How can they help?"

"People outside other schools laugh at us because our buildings are not completed...but we have good teachers and are very respectful students. We are also well educated," a student named Jasper spoke.

"Our school is not perfect, yet it feels like home to us," Rebecca shared shyly.

Not perfect.

Home.

She paused and stared at the board, seeing the truth side by side.

***

"Hi, Pumpkin. How are you feeling? Is your malaria better?"

Her father's groggy voice sounded as far away as it was, but she needed him. Her three month visa was almost up. Originally, she'd planned to fly back to Paris after New Year's but she couldn't imagine doing that now. She saw the effect when the other volunteers went back home after a week or two, barely enough time to take photos, and learn a few names. But long enough to make the children cry at another goodbye.

"Hey, Dad. I'm okay. My malaria is pretty much gone. They gave me some medication at the clinic. How are you? How was your Thanksgiving? Did you and Grandpa do anything?"

"Yeah, your brothers came over on Friday, and we had a nice dinner. Jeremiah's girlfriend made apple pie and Micah brought some green bean casserole from Hy-Vee. A bit of a bachelor's take on Thanksgiving, but we did our best." He laughed. "We definitely missed you!"

"I miss you too." She tried not to let her homesickness show. "Dad...?"

"Yeah, honey. What is it?"

"I don't know if I can keep doing this..."

She wanted to change it. She was doing it wrong. She was loving too much, too soon. Or, choosing ones that didn't have the capacity to love her back, not the way she needed.

"I don't know how to say goodbye. The kids here," she choked. "I'm not ready to leave."

Eleanorah looked down at the traffic below the balcony of the fast food restaurant where they came for the fried chicken and free Wi-Fi, waiting for his response.

"You love with your whole heart, Pumpkin. It's just who you are. It's how you were made. I know it doesn't always feel like it but it's a gift.

"I know it's scary when you don't know what to do next. But I love you. Your brothers love you. Your Mom loves you, too."

She took a deep breath. Hearing it through her Dad's voice made it somehow softer, easier to accept. Lowered the barbed wire fence between her and her mother, a cautious barrier she avoided often.

"Have you called her, lately? I know Christmas is one of her favorite times of the year. I'm sure she'll be missing you."

"I know." Eleanorah sniffled, louder than she intended. "I'll try to call her soon. I miss her, too."

"Okay, Pumpkin. I know it's late there. We're all here for you, no matter what. I've gotta go get some breakfast for Grandpa and I. You get some rest so you can keep loving on those kiddos, okay? Give them all big hugs for me."

"I will, Dad. Tell Grandpa I said hello, and I love him, too. How is he really doing?"

He paused. "He's okay. Some days are better than others. He asks about you a lot."

Her father didn't admit it directly, but there were hints he was in the early stages of dementia. He'd recently sold the pattern shop and all of the mold-making machines, but when she closed her eyes she could still smell the fiberglass and resin, hear her grandfather's voice echoing through the dusty aisles. He had just turned eighty but to Eleanorah, he was frozen in time. When she pictured them together, she was, too.

How many of his stories had she never heard? How much time was left?

***

"Barges, I would like to go with you, I would like to sail the ocean blue," her mother hummed a little off-key, behind the wheel.

They'd passed over an unnamed bridge, speeding through the night. Eleanorah's feet were bare and propped up against the windshield, the passenger seat reclined as far as it would go. Splotches of insect remains dotted the paned glass, each one marking a hundred miles, more or less.

It was her favorite place to be, next to her mother. No distractions. Just the two of them, and the road ahead. Her mother had surprised her by offering to pick her up in Chicago to drive back to Independence together so Eleanorah could store a few belongings in her basement before flying to Ecuador.

"I always wanted you to know there was more to the world than what you grew up with. What I grew up with," her mother admitted. Like Eleanorah, her mother had left her small hometown for college when she was just seventeen, and never looked back. It was one of many things they had in common.

"Don't cry little child, don't cry little child. Your mother isn't home? Who are you crying for? My poor little child, please sleep peacefully."

Another mother hummed outside the window of PK's new house, a home base for the increasing number of volunteers who came to stay. Eleanorah loved the camaraderie they shared—all sleeping together in one room for the girls, and one for the boys, cooking curries, and making fried rice while practicing French or Twi. But part of her missed Auntie Yaaba's house, just a few miles down the dirt road by the big tree. After living there for three months, it was hard not being closer to Mary, and seeing Kofi and Amma in the mornings before school.

The new house was salmon colored, like the earth that remembered the indentation of their footprints until the next hard rain. Sometimes, after a downpour (the kind that you could feel knocking at your door all day until it finally burst in), the floor of the entire house would be covered with ants. Big, winged ants. Ants that crawled out from their tunnels in the now-clay earth. Dying ants. Flying ants. The neighbor kids would laugh and squeal, running to avoid stepping on them, adding to the chaos.

Eleanorah surveyed the plastic chairs stacked on top of each other to prevent them from crumbling beneath their weight, next to the makeshift table. Crayons littered the floor, and a mattress with no sheets on it lay propped against the wall. Dishes left from last night's meal filled the small sink and fruit flies hovered over the plastic bag hanging on the kitchen door, feasting on mango peels and rotting pineapple.

Outside, the fading twilight gave no indication it was Christmas Eve, the night Eleanorah's family celebrated together. Earlier in the day, she'd gone to the market with Béatrice to gather ingredients for a special curry. "Three tomatoes, two cedis, two cedis," the women with carefully balanced stacks of ripe red fruit called after them.

Together, they'd purchased a few candles and a string of red lights to go with their small, Charlie Brown Christmas tree. After dinner they'd sung carols in German and French and English, ending with an acapella version of Silent Night before exchanging small gifts.

She padded softly through the candle-lit living room, through the tiny kitchen, and out the back door, torn between her unexpected contentment and the uncertainty that came with staying in Ghana, not to mention her longing for Lucas—the recognition in his blue eyes, how they could say so much without any words at all.

She sat on the small stoop facing a brick wall. Beyond the wall, there was an open field and sky.

"Mama?"

Eleanorah held the phone she'd bought in Spain after saying goodbye to Lucas. It was simple, but had two SIM cards. One for France and one for Ghana. Both numbers were programmed into her contacts with ME GHANA, representing her newest location, a pin on the map so she couldn't forget.

"Hi honey." Her mother's voice was clear, despite the thousands of miles between them.

"Merry Christmas!" Eleanorah's vocal cords wobbled in response. Tears fell involuntarily. She tried again to sound cheerful. "Are you still up?"

"Yeah, it's still early here. I've just been cooking all day, getting ready for dinner. I'm so glad you called, I've been thinking about you a lot."

"Me, too."

She had a flight back to Paris in less than a week she hadn't changed yet. She was supposed to leave on New Year's Eve. She could return to Europe any day now with a new visa. She could look for a job in France like she'd planned. She could take a hot shower. She could see Lucas.

Or she could stay.

With Béatrice and Mary and Wegina. With Hannah and Adam and Izaak. With arms that wrapped around her arms and legs every day.

"Honey, I have something I want to tell you." Her mother exhaled a sigh that sounded like the relief that comes when the tornado sirens finally turn off and it's safe to come out of the basement again.

"I know I wasn't always the best mom to you and I'm sorry. I wish you could've been raised by the mother that I am now. I would've done things differently..."

"Mama..." Eleanorah swiped at her eyes. She took several breaths before she could speak again. "It's okay. I forgive you. I honestly wouldn't be here if it wasn't for you."

"Thank you, honey. I know you're worried about what to do, but if you're not sure where to go, or what to do next, it's okay to stay until you figure it out."

"Thanks, Mama."

"You're welcome. You know we'll support you whatever you decide."

"I know. Tell everyone I said Merry Christmas, please. I love you, Mama."

"I love you too, Ellie. I'm proud of you."

"Out of my window looking in the night, I can see the barges' flickering light. Taking their cargo out into the sea, how I wish someday, they'd take me," Eleanorah sang quietly, a weight lifted from her shoulders.

Tonight, there were no bridges to pass. There were no highways for speeding through time, and space. But the breeze carried memories across the sea. Banana leaves rustled softly. Vibrations of grandmothers and mothers soothed children to sleep, singing under the upside-down moon.

***

The sky hummed with the noise of planes taking off, returning foreigners to where they belonged. In a place designed for movement, they waited. Eleanorah observed the clouds and smelled the warning of rain in the air.

They were at the airport to meet Otumfuo, which was not his real name, but an important one—shared by the ceremonial leader of the Ashanti Kingdom. His true identity, however, was a mystery. During their meetings, he wore his official name badge tucked into his collared shirt. His uniform was forest green, the standard attire of an immigration officer. A yellow sash draped over his shoulder to his left hip, just brushing the hidden gun at his side.

Otumfuo made her feel uneasy, even with PK at her side, confident, and charismatic. This was to be their third and final meeting with him. Today, on the day Ghana celebrated its 57th anniversary of independence from the British Empire, she would obtain her last visa. It would be stamped with green ink into her newly minted passport printed with a caveat, "This is a replacement for a lost or stolen passport."

In fact, hers was stolen. The entirety of her wallet, passport, and a brand new, unopened packet of cigarettes were snatched from her purse at a busy tro-tro station outside the mall in Accra. Her new passport, obtained from the U.S. embassy, was empty. There were no stamps or visas or proof she had been anywhere at all. Since she couldn't leave Ghana without proof that she had arrived, Otumfuo agreed to forge a fake arrival date. At a cost, of course.

She'd be lying if she'd said the empty passport hadn't made her question everything.

PK looked at the sky. "Looks like the season of Harmattan is over," he commented as the first few raindrops began hitting the windshield. "Sssister Eleanorah, have I tttold you the meaning of our word sankofa?"

She gazed at the airplanes flying through the clouds.

"No, I don't think so."

"Ssssankofa is a sacred word. It's from our Akan language. Ittt means, 'go back, and get ittttt.' The proverb says, 'It is not wrong to go back for thattt which you have forgotten.' The ssssymbol is a bird, looking behind, and fetching an egg in itttt's mouth. We cannnnot look to our future without knowing our past. Now, we will be part of your passst. Annnnd we will also be part of your future." He smiled.

Eleanorah thought of the monarchs, how entire generations were born away from home, yet somehow they remembered.

The rain came heavy. He opened the taxi door and she ducked inside. On the radio, they heard the crackle of the Independence Day speech given by President John Dramani Mahama.

"My brother and sisters, this is a most extraordinary Independence Day celebration. When it rains we call it showers of blessing..."

They were only a few miles from Black Star Square where the ceremony was. She imagined the crowd, gathered in the wide plaza where there was no shelter from the storm. It could be hours before the rain passed and her passport was safely in her own hands again.

The gesture of "gifting" was a sleight of hand she'd never mastered. It was done among men for her benefit, or expense, she could never tell which. The last time they met Otumfuo, he'd teased her relentlessly.

"So..." He'd thumbed through her passport, relaxed and deliberate.

"You've been here since October, eh? Have you found a man here in Ghana yet? A nice, strong man to be your boyfriend?" The words oozed out of his leering smile, coating the air around them with insinuations.

"No, not yet." She'd forced a coquettish smile, reserved for those instances when it helped to be seductive, when it helped to ignore the repulsion forming goose bumps on her skin. If her disgust bubbled too visibly to the surface, the deal could be over.

"How are your people in America, Obama's people?" he continued, holding her passport securely in his grasp. "You know, the white man was the one who taught us how to offer gifts." He patted his shirt pocket. "Now it is part of our culture, it is how we show respect to each other. You cannot blame the black man if you do not want to give a gift. It is how you show appreciation."

It was also how you got a police report filed, she learned. Without this "gift" there was no report, no crime, and no missing passport. Without the report, there was no replacement passport. Without the wallet and the passport, there was no "gift," because her capacity to "give" had been stolen.

No matter the logic. In the shadows, it was impossible to connect all of the dots. What Otumfuo said was true. The white man played the game of appreciation, too. And mostly won. Fourteen former colonies still showed "appreciation" for their liberation by allowing the French to retain control over 85% of their foreign exchange reserves.

Rain pelted the pavement, coming in sideways like sheets of invisibility. "Do you mind turning that up?" Eleanorah asked.

The president continued his speech in the downpour of blessings. "Ghana was the first black African nation to win independence, and so the world's eyes were on us. If Ghanaians could free themselves from colonial rule, then so too could the rest of Africa. And, despite the cost," the voice continued over the radio, "freedom proved to be an extremely contagious condition. In 1960 alone, seventeen African countries gained their independence.

"Dr. Martin Luther King, Jr., the leader of black America's Civil Rights Movement, travelled to Ghana to witness our Independence Day. When he returned to America, he delivered a speech called "The Birth of a Nation," in which he said:

'Ghana has something to say to us. It says to us first that the oppressor never voluntarily gives freedom to the oppressed. You have to work for it. And if Nkrumah and the people of the Gold Coast had not stood up persistently, revolting against the system, it would still be a colony under the British Empire. Freedom is never given to anybody.'

"My brothers and sisters, what we are celebrating today, and what we celebrate on every anniversary of our independence, is not just the attainment of freedom; what we are celebrating is what that freedom meant, and still means—to us and to an entire world.

"The door we opened on 6th March 1957 was not just to our future; it was not just to our freedom. To countless people across the globe, that door was an opening to the possibility of their own freedom."

Eleanorah wondered what the doorway to her freedom held.

A cell phone rang.

"Yesss-a, hello?" PK's voice stuttered. "Okay, thank you very much sir. Please, I'm coming. Yesss, okay. Medasi."

Eleanorah's heart fluttered. Her new passport was ready.

***

"What if I'm kidding myself?" She looked out the window at the passing scenery.

The driver raced over dips and caverns, ignoring speed bumps and curves. The badly paved road was unforgiving. She laughed as passengers raised their voices in protest. "Driver, driver!" they shouted. "Driver, you are going too fast!" they admonished.

The view from the bus at this speed was flattering. Banana plantations and mango farms, hills with forest still intact. The blurred landscape was lush, and green. Truthfully, Eleanorah was scared of how happy she felt. Terrified that her growing contentment would be shaken. That she was fooling herself. That this couldn't possibly last.

Béatrice looked at her incredulously, her dark eyebrows raised. "Everybody is kidding themselves. People back home are kidding themselves!" Her chuckle was chiding, dismissive.

Eleanorah laughed with relief. She had been in mourning for so long, the taste of joy felt foreign on her tongue. More than her own gladness, she trusted Béatrice's confidence, and sturdy, sure-footed Grace.

"You're right." She leaned her head on her shoulder. "Thank you for being my sister. I'll really miss our pillow talk! Who's going to keep me up late at night watching pirated Friends episodes when you leave?"

"You'll be alright, my love," she said, patting her head. "Besides, we have the next four days, just the two of us!"

They were on their way to Kumasi to see the largest market in West Africa, taking a mini vacation together before Béatrice went back to Belgium. From there, they'd visit Cape Coast, historically significant as a major destination for the slave trade, first established there by the Portuguese in 1555.

It was the first time Eleanorah had traveled since the night she arrived in Ghana, dressed in black. Finally at peace in the place she'd been avoiding, there was no reason to go anywhere else. After almost six months, the days passed in a comfortable routine marked by the coming and going of new volunteers and trips to the airport. Being the only one who wasn't leaving made her feel special, somehow. Like she could trust herself not to run away, even when it was hard.

But it was nearing the end of February, and while the agent at Air France was able to change her original flight to Paris for a hefty fee, there was no way to cancel it completely. Eleanorah hadn't wanted to, anyway. Lucas and Camille were finally over. She needed to find out what that meant, if anything, for her.

"The only plan I have left is to see you once more," Lucas said when she told him the news that she was coming back. "I'm sorry I have nothing more romantic to say."

For once, she didn't need him to be the one to plan anything. She'd leave for Paris in early March. Three more months in Ghana had given her the courage she needed to make a decision about what came after, regardless of his choice.

The bus made an abrupt stop down a side street near the outskirts of Kejetia, the largest open-air market in Western Africa. The other passengers gathered their belongings, bustling into the aisle. Béatrice and Eleanorah were the last ones off the bus.

"Medasi," Béatrice acknowledged the driver before stepping down onto the curb. Eleanorah followed closely behind her left shoulder. The crowd opened and then circled them again, pressing inward as they walked toward stalls illuminated with flashes of richly dyed fabric, patterned with ancient symbols they were still learning to decipher.

An older woman sitting next to a stack of kente cloth inspected Eleanorah's bare white legs with disdain. Laughing smugly she slapped her thigh, making a motion with her hands, indicating her shorts were too short to be proper. A young, naked boy heard the smack and started crying when he caught sight of them.

Eleanorah wanted to cry, too. The streets were a maze, narrowing like a tunnel in a mammoth cave, each one going further in, in, in. She was lost in its enormity, in the topsy-turviness of it.

Life and blood spilled out from all sides. The smoke coated her hair and got underneath her fingernails. It stuck to her skin. It was pure madness, but there was a surety and purpose to the chaos. She was frightened, yet enthralled by the implications of it; life lived so close to its essence, stripped bare of any pretense.

A building with a stairwell appeared and Béatrice leapt up, up, up. Past the hawkers selling football jerseys and men's boxers. Past the shadows and into the light. Eleanorah grabbed Béatrice's hand and held on until it opened into a wider avenue full of tro-tros and foot traffic.

"Peace Ghetto," a sign read, in orange, red, and white. A small patio ran up to a bar under the slightest shade. Béatrice nodded to the pair of chairs next to an empty table.

"Yeah," Eleanorah agreed. "Let's sit for a bit." She leaned back in her chair and shooed the flies landing on something sticky, lapping up the leftovers. Her head throbbed. Probably due to dehydration, and too much nicotine. She pulled out a cigarette, anyway.

"Everything happens for a reason," a woman's voice said confidently. "Sometimes people come into your life to teach you something about yourself." The woman behind the counter continued telling her friend. "You lock eyes with them, and you know."

Eleanorah thought about the moment on the ferry. Maybe she'd made it mean something it hadn't. *But it wasn't nothing.*

An idle breeze stirred the air. It loosened the sweat-soaked strands of hair plastered to Eleanorah's forehead. And then, it was gone.

***

Strands of bamboo clanked together in the gentle ocean breeze, a welcome distraction from the harsh surroundings. Béatrice and Eleanorah had arrived in Cape Coast only to discover it was covered in feet of garbage leading to the shoreline. Heaps of it. So deep it created an artificial hill that had to be climbed over to reach the water. And then there were the pigs. Crusty and large, nosing their way through the remnants, uncovering a perfectly pristine shoe, its laces still tied, next to cracked pots with missing lids.

Far from the beach, the despair stretched toward them. Small children gathered on the outside terrace of the restaurant where they sat, begging and pleading with their eyes. Their clothes were dirty, bellies round, and taut. They wanted attention but they really needed something to eat.

The words from their blistered lips were few but insistent. "Please Madame, please."

Eleanorah watched the waiter shoo them away with one hand and serve the tourists with the other. It was a hot day. The ice in her freshly squeezed pineapple juice was already beginning to melt. The air was weighed down with dust. Fumes from burning trash and exhaust overpowered the salty fragrance of seawater. Her chest was heavy, lungs darkened with each breath.

After two days exploring Kumasi, they'd made it to the place where slaves boarded ships for centuries. Where a castle was a fortress, a refuge, a prison. Where it sat upon a ridge overlooking the tan-colored sea. First Swedish, then Dutch. Then English, and now finally, Ghanaian.

A museum for the darkness. A ticket to see. The men and machines that kept repeating the same patterns, over, and over.

And yet.

"If you're looking for trash, you'll find it. If you're looking for beauty, you'll see it," Béatrice said, reading Eleanorah's thoughts and nodding to the girl.

And then there was her smile.

Her white, glistening teeth, not yet decayed from the effects of chewing on sugar cane and lack of dental care, were perfect. Her dress was faded, gray. A worn washcloth wrapped in a circle rested on her shaved head as she ran toward them.

An hour ago, her shoulders were hunched. Her body moved heavily, eyes wet with despair. "Please Madame, please. It's been a hard market day," she confessed and took the full bowl of water sachets from her head as evidence.

It was always a hard market day. There were always hungry children with empty stomachs. And not enough. Never enough. Eleanorah and Béatrice fished some pesewas out of their purses anyway, the smallest act of fragile hope.

Now, she'd come back.

"Madame! Madame! Look-at!" The bowl was empty. "I sold everything, I sold everything!" She skipped around them gleefully, a child once more, her face transformed by the afternoon light.

Her smile charted the chance of another path, a different pattern. Redemption. Or at least, the possibility of it.

***

The phone in her back pocket vibrated. She shifted her hips to the side of the slatted bench, and answered. It was him.

"Salut, Eleanorah! Where are you? I'm here, by the station!"

She turned from her view of the small garden near the Gare de Lyon where golden daffodils opened their delicate petals and delicate violets carpeted bright blades of grass. Bushes of pale purple hydrangeas wafted the delicious aroma of spring. With each minute that passed her heart raced to keep time, exhaling all of its nerves into the sweaty palms of her hands. She wiped them on her faded jeans, now patched with brightly patterned cloth, and stood, shielding the light from her eyes.

"Bonsoir, Lucas! Ça va? Where are you, I can't find you!"

She'd been sitting there for hours after landing in Paris, the dust from Ghana still on her skin, a new map of the world inked on the tops of her feet, a farewell gift to herself. A talisman inscribed on her body so she wouldn't forget. She belonged to this world.

The crowded plaza spilled over with people clamoring out of taxis and waiting for the train. A dark van pulled through the sluggish roundabout. She crossed the street looking for his smile, knowing she could feel it if she just got close enough.

And there he was. He waved shyly and she hung up the phone, basking in the last beams of light. "I'm so happy to see you." She hugged him, her whole body melting with relief.

***

Swing music played loudly. Couples leaped across the upper floor of a Parisian apartment-turned speakeasy. Speak, easy.

Eleanorah and Lucas sat together in the stairwell, blocking the only pathway to *les toilettes*. Eyes only for each other, cocooned against the storm. He looked different, she noticed. Tired. Worn out. Pudgier around the middle. Like he was battling ghosts he was not sure he would win.

"I'm sorry to tell you, I can't give you something stable. I have nothing to offer you," he began. "I need time."

Eleanorah tilted her head sideways, searching his blue eyes. "Please wait for me," he'd said while she was still in Ghana. *How long would the waiting last?*

He'd broken up with Camille, just after New Year's. "I can't, I won't last another year this way," he'd told Eleanorah. Since, he'd moved out of their shared apartment into a small vacation rental his parents owned, by the ocean. He'd let his beard grow long, and tangled.

She sighed, squeezing his knee. He wasn't ready. Maybe never would be. She had been trying to build a home inside someone else's bones. But she was strong enough now to stand on her own, to go without easy answers and predictable outcomes.

"I get it. We agree on everything but this," she said. "You need time to be single, to figure out what you want. I've already been single. I'm ready to settle down with someone, and share a life."

She waited.

I have desire for you," he admitted. "That time San Sebastián, the first time we kissed, I have it memorized. You know you're always welcome to stay in Brittany in my parents' cabin. There's a nice room facing the sea you could write..." His voice trailed off.

She smiled but said nothing. Held her ground. It had to be different this time. "I'll go get us some water, be right back."

She watched him go and moved to sit down on the couch, next to a stranger sipping a chilled Kronenbourg.

"Salut, comment ça va? Êtes-vous américain?" the stranger asked, scooting closer to Eleanorah hopefully.

"Oui..." Eleanorah hesitated, finding the correct answer still slightly uncomfortable on her tongue. She'd always imagined feeling relief at being properly identified in the right category, at the right place, and time—but the need to label things, including herself was fading. Who she was wasn't tied to her country or career anymore, it wasn't even to Lucas.

"Is he your new boyfriend for the evening?" Lucas returned with two glasses of water, glaring.

"Is that *your* boyfriend?" the stranger asked, eyebrows raised at Eleanorah.

She looked from the stranger to Lucas and back again. "No. We're just friends." She raised her chin defiantly, mirroring his words from earlier. If those were the terms, they applied both ways.

"Just friends!" Lucas retorted, incredulously.

Eleanorah let out an exasperated sigh, frustrated by their game of awkwardly twisting around the truth. "Come on, let's dance." She put both hands on his shoulders, facing him squarely. "Look, you can't just do that. You can't interrupt me when I'm talking to someone. You have no right." Her eyes flashed.

"I'm sorry," he said softly. "I thought he was bothering you. I was trying to save you. We call that kind of guy like a 'wolf,'" he said, backpedaling.

"I don't need rescuing!"

"I'm sorry. You're right."

He held her hand, leading them toward the wall where they could sit. Everything reeled around them, a merry-go-round of music and intoxicated movement. He rested his arm on top of her thigh and nestled into her shoulder. She leaned her head gently against his.

Balance. Their bodies, a natural alchemy. For a brief moment, they forgot about holding any other pose.

***

She got up early and tiptoed downstairs, her ears still ringing from the noise the night before. The smell of coffee brewing was comforting. Coffee, and cigarettes. No matter where she was, this morning ritual anchored her in place.

But something was different about today.

The house was quiet but not empty. Benoît had just moved to the outskirts of Paris and invited them to stay, or maybe Lucas had invited them, and Benoît agreed. She couldn't be sure. She heard the door of the bedroom they shared the night before creak open and waited for him in the kitchen.

"Are you looking for the sugar?" Lucas wrapped his arms around her waist and kissed her neck, resting his chin on her shoulder.

He emptied the carafe, and they moved outside to the small balcony, overlooking the yard. Laundry hung on the line, and a few chickens ran about, clucking. One of the roommates sang, softly strumming his guitar. The sun peaked just above the red chimney tops of neighboring houses.

Lucas lit a cigarette and offered one to her.

"Non, merci," she said. She wanted her lungs, her heart to be clear.

He watched the emotions on her face change with the subtlety of a wind sweeping across a desert. He didn't argue, didn't try to make it better. He just pulled her close against his royal blue sweatshirt and held her, without saying a word.

"You know, you're someone important for me." He tucked a stray, strawberry golden hair behind her ear. "All this time, you've had an impact. I'm thinking about taking some time off from work to develop the travel eco-project more. You've paved the way..." He smiled.

"You've had an impact on me, too." She leaned back over the rail, contemplatively. "I think I've kept in touch with you more than my family, or friends. You've been like this safe harbor for me, whenever I'm away. I think that's why I keep coming back."

He wrapped her in his arms and she turned her ear, listening for his heartbeat, echoed in hers. The symphony of all things. She wanted to memorialize this moment in time forever.

"What will you do when you get home? You will find a job so you can save some money and begin traveling again? Will you write a book?" he asked, purposely.

"I honestly don't know. I thought maybe I'd find all the answers while I was away." She nuzzled her chin into his shoulder. "I miss home, the sense of it, at least. I've been avoiding it for so long." She watched the trees sway, their branches carrying messages yet to be heard. Memories of ancient flight patterns and wings, learning to trust the currents, and herself.

"I feel like I need to go back before I decide what my next steps are. There's a saying PK taught me before I left, 'Se wo were fi na wosankofa a yenkyi,' it means something like 'It's not wrong to go back and get what you've forgotten.' I'd like to spend some more time with my grandfather, hear as many of his stories as I can while he still remembers. I think there's a chance for my mom and I to have a different relationship, too."

She pictured her mother's kitchen—the recipe box with hand-written notes and a jar of sweet tea in the windowsill.

"I'm sorry I keep changing my plans." She tried to keep her throat from closing.

"I haven't noticed. If anything, it's not a drawback, it's an asset." He cupped her face in both hands, kissing her lightly on the forehead.

"I don't know if I can do this."

She thought of all their train station departures and the one yet to come—the sing-song ringing of the doors open and closed. The weight of her belongings, squarely on her shoulders. The step up from the platform into the car. The seat she chose so she could see him through the window, waving until he was out of sight. Their last kiss, sent through the air in a playful gesture. They rehearsed the ritual to avoid its finality, repeated the pattern to ensure there would always be a next time.

Yet.

Some endings can't be predicted or postponed.

And some beginnings happen over and over.

"*We* can do this." Lucas wiped the last of her tears on his sleeve. Kissing her saltwater lips, he lifted her ever so slightly off her feet. "Sometimes in life it's good to lose control." He spun her in the air, gazing lovingly into her bright, golden eyes.

She spread her wings, giggling with delight.

The root. The trunk. The branch. The tree. There are things which we can't possibly know *but we do*.

Eleanorah would see him again. And, she was finally going home.

The rest was to be lived.

Acknowledgements

It took me over ten years to write this book. It wouldn't have been possible without the many, many voices of encouragement and love along the way. These stories aren't mine, they're *ours.*

To Jónsi, whose soundtrack to *We Bought a Zoo* was the music I listened to on repeat while writing, and all the coffee shops whose buttery pastries and caffeine helped fuel these pages. To my early beta readers—Cindy, Sarah, and Mary. Thank you for believing in my writing enough to tackle that early draft and offer feedback. To Mandy, who reminded me, "We are the generation that tells the truth."

Special thanks to Peter, who understood the heart of this story and designed a cover that captures its essence perfectly. And to Eva, who sharpened this story with incredible insights and reminded me to give Eleanorah agency. Your professionalism, patience, and polish come through on every page. To Dominic, who saw an early version of what this could be and gave me a first glimpse of its potential. I came back to your words of encouragement during every revision and setback. To Ashley, whose photoshoot for this book was a literal dream.

To Lena, Matthias, Elisavet, Jennifer, Ciska, Jenny, Peter, and so many more, you became the family I needed on the road. I carried your authenticity and courage in my heart every step along the way. To Pastor Charles, for helping me to look for and finally see the light. To P. Laud and all the children at Wisdom Academy, you taught me the taste of joy and reminded me that hope is never finished.

To Meghan for helping me brainstorm comps and Minnie for reminding me that this story was NOT about a boy (even when it kind of was). To Lydia, whose friendship and practical wisdom about everything from motherhood to building a business is a grounding force. To Keva for giving me the tough love I needed to choose self-publishing and to all the creative mamas on Substack who keep showing up every day, letting me know I can, too. To Jordan for reminding me that play and creativity go together, and Joe, for all the kitchen conversations that nourished my soul. Your dedication to your art continues to inspire me.

To all the ICU nurses who are on the front lines every day and my friends at SLE, thank you for continuing to fight when I couldn't. To Nick, for knowing I was a writer before I did and caring about what I had to say. To Marlise, for letting me crash in your apartment for months while I hopscotched around coffee shops in Chicago, writing early versions of these stories, but more importantly, for always being the friend I needed and the best adventure buddy. To Marina and Eliza, for being my anchors across space and time —your friendship is a lifeline. To Victoria for being my adopted older sister and holding me through some of the hardest times.

To my Dad, who always gave me wings, and Mom, for teaching me that the world was bigger than our small town. To Rebekah, my compass when I'm lost, and Annie, the one who blazes ahead and waits for me to catch up. To Prasunjit, for being the partner I always hoped I'd be lucky enough to find. Thank you for believing in me. You are the steadiness I need. To my grandparents—your love is still my shelter from the storm. I miss you every day.

And for Noah, may you always find your way back home.

About the author

Mariah Friend is a former ICU nurse who traded her stethoscope for a pen. She spent her twenties teaching in rural Ghana, volunteering in Ecuador, and falling in love in France, searching for a place to belong. After realizing she has a suitcase heart, she decided that home isn't a place you find but a choice you make.

The Pattern Shop is her debut novel, born from re-telling the stories that continue to shape her—from her grandfather's pattern shop to conversations with strangers on the road over a shared cigarette. From Missouri to Morocco, the places, textures, colors, and people she's loved are inscribed on her chest. She hopes she's done them half the justice they deserve.

When she's not writing, Mariah can be found with her husband chasing their toddler through the hills of Chattanooga, Tennessee, digging in her garden, or writing her newsletter *Heartbeats* for creative caregivers.

She believes we belong to each other, and that it's never too late to choose home.

Connect with Mariah

Thank you for reading *The Pattern Shop*. These stories are deeply personal and sharing them with you means the world to me. Research shows that when two people listen to the same story across time and space, their heartbeats begin to synchronize. *That's* the power of storytelling.

I'd love to hear yours, too!

If you'd like to stay in touch, I write a weekly newsletter called *Heartbeats* for creative caregivers—subscribe at thebarefootbeat.substack.com. My archive of original travel and lifestyle blogs lives at thebarefootbeat.com. You can also find me on Instagram (@mariah.m.friend) and Bluesky (@mariahfriend.bsky.social), where I share writing updates and glimpses of the creative life in process.

For media inquiries, creative collaborations, signed copies of *The Pattern Shop*, and other merchandise, visit mariahfriend.com.

Loved *The Pattern Shop*? Please consider leaving a review on Goodreads or your favorite book blog. Reviews help indie authors reach new readers, and I'm so grateful for your support.

Warmly,

Mariah

Discussion Questions

The Pattern Shop explores themes of belonging, inherited trauma, privilege, and the search for home. These questions are designed to spark meaningful conversation about Eleanorah's journey and the choices she makes along the way.

1. Eleanorah mentions her grandfather has told her about *The Manual* but never shown it to her. Why do you think he chooses to keep it from her, despite their close relationship?

2. How does Eleanorah's relationship with intimacy shift throughout the book? What rules does she make and then break?

3. Early in the book, Eleanorah wonders if her dream is really a memory. What do you think is the difference, and how can we tell?

4. When do we first see evidence of Eleanorah's voice being silenced, and when does she start to regain it?

5. How does Eleanorah's profession as a nurse reinforce or question her need for control?

6. What does bleeding come to symbolize for Eleanorah throughout the book?

7. How are nature's patterns and cycles different from ones created by humans? What purpose do they serve?

8. What role does fate play (or not) in her story as it unfolds?

9. What's frustrating about her relationship with Lucas? What's redeeming about it?

10. How does Eleanorah begin connecting the dots between colonialism, the medical industry, and voluntourism? What questions does she not ask that she should?

11. How do the characters she meets along the way—Hans, Poppy, Daphne, Izaak, and others—shape and change her perspective?

12. How does her inherited trauma and family history show up in her body? How does she learn to carry it with her?

13. With Lucas and her mother, how does she leave room for reconciliation while also choosing herself?

14. What shifts for Eleanorah in Ghana so that she's finally able to choose home?